Immortal Bloodlust

By

Catalina Chao

ISBN: 14033-8276-X (e-book)
ISBN: 1-4033-8277-8 (Paperback)
ISBN: 1-4033-8278-6 (Dustjacket)

This book is printed on acid free paper.

1stBooks – rev. 11/1/02

PART ONE

Catalina Chao

THE VILLAGE 1603

I want to thank my family, especially my little sister Nancy, who endured a blazing hot summer sun to help me find my contract. My father, who turned my dreams into a reality. All my English teachers who knew that I would succeed if I never gave up. Kim Wright for her caring and putting up with my endless questions. I miss you and I hope that we can talk soon. Ms. Haworth, you've been a mountain of support for me. Brien Jones, I thank you for your bluntness, which always keeps me on my feet.

Deep appreciation goes to Carly Alfonso who was the first person to ever read my stories and encouraged me to keep on writing. Carrie Case, for breaking me away from the same old tedious routine of everyday life to experience fun. To Gurpinder Nagra, who has been one of my most loyal readers and has read stories from my first series and told me that they were incredible—even when they weren't.

Mellissa Pelster, who continues to strengthen me when I have doubts and plants seeds of faith within my heart. Erich Schaub, who always makes my writing sound so sophisticated and wonderful. Thanks for all your help on everything. Good luck with your work. I know you will be successful. Jonah Gojar, my fellow Libra chick, you gave me one of the greatest honors when you allowed me to co-write the sequel to *Eternal Craving*. (Jethro's so hot!)

And where would this story be if I hadn't gone to the graduation party on that fateful Sunday afternoon that inspired the creation of one of my best stories ever? My endless appreciation goes to my delightful friend since elementary school April Jacobson, my "little brother" Andrew Cheng who gave me the marvelous idea of having one of my characters cross-over, and my own private court jester Michael Ma. You have no idea how big your roles are in this story and this book is mostly dedicated to all of you.

I would also like to dedicate this book to Crystal Heath, my best friend in the whole entire creation of the universe who made all of Heaven envious of me when you became my angel. I love you more than words I can ever write, even if I had an eternity of paper to write on. I would not be who I am today if it were not for you. You say that you are so lost sometimes, but I am never lost when I am with you. You are my way—to peace, to love, to happiness—and there is no one else I would follow.

But above all, the heart and soul of this book belongs to Sophia, who dragged me into the story and threatened to blind me if I didn't finish it...It wasn't a hard decision to make.

Abrasion to the Soul

It feels like glass
Against my skin
It hurts like a thorn

Catalina Chao

Pricked by my kin

The demons tried to take me
The beast is trying to chain me
But I refuse to let them break me
I will not allow them to reign me

The blood seeps through my flesh
It hurts even deeper inside
I seek peace, but they will not allow me to rest
I want to live, but instead I die

I weep tears and I fall apart
I am fragmented and broken
They tore out my still beating heart
And my damnation was spoken

They cut me even deeper inside
An eternal wound that can't heal but grows old
She stabbed me once, but it felt like a thousand knives
An abrasion to my soul.

—Catalina Chao

Catalina Chao

CHAPTER ONE

εφ

I WOULD LIE AWAKE SO poignantly at night wondering if I had been cursed, damned, or doomed. And then I would see *her* face. The face of both, my salvation and damnation, laughed at me. The hazel brown eyes of my savior, my deliverer, and my taker stared at me. The lips of my god and my devil taunted me. The memory of my creator and destroyer plaguing my thoughts even now in the dark recesses of this room where not even light, of *any* sort, touches the cold and bitter stone. Her last words left me with the lust to seek out retribution to avenge the deaths of those whom I have loved and lost and to requite the darkness in my own immortal soul.

That is not even equidistant of how much I hate her, her, whom is all those things and more. Her, who still calls herself "Kathleen".

If she has forgotten about me and assumed that I've of her, she must be foolish beyond her years, beyond even mine.

How can I forget about this Kathleen personage?

I can easily cite the eerie soundscapes of which I had met her in. My first encounter, but not my last. This image of Kathleen sometimes remains still in my mind, even when my soul is restless and moving.

She was displayed in a velvet crimson gown with a black lace mantilla concealing her white face and blood red lips. And I, I was but plain, in a simple wintergreen dress. Reminiscing, her first presence upon me was grand and sublime. Now, should I have the displeasure of being in her company again, it would sicken me to the core of my still heart. And for me, that is saying much.

Not much can disgust me. I am a vampire of centuries, but Kathleen is an exception.

The night had shrouded me in its dark shadows when I had first stepped out from the theatre only miles away from my humble, tranquil village in Paris. I had come out from a new play, written by a mysterious new playwright. The play intrigued me. The scenes were enigmatic, but something, right from the start, drew me in like a spider closing in on its prey for the kill.

The play had been simply titled *Immortal*, for whatever reason. The main character, a young woman dubbed Sophia, was an "immortal" as she was called throughout the play. (The conventional word for it now would be "vampire".) Sophia had been seduced by a stranger, whose name was mentioned only once throughout the story, though she had many names: Bridgette or Darkangel.

And Sophia had been "brought across". She died only to wake up the next night with the seducer by her side, and then she returned home, searching for her infant daughter. But she was gone.

(Little did I know at the time that the gothic script had been scenes, events, experiences, and moments from Kathleen's own gory life.)

I felt myself wholly consumed by the poetic language in which the play had been prose.

And after the play, as I was leaving the theatre, that was when I would first lay my eyes on the one woman who would promise me everything and leave me with nothing.

THOUGH I HAD BEEN BORN into a somewhat haughty and wealthy aristocratic family, I cared nothing for the wealth, the fame, or the money that was to be my heritage, my future claim. I often found the money unfulfilling and unimportant, to say the least. I was more of an artist, dabbing into the creative arts that dealt with the matters of the heart and soul, rather than the physical matters of the flesh.

My mother, the lady of the household, cared little for her only daughter. I was her firstborn and she had always been resentful of me, living in constant fear, terrified that her only daughter would grow up to become more beautiful than she was. Oh, my mother was beautiful; she just didn't have enough beauty inside.

I had two brothers. A ten-year-old pious brother named Peter, who preached the teachings of God more often than I needed to hear, and a seven-year-old feminine brother named Jacob.

And even though I had all these family members, it was my father who stood up for me against my mother. My mother, Lady Opaque, was only rich and wealthy because she had married my father, Sir Wesley Opaque. He hailed from Scotland, but my father left the emerald valleys of home to claim his fortune waiting for him in the gold-ornamented halls of Paris, France. That was where he met my mother, a seventeen-year-old country girl, and he, a twenty-three-year-old man. Married in two and a half months, my mother became pregnant with me within a year of their marriage.

My brothers, evidently, came later.

Oh, that is enough of my family. They are no longer important. They are dead. Dead for a matter of a couple centuries I assume. They've long since rotted in their damp graves under the moist ground of a Paris cemetery.

I speak not of my own past, before I became what I am today, because I find it much too shameful.

These are the moments when I ponder about the afterlife, if there really is a Hell or a Heaven, and if there were, would I be accepted in either one of them?

Or would I be forever cursed with rejection and doomed to live here on this forsaken plane for eternity?

If it hadn't been for Kathleen, I would not be in here, musing my morals from my past and my morals now in the present.

I never believed in vengeance, thinking it was a terrible sin against God, and now I live for it.

I can tell that it is night outside. The sun has just set and the coolness of the moon alleviates me, though it does little or nothing else.

I seek solace in the darkness, because the light refuses to accept me.

I seek solace in knowing that I will one day be let loose and free to assassinate my enemy, take her out, as she did me.

I SHALL NEVER FORGET THE precise words Kathleen uttered to me as I exited the theatre. My horse-drawn carriage waited for me a few yards away, waiting to take me back home.

A voice called out from behind me and I turned to see a slender and attractive female standing in front of me, adorned in a scarlet gown and her chalky face masked behind a lace curtain.

I was about ready to turn and make my way to the carriage, but her presence was potent enough to silence even *my* will.

"Did you enjoy my piece?"

Of course she was referring to her dramatic play.

"Yes," I affirmed, "I found it riveting and detailed."

She took a subtle step forward, a step so filmy I would not have noticed it save for the shift in the darkness. "'Riveting and detailed', those are two words I have never heard formed into the same sentence together. I am pleased."

Uncertain about my next move, I curtsied and courtly darted around, so as not to cause the woman suspicion or disrespect.

"Wait!" she frantically called out for me. "My name is Kathleen. I would like to know yours."

I answered her request, though I found that it was more of a demand. I looked her dead in her eyes, though they were hard to find under the veil. "I am Catherine Opaque." It was perhaps the last time that I would ever say my name with conviction and truth of my identity. "It is an honor to meet you, Miss Kathleen," I added.

She shook her head. "No, please, it is merely 'Kathleen'. I have no unique title," she insisted. "Do you come to these plays often?"

"Yes, I do," I proudly replied with extreme precaution not to reveal too much to the stranger. "I have not come to this theatre before, but your play has received such high reviews and remarks that I thought I should come see it for myself."

"Where do you live, Miss Opaque?"

That was a question I had not expected.

For a second, I stumbled, fumbling around like a bumbling idiot to find the correct response.

"Paris."

She scratched her chin in a ladylike manner. "Ah ..." She looked pensive. "I will be coming to a theatre in Paris soon. Perhaps I shall meet you again there."

"Perhaps we shall."

Once again, I curtsied, making a break for it and stepped into my carriage without further incident.

Kathleen stood still while my carriage passed her by. I watched her through my window. She said nothing, did nothing. She just plainly stood there, vigilantly gazing at me with those hazel russet-brown eyes that would soon shudder my spine and that I would learn to despise.

HOW LONG HAVE I BEEN here?

This sudden thought interrupts my nostalgia.

It brings me back from my time-warped reflection to this hideous place of despair.

I gaze around the circular stone room. It is tiny in diameter, perhaps large enough to fit one average-sized male. There is barely enough room in it for myself. It is difficult for me to stretch my body straight because the room does is so confined, but not impossible. Usually, I stay curled up to a section of the room.

On my left, there is a long wooden box. It is long enough to fit my body. The story of this box will come much later.

And there are chains. The chains, like the box, will come much later.

Across from me, there is a certain stone that is large and written on with blood. There are tally marks, one hundred twenty-one to be exact, smeared onto the stone. The blood has dried and faded, though it is still near visibility. A mortal would have to squint his eyes to read it.

The tally marks are the only things I can focus my eyes on. There is nothing else except for the cracked stones that sometimes tell a story.

I see faces in these rocks.

I see the faces of all those whom I have loved and lost.

I see Michael, Christine, Peter, and Jacob, not all who I have lost at the hands of Kathleen. Some blood has been shed on my own skin as well as hers.

At that moment, I see Kathleen's Greek/Portuguese face.

Her face is the one I see most often.

The one I see before I fall asleep at night and when I wake up in the morning. Unchanging thoughts of her reside in my mind, devouring me like a tiger to a wildebeest's carnage.

And still, that is not even the beginning of my hatred for Kathleen. It is much deeper than that.

OUR SECOND ENCOUNTER CAME WHEN I heard of her play coming to an ancient stadium in my hometown.

I convinced my father and mother to come with me. Peter and Jacob were to stay home with our nanny.

My mother, in spite of our differences, did enjoy the same theatrical productions as I.

As my mother slipped her gloves on in front of the carriage, Kathleen approached us.

I greeted her and introduced her to my family. "Mother, Father, this is the friend I have been telling you about, Kathleen, the playwright of *Immortal*."

Kathleen shook my mother's hand and my father, in a courtly manner, kissed the back of Kathleen's pale hand.

"I have hoped that we would meet each other again," Kathleen remarked. "Your daughter is quite the interesting young lady."

How could she have known that I was interesting? We had met only once before and I hardly said anything about myself.

"Thank you," my father said. "Interesting young lady or not, she will always be my darling little baby girl."

I remember feeling my cheeks flush at the comment. It wasn't just from embarrassment, but from astonishment. My father had always loved me more than my mother did.

For a twinkle of a second, after my father made that cheek-blushing comment, something flickered in Kathleen's eyes like an unstable spark—was it rage?

"I would like to hear more about this play and your inspiration for it," my father went on. "Please, join us for dinner tonight."

The moment my father said that, I did not know whether to feel excited or terrified. Kathleen was a stranger who wrote a very detailed, gory gothic play. Could she be trusted?

I have learned now, several years later that Kathleen could not be trusted and I should have never allowed her into my home. But I was young at the time, foolish and unwise. And my family and myself paid the ultimate price for my senselessness.

I invited Kathleen into my home several times, allowing her to meet my brothers, who were as drawn to her as I was. She was always so humane and refined. I would have never guessed, at that time, she was far from the definition of "human".

Two and a half weeks after the night that Kathleen accompanied us at dinner, was when she introduced me to the dark underground. I never asked to know the things she told me. She simply did it out of, what she called, "friendship".

I call it malevolence.

MY HEART CONTINUES TO ACHE when I think about my family. My handsome father, attractive mother, and innocent brothers. Regardless of the fact that they are dead, I was their daughter and I belong with them. I should be in a coffin decomposing six feet under a Paris cemetery like them. Instead, I am trapped in my seventeen-year-old mortal body for the rest of my immortality, however long that shall be.

Momentarily, I feel that the moon has risen to the sky and its radiant light shines down on me.

I am shrouded in perpetual darkness, just like how I was when Kathleen intruded my peaceable noblewoman life.

"OPEN YOUR EYES NOW."
I gradually unsealed my eyelids.
"Do you like it?"
I was surrounded by continuous darkness. A fire roared in the center of all the blackness.
"I don't understand," I told Kathleen.
Kathleen snapped her fingers and torches attached to the gold red walls fired up. There were dancers. They were all scantily clad, wearing little strips of undergarments to cover their genitals and, for the women, tiny leather tops that stretched around their bosom.

On a lavish table scattered with gold coins and silver bars, were platters of food. There was a brilliant crystal-clear punch bowl. It had something dark red in it. In fact, I wasn't even sure that it was wine. It was darker than the ordinary moonshine.

But to compliment the crystalline bowl were light green grapes, rich purple and burgundy grapes the color of blood.

A diamond chandelier was suspended from the high-raised ceiling, which was painted with a beautiful mural. The artistic scene featured dozens of white-winged and blue-winged angels gathered around the Virgin Mary, while She cradled Christ.

"Come," Kathleen invited me, "sit and eat."
She clasped my hand and led me over to a velvet-covered bed where she laid beside me.

"Where am I?"

"Some place beautiful," she briskly replied. "Do you like it?"

I beamed. "I've never seen such raw beauty before."

Kathleen cackled at me. "Young child, you must get out more often and see the world." Then her face grew serious and intense. Her eyes narrowed down at mine. "I can show you the world, if you let me."

To take the pressure off, I jested a bit. "I'm afraid, being the heiress of a fortune, that I am under the strictest security."

"You are the daughter of a wealthy family. You are your servant's master. They can't tell *you* what to do. Tell *them* what to do," Kathleen said.

It had worked. She became looser.

Nonetheless, I was meek. "I do not like to think of them as my servant and me as their master. I do not like making myself sound superior. We are all equal human beings in this world, are we not? That is the way the Lord intended it to be."

Kathleen's playful smile turned wicked at the mention of the Lord. It was obvious to me that she was not a believer. She proved me right with what she said next.

"If the good Lord intended us *all* to be humans," she challenged, "then why did He make some of us superior than others?"

"No one is as superior as the Lord," I argued on His behalf.

Kathleen chuckled softly, reaching for a clump of ruby grapes and plucking only one. "Your faith should be reserved for yourself," she prodded.

For a moment, I had believed her and swore at myself for forsaking my faith.

"If I trust in the Lord," I voiced, "I confide in myself."

Kathleen and I discussed no further implications of the Lord for the rest of the night. We watched the dancers who seemed in sync with the wild spirits.

I stayed there all night with Kathleen, opening my mouth once in a while to praise the splendor of the party.

When I came home, the sun had almost risen in the horizon and my family was not very happy to see their daughter come home in a drunken stupor with half of my clothes ripped and torn.

I suffered a sound lashing, though I hardly remember the pain because I was so intoxicated. I hardly even remembered the wild night I had spent with Kathleen.

I had no memory of the gala until much later on.

And to this day, I truly believe that I would have been better off in the dark, not knowing the truth of what happened.

KNOWLEDGE IS A TERRIBLE THING sometimes. Kathleen made me a part of something I had never known before. She seduced me with her promises of the universe and now I'm merely a small part of it. I played a bigger role when I was opulent. I could have done something great and extraordinary with my life, but I allowed Kathleen to take control of it and when I regained authority, it was too late.

I WANTED KATHLEEN TO LEAVE me alone after I received cruel punishment for staying out beyond my set curfew. But she did not want to leave me. In fact, two days after the social, she came back in search of me.

"Catherine …"

I turned in my bed before I woke and found Kathleen sitting on a chair in front of me.

I gasped and bolted upright.

"*Kathleen*," I hissed. "You are taking liberties with me, showing up in my bedroom and in the middle of the night!"

She grabbed my hand without me even seeing her own hand reach out for mine. "I want to show you something." Her smile was secretive.

I pulled my hand away. "I want to see nothing of yours. Thanks to you, I received a lashing after I came home."

Kathleen reached out and stroked my chin.

It was only then that I realized for the first time how chilly her hands were. But I welcomed her touch. I felt comfort in it.

"I apologize for getting you in trouble," she commented; though I did not think she meant it. "This time, I promise I will have you in before your parents even know that you are missing."

I gazed deep into her cinnamon brown eyes. They appeared sincere and honest, but the key word there was "*appeared*".

Just one more time, I had thought to myself. *You had so much fun last time. Maybe this time will be even better.*

I threw the sheets off of me. "Let's go," I prompted.

I went to throw on one of my favorite blue gowns, but Kathleen did not allow me to.

Instead, she jerked me away from my room, towards the window.

"What are you doing?" I demanded.

"You're wasting time," she whispered at me. "What you have on is fine."

I examined my thin body. I barely had anything on. I wore a silk peach slip. Yet, Kathleen goaded me on.

"You look beautiful," she exhorted. "People always look better in their natural form."

I listened to what she said and believed her. I followed her out of my window. We hopped a foot down onto the drizzled grass and she went ahead of me, yanking me along by holding my hand.

I am not certain if she owned the house or not, but she definitely had some control over what went on within the silent walls.

It was another soiree, similar to the one that I went to before with her, the one that ended with me on the receiving end of a sound lashing.

But in some deranged way, I trusted Kathleen. I trusted her in a way that I will never understand. Perhaps that is what trust is: Not understanding, but believing.

I believed in her, with all my heart and soul I truly did.

Her grip on my hand was comfortable and consoling. In her silk touch, she promised me that no harm would ever come to me. I trusted her beyond the expression of any words.

And she led me here.

I watched, bewildered, at the void of colors.

It was as if I had entered a warped frame of mind. Everything seemed twisted, including the metal statues of contorted beings. Oh, they were in so much pain; so much writhing agony. Naturally, I felt the need to deliver these gnarled dead, lifeless things that felt tormenting—almost blinding—pain from the clutches of oblivion.

It was almost as if they were formless pieces of clay; without a shape, except for what one molded it to become.

Humans are empty statues, I mused suddenly. *We have no form, no shape. But our sculptors come and carve us into their liking.*

These bronzed silver statues rested, inanimate, on a table surrounded by many other beings like them.

I wondered what it would feel like to be trapped forever in a moment of intense agony with no hope of ever being freed. Now, I know.

Moaning broke me away from my unrelenting chain of thoughts.

My eyes fixed on a piece of plushy furniture where a young man and young woman sat. The woman's dark, shimmering eyes stared blankly into the shade-less room while the man whispered sweet nothings into her ears, ever more edging closer towards her.

For one brief moment, I could have sworn that I saw the man bare his gleaming fangs.

He came closer to nuzzle her neck, but before he did, he looked in my direction and his eyes caught mine. He winked at me.

I gasped and the force of his mind pushed against mine and caused me to lose my balance for a split second before I regained it.

I felt Kathleen tug at my hand and it pulled me. When she had my attention, she displayed a thick-bottomed crystalline wineglass with a pure black liquid inside.

Within the lightlessness of the room, I thought it to have been some kind of dark wine, but when the faint glimmer of light hit it, I saw that it had a scarlet tint to it.

I cupped my hands around the wineglass—and though I had seen my parents drink from glasses such as these—I did not know how to drink one myself.

I sipped from it and instantly spat it back out.

"Good God!" I exclaimed. "What kind of devil elixir is this?"

Kathleen frowned. "You don't like it?"

I wiped my mouth with my exposed forearm. "Lord, no."

Kathleen shrugged. "Ah, well. Everyone's tastes is different from the other." She held the wineglass to her lips and consumed the devil elixir before three seconds was up.

Recklessly, she tossed the wineglass and the distinct shattering of glass echoed forever in my mind.

"Who are these people?" I questioned her, looking at her.

"Friends of mine," she told me. "Good friends, from long ago."

As if on cue, the same man who had winked at me shook Kathleen's hand. He had pitch black eyes, yet they appeared to sparkle with brilliance understood by no living creature on this earth.

"Kristoff," Kathleen chirped. "Where have you been?"

He replied simply, "I've been around. You know how I am. I can never stay around for long."

"You've never been the kind to stay put," Kathleen pointed out. "Don't even follow tradition."

Kristoff smiled wickedly. "The thing with tradition...is that it gets boring after a while." He glanced at me, as if acknowledging that I was accompanying Kathleen for the first time. "Who's your friend?" he asked.

"This is Lady Catherine Opaque," she introduced. "Pretty little thing, isn't she?"

"Hmm...Enjoy your stay," he said before he turned around. I thought I heard him whisper: "You'll never leave."

Kristoff was intimidating, but everyone else that I met did not rattle the same bones that Kristoff had done.

In fact, I met a man. His name was Hutton. Bronzed skin and mahogany eyes were a comforting sight, and though he was nowhere near as elegant and muscled as Kristoff had appeared, he was still a rather handsome man.

I sat down with him where I had seen Kristoff with that unknown young woman. He and I spoke for what seemed like an eternity, spinning the most elaborate tales from Egypt, where he insisted that he had hailed from. Of course I did not believe him.

I remember falling asleep a few hours before the sun had risen, out of exhaustion. Being surrounded in that house wholly drained the energy out of me. I was stunned by it, the amount of exuberance stolen from me, from staying in a house clothed in black-and-white with individuals who could have been the inspiration for the infamous comedy and tragedy masks.

And I remember waking up that morning.

It was the last morning that I would ever see as a human.

CHAPTER TWO

εφ

I HAVE LONG SINCE FORGOTTEN what it feels like to take in a breath of air. My lungs contract subtly, and my heart beats about twice an hour. I don't feel my breath, though I know I take but one every once in a while. Even vampires need something to sustain them, besides pleasure, adrenaline, and blood. I breathe rarely and in the face of terror, breathing can become much more rapid and frequent.

My mind is surging again with haunting recollections.

Kathleen played her first cruel trick on me on my seventeenth birthday.

After that frozen moment in time, I replayed it over and over again, coming up with different theories of how things could have been different if I had done things differently back then.

In my chimera, more people lived happily ever after. What's more, people *lived.*

My family might have lived. My untainted brothers, Peter and Jacob, would have been given the chance to grow up, marry, have children and continue the Opaque lineage. Now, the day that I die, the Opaque lineage will die with me. The end of a whole line that goes back to hundreds of years ago in the early twelve hundreds will be exterminated, either from suicide or murder, whichever comes first.

Would Michael have received the chance to live as well?

In my reverie, Michael married me; we had many children together, lived on a peaceful vineyard by the sea, and died old together.

Who am I fooling?

None of those things happened and will *never* happen.

It's too late for us.

It's too late for them.

It's too late for me.

But it may not be too late for my reprisal against Kathleen.

In fact, I will not allow it to be too late for requital.

It's never too late for vengeance.

MY FAMILY NEVER FOUND OUT where I had been.

Kathleen, on a technical advantage, did keep her promise. I came home at the first light of dawn and my family still slept under a warm blanket free of suspicion.

Lucky them.

For the first time ever, I realized how cold my room actually was.

It chilled when I entered the vacant chamber.

The bed itself seemed untouched for centuries, though I had only left it a few hours ago.

I found myself removing my nightgown from my body before I even had time to take control of my action. I was in such an urgent rush to rip it off of me and throw it on the ground. I scrutinized it for several minutes before I, in a fit of unwelcome rage and fury, stomped on it, thrashing it all over the room. The light of the daystar beamed in through my window and I quickly ran to shut the panels, revealing my bare body for the public to see if they had been outside my window.

"Catherine!"

My mother beckoned me, but I did not want to answer her.

What was the point in doing so anyway?

My mother never heard me and when she did, she did not pay attention.

For the first time in my mortal life, I rebelled.

I went against the unwritten code of honor for daughters all over the European nation. I refused to obey and do another's will without question.

What's happening to me?

I sharply remembering pondering that question, however, in the end, I knew there was no answer but the one Kathleen could offer to me and I did not want to accept it, even if it was the truth.

I threw temper-tantrums throughout the whole day, behaving in a terrible fit, something I had never done since the first two years of my childhood. My servants ran back and forth trying to calm me down. They brought me gemstones and jewels of all kinds, knowing that I had a soft spot for anything that sparkled or shimmered.

I was so dangerous, or threatening to my mother, that I was locked up inside my room for the rest of the morning.

When Peter was sent up to read me "teachings" from the Bible, I hurled things at him, things like my priceless

Chinese vase from the Byzantine era and the precious stones my servants brought up to me.

Peter came out of my room alive. Nonetheless, he was bruised and battered, drained of all his strength, and his beloved Bible had been torn into unreadable shreds.

Worthless was what I thought of the Bible. They were not even worth the pages they were printed on.

Nothing could console me and that was when I realized that the only condolence I needed could only come from Kathleen, my mysterious and comely friend.

I dashed around in my room, breaking things, causing destruction everywhere I moved and I moved unclothed. I had not dressed and declined to.

I screamed all day. My throat had become hoarse and my cheeks were rosy pinks from all the shouting. I roared unimaginable and unspoken curses at my father and bellowed out how valueless my mother was.

I continued to bark comments and mock the Scripture. I did not allow anyone in my household to have one second of peace or silence. No matter what, the blasphemous declarations of mine became bolder and louder. No one could do anything. After a while, no one *did* anything. They all gave up on me.

Maybe that's why I learned to give up so easily on myself.

Everyone had forsaken me. My own faith had relinquished me and my own family disowned me.

The funny thing was, after all was said and done, I meant everything I said and regretted not one bit of it.

About an hour after the sun had set on the skyline, I finally put on a white gown and crawled quietly out of my bedroom window.

Cleverly, I moved my mattress and chiffonnier to the door and stacked chair on top of chair to prevent anyone from entering my room.

I knew that at the moment I would stop screaming or creating endless noise, someone would unlock the door and come to check up on me. I did not want them to know I was gone, though I knew they would figure it out. I just wanted my disappearance to remain a mystery. I looked at it as a test, a challenge to my family to prove their love for me.

They failed miserably.

IT WAS ALMOST AS IF Kathleen knew what was going to happen. She waited for me at the local cemetery, the cemetery that my family would be buried in, in days to come. I passed by it on my way to nowhere and I heard her call out my name. I heard her tone and I instantly recognized that it was Kathleen.

I barged into the cemetery, stepping on fresh graves as well as old ones, destroying the artistic flowers that had been placed on the crisp dirt. I sprung above tombstones, ignorant of whose it belonged to.

I found Kathleen deep in the heart of the graveyard. A gentle mist was lifting as I arrived at a mausoleum where Kathleen was perched, grinning knowingly.

"I knew you would eventually come," she announced. "I just didn't think you'd come as quickly as I thought you would."

I attentively approached her. She was so high above me. "I surprise many people, even those who think they've seen it all."

Kathleen's eyes were focused on her nails. I assumed she had just gotten a pricey manicure for them.

"Why have you come?" she asked me.

"You're the one who knew I would come sooner or later," I countered wittily, "you tell me what I'm doing here because I would like to know as much as you."

A moment of silence passed over us.

"You shouldn't have been so cruel to your family," she suddenly declared. "You might need them more than you think."

"What do *you* care about my family?"

Kathleen hardly even shrugged, but kept her eyes on her nails. "Nothing. You, on the other hand, will find them quite important."

My eyes narrowed in suspicion. "What are you talking about?"

"It was too late when I realized that my family was more important than I ever thought. Now they're dead." She said this with a cold, nonchalant voice. "They've been decomposing in their graves for aeons."

Eons? I had no idea what she meant. Certainly, she could not be that old. I was so wrong and that mistake cost me my life.

"What am I doing here?" I suddenly asked, as if waking up from some sort of interrupted and hazy somnambulism. I looked at my own hands. *So dirty...almost as if they were tainted with red blood.*

Kathleen, finally diverting her attention from her nails to me, sprang down from her high pedestal. She grabbed my wrists while I was examining them. Her hazel eyes stared deep into my soul, shedding all the layers mortals use to hide what they do not wish others to see.

But she stripped all of that away.

All pretensions gone.

She took a good, hard look at me and found weakness and vulnerability, and she saw herself, I know she did. She hesitated for a moment, perhaps contemplating her next action, though it seemed like she had already mapped out the future. Maybe she saw a part of her in me.

Whatever I *think* she might have seen I know what she *did* see.

She saw my long yearnings and unspoken desires.

"I can give you *everything* you've ever wanted," she whispered into my ear. "The whole world can be yours. Everything you've ever wanted can be all yours."

Her lips were pressed against the lobes of my ears.

It was tempting.

But how could I forsake the Lord and the promises of Heaven and an eternal paradise where happiness reigned?

If I agreed to her, I knew that my soul would be lost forever.

I took a good hard look at my hands again. "What have I done?" I asked, baffled. "The things that I said to my family, my mother, my father, my brothers."

Kathleen released me.

I took a seat on a fallen marble pillar. I needed something firm and sturdy underneath my lack of stability.

"It does not matter anymore," Kathleen prodded. "You are here, now."

I met her chocolate irises, intently. "I have to go back home, Kathleen." I rose from the pillar. "I have to repent, make amends for my behavior."

Kathleen blocked me from my desired destination. "You can't leave, *ever*."

Her eyes bore into mine once more and I found that she had shed all my mortal layers, the physical coating that prevented me from being free.

"I never want to see you again, *ever*," I hissed into her ears. "Don't ever come near me and mine again, otherwise I *will* have to take drastic action."

"You don't scare me," she breathed into my face.

My own breathing was becoming scarce and few in between. The breathing pattern was rapid and inconstant.

Kathleen gripped my right hand. "Now, we'll be together forever, just like how we should have been from the beginning."

My brows knitted. Forever is such a big word. Surely, she did not have forever. And what did she mean "*should* have been"?

"What are you talking about?"

Kathleen's humanly face shifted into something darker, more malicious. Her teeth became unto fangs, canine-like. Her eyes were not the ravishing brown eyes. They had become bright reds, the color of sanguine fluid—blood.

"I'm talking about eternity," she informed me. "I promised I would show you everything, Catherine, and I will." She leaned in closer towards me.

I felt frozen solid.

I was numb.

How could I have ever guessed that I would remain that way forever? If it hadn't been for Michael, I would be a statue of glass—fragile, transparent.

I could feel Kathleen breathe onto my neck.

"There's darkness in every man, just as there is a demon in every soul. I'll show you yours, Catherine Opaque. Life is brief, but death is eternal."

My eyelids would not close.

My terrified eyes remained opened.

I wished that I were blind.

Kathleen would have never shown me the temptations of iniquity if I had not been able to see.

It is just the same as the ancient enigma: *If a tree falls in the forest and no one is around to hear it, does it still make a sound?*

No, it does not.

"Death is only the beginning," she whispered into my ears before she tasted me.

IT WAS TRUE, WHAT SHE said, about death being only the beginning.

Death opened doors for me.

No matter what assurances anyone gives you, death is painful.

It may be a sweet release for some, but there is always an evanescent moment of pang.

I remember my moment of pain vividly.

You do not forget your own death as easily as you forget the deaths of others.

I felt my knees go weak as my blood was drained from my young body. Kathleen's lily-white fangs pierced my delicate skin and though I wanted to sink to the ground, she held me up. And I had seen a vision.

An eerie image flashed in my mind's eye.

I saw an arm, a pure snow-white arm holding a black scarf. In slow motion, the black silk scarf slipped from the fingertips of the bloodless hand and hit the ground gently.

I blinked my eyes and shook my head.

Where had such an image come from?

(*Like silk slipping, falling to the ground.*)

She took so much of my blood that I was certain I had probably gone delirious and was just creating things that I had never seen before.

I was certain that she was going to kill me, but then she did something that even the devil had not expected.

"DRINK," THE VAMPIRE TOLD ME.

I am not absolutely certain, but I think that I shook my head in a futile effort of resistance to her commandment.

It did not matter to her, though. Of course not. She was a vampire, a demonic entity and much stronger than I—at the time. She could do with me whatever she pleased and I truly had no say in it.

Kathleen chuckled softly, though there was doubtlessly a tinge of cruelty in her tone.

She tilted my neck away from her and with a sharp nail; she cut herself an inch or so on the side of her neck.

"Drink," she ordered.

No, I had said in my mind.

Drink.

I gasped silently.

Once again, she had invaded my mind. The privacy of my thoughts was violated.

"You'll feel much better," she promised me.

At the moment, my head throbbed from the massive amount of blood loss and I was ready to falter down.

"No," I intoned in a solid voice.

Kathleen laughed and her grip around my neck became tighter as her nails dug into my skin and she pulled me to the open and bleeding wound on her neck.

PREPARING MYSELF FOR THE WORST, I closed my eyes and I felt the jagged rocks and smooth pebbles beneath my bare feet. I opened my eyes and I found myself in a new place. To this day, I haven't a slightest clue of where I was.

I stood in the middle of nowhere.

There was a gentle mist lingering throughout this desolate—and cold—destination.

I shuddered, rubbing my arms.

This was a mysterious land.

My eyes scanned my new surroundings, trying to determine where I was, but I had never been there before.

From out of the mist, right in front of me, two gleaming emerald eyes pierced through the cloudiness.

I was startled and I jumped back.

The two eyes moved away from the mist and towards me. They took on animal form, the form of a beautiful silver-snow wolf.

The silver-snow wolf gazed at me, its otherworldly eyes penetrating my soul.

I was caught in a trance that I could not break away from. The wolf had mesmerized me.

Follow me.

My feet hopped back again. I felt my heart beating rapidly, and then suddenly, the beating slowed down. All I could hear was the beating of my heart, its sluggish pace.

The voice in my mind belonged to the wolf. I know this for sure.

But should *I follow it?* I asked myself.

Follow me, the voice whispered in my mind again.

The wolf turned, as if it knew that I could not refuse, and I faithfully followed it.

The silver-snow wolf disappeared when it gracefully descended a mound. I felt lost when I could no longer see the wolf, my guide in this strange land.

My steps were done with caution as I approached the peak of the mound. I saw the wolf already on even ground. I took a deep breath and began my gradual and wary plunge to the smoother surface where the wolf's powerful paws touched.

Follow me.

I was getting tired of hearing that same utterance. Could it say nothing more, I often wonder. *Certainly a creature as intelligent and cunning as the silver-snow wolf has more to say.*

When my feet were firmly planted on the ground, I looked ahead to see the wolf leading me forward, never once stopping to look back on its trailing traveler.

The mist on this side of the mound was thicker and the wolf disappeared into it.

I entered the mist and all I saw surrounding me were clouds near the ground. I could see nothing beyond the mist, and I nearly missed the soft swaying of the wolf's tail.

Unable to see anything else, I followed the wolf's tail until it finally led me out of the mist.

The place I was now in was the same as the place on the other side of the mound. It looked no different, except for one significant thing: there was a river.

The silver-snow wolf rested on the other side of the river, licking its paws.

The moment it saw me, it put down its paw and stared into my eyes. I wanted to turn my gaze away, but I was under the silver-snow wolf's thrall. There was no escape from it unless it allowed me to.

Drink from the Fountain of Immortality, it instructed.

I thought, *If I do, I would be damned, wouldn't I?*

Drink and unite with the Goddess.

Answer me, I demanded.

Drink and you will know.

I scowled at the wolf. *That does not help me.*

I am not here to help, only to guide.

Guide me to what? I inquired.

Drink and you will find your answers.

I was reluctant to drink from the river, yet I wanted answers. Above all, I wanted to leave that place, wherever I was.

I advanced upon the river.

From a far away distance, the river appeared to be gushing out dark waters, but when I got close enough, I saw that the color of the river was a dark crimson. The color of blood.

Is this blood? I asked, and then looked up at the wolf to receive my answer, although I knew by now that it would answer me in my mind.

The Blood of Life.

I shook my head briskly. *I cannot drink blood. It is against my faith.*

It is the same blood that flows through the veins of all Her beloved children.

I refused to drink it. Preachers had always warned me against any creature that offered me blood. It was a sin to take it.

You will die if you do not drink.

I was terrified. I did not want to die, especially in such a forsaken land. More than ever, I wanted to leave.

Hesitantly, I knelt down beside the river. I looked to my right, to see where the river began, but it only continued. I turned to my left, and still the river seemed to go on and on.

A river of never-ending blood, I thought.

Seeing no other way out, I cupped my hands together and reached into the river.

The silver-snow wolf never took its eyes off of me as I brought my hands to my mouth and swallowed the blood.

The first taste had an odd flavor to it, something quite difficult to describe. But when I swallowed the rest of it, it had the sweetest flavor to it and I suddenly craved for more.

My hands hungrily shot out to the river to gather up more of this luscious liquid, but the eerie howling of the silver-snow wolf stopped me instantly.

The howl echoed back several times before it finally faded away.

I watched the wolf curiously, waiting for an explanation.

Come across the river now, it told me.

I rose to my feet. The river was so wide that I would not be able to make it across in one leap. For me, it would take perhaps three or four leaps before I could make it across.

Step in the river, it said.

I raised my right leg up and plunged it into the warm blood river. I did the same to my left leg and repeated the process until I was nearly across. I paused before I lifted my right leg to land on the ground, contemplating whether or not I should make the final step.

I swallowed my fear and the moment my leg touched the pebbles, I suddenly woke to darkness with no memory of who I was or what had happened.

Everything had become black.

Everything had faded.

I DO NOT REMEMBER EXACTLY what happened during that last moment of my short-lived existence. But I have made assumptions.

Everything seemed blurry when she began to draw blood from my neck. I could not see as clearly. And when I drank the blood she drew from her own neck, everything became pitch black—until my travel to that peculiar world interrupted oblivion.

Now that I think about it now, my opinion has never mattered in anything. As a human, I was born to a rich family; thus, I was showered with gifts of gold and dishes full of diamonds. I was taught what a young woman should learn: knitting and sewing, and my parents even had me learn some opera. Because my family was also prosperous, I was taught how to read and write, whereas most of my peers, females and males alike, were denied of such an education.

I was fortunate, but I never asked to be moneyed nor did I want an education. All I ever wanted to do was watch plays, from comedies to histories to tragedies.

As a vampire, I was changed against my will and forced to commit sins against my faith, for example: murder, the exchanging of blood and the worst crime of them all...forsaking my faith.

Fate has played a cruel hand in my destiny.

LIKE I SAID, I DO not remember the exact details of what happened before I died and was reborn in the same mortal body, but enhanced with preternatural strength and the fluid of immortality.

But I remember what I felt.

I felt...*free.*

The cage of flesh and bones that I was detained in held no meaning when I tasted Kathleen's blood.

Whatever physicality of the human body that I had once possessed vanished and I was floating with no form, just floating through a sky of pure white clouds.

I was happy.

My mortal cell could no longer hold me, keep me captive, and trap me within the walls of skin and blood.

I was free.

I was flying—no, soaring through the air, until I woke up.

That was when I crashed back down to the hell that is Earth and the curse of immortality.

MY HEAD WAS ONCE AGAIN stinging.

I felt the cold ground underneath my dirty fingers.

My eyes were barely even slits.

Darkness enveloped me.

I saw no figures, no faces, no shadows, and no light.

I was hazy. My brain felt literally foggy. It was clouded and I could not think or remember anything. I did not know who I was.

My name escaped my lips, an elusive and lucky rabbit that just barely misses the clutch of a starving and drooling fox.

I licked my lips suddenly.

I tasted a strange flavor on them. It tasted delicious.

I licked my lips again, hoping to savor it, yet craving more and more of this precious liquid that mixed with my own saliva.

"You must eat."

My eyes darted up to the shadow that moved within the shadows taking on substance towards me.

"You are hungry. I can tell. One is always hungry after death."

"Who are you?" I asked the shadow.

There was a momentary pause, as if the shadow was trying to contemplate its answer and with an extreme caution as well.

"The question you should be asking is who you are," the shadow corrected me.

That was when it truly hit, when realization finally sunk in with horror. I did not know who I was.

"Who am I?"

"One of us," it told me.

At this point, the shadow had come close enough that I was now able to see it. It wasn't even an "it" at all. It was a female figure. She was slender, thin, and a shapely young woman, perhaps no older then twenty-five. Her Greek/Portuguese features made an intriguing combination.

But it was her eyes, her chestnut irises that seemed to damn me.

She knew something that I didn't know.

She knew something that she wasn't going to tell me.

"Sophia," she unexpectedly declared.

"Sophia?" I repeated under my breath.

She half-turned, her purple gown swaying behind her.

"Wait!" I beckoned. "Where am I?"

A heartbeat of soundlessness passed.

"Home."

I WAS HOME. I TRULY was.

I was in a state of perpetual darkness and I have remained that way for decades, endless centuries perhaps.

As I have once said, I do not know how long I have been trapped in this prison of stones.

It is impossible to tell now.

The nights and days have merged in a seamless landscape, making it hopeless for me to determine the date from the year that I was caged here to whatever year it is today.

The tally marks in front of me are evidence that I had once attempted to keep count of the days that have passed since my entrapment.

I counted for one hundred twenty-one days, hardly a year, and then I stopped. It was an exercise for me to keep my sanity, but that was unfeasible in a place like this.

It is my torment here.

I have to give Kathleen credit.

Bravo! Bravo!

She is much more intelligent than I have ever given her merit for.

Her plan to isolate me in this stone cell was brilliant!

I, myself, would have never thought of it.

She knew that she could not torture me, not like how *I* could torture myself.

Therefore, she threw me in here and sealed up the wall. And my past and memories keep me company here, while tormenting me at the same time. Bitter comrades we are.

Kathleen sent me to the slaughterhouse so that I would die by the only person who knew how to kill me: myself.

Kathleen would never be able to agonize me as much as I would be able to agonize myself.

Now I am beginning to question my sanity.

Am I crazy?

I am not able to differ the lines between sanity and *in*sanity.

It is only now that I have realized that I have not spoken out loud since Kathleen put me in here.

I have said no words out loud.

I have only spoken in my mind, via my thoughts.

But even in my mortal life, I never used my voice as much as I used my mind.

I think much.

Perhaps I think too much.

When I watched plays in France, I never once spoke during them. I remained utterly silent. I only contemplated the actions and language in my mind. I made no comments about the piece and kept all of my private thoughts to myself.

Yet in this place of vexation where recollections bleed, I think only of my past and the future, never of the present.

I think of how I will meet my maker once again and how I will slaughter her to make even the ones I have loved that she has slaughtered.

Kathleen has butchered many, no doubt, and though she is but one individual, I will make her death equal to the countless deaths suffered at her hand.

My family will be avenged.

My love will be avenged.

My soul will be avenged.

I REMAINED IN THAT PLACE of darkness for perhaps two or three days before my anamnesis returned to me.

It was then that my seething animosity for Kathleen returned and it burned hotter than any fire in hell that preachers in church had threatened me with.

It was also the day that I would see light once for the first time after being brought across the darkness, through the land of the living and the realm of the dead.

Since I woke from my slumber after Kathleen killed me, I had not eaten. I had gone for at least three days without any kind of food and now I was starving.

I was weak from hunger.

My stomach craved for something that I did not understand or know of.

It was not food it wanted.

It was not wine.

There was some other fluid, some other sort of cuisine that my stomach yearned eternally for.

I had found something to sit on, regardless of the fact that this place of darkness was still unnamed to me.

What I sat on was cold and unmistakably, it was made of stone as well. I could smell it; I could smell the musky stones and I could almost taste the dust on my tongue.

Kathleen opened the door.

That was the first time I had ever heard a sound besides my own voice and even then, I did not speak much, little if all.

It was my second day in here that I realized not only could I feel the sun rise and set—though I did not keep count—but I also discovered that I could not breathe. At least, I did not breathe a lot. I tried to inhale the air, but it hurt my lungs to force a contraction in such a manner, as if my lungs had never done so before.

I tried to exhale, but next to nothing came out.

I felt *some* air, true, but not much at all.

Kathleen closed the door as quickly as she had opened it in a lithe movement seemingly reminiscent of a cat. She stalked towards me and I immediately sensed her presence.

Enraged, I rose and picked up the stone bench I had sat on and heaved it above my head.

I threw the stone, aiming for Kathleen, and then missing, although I could see her distinctively amongst the myriad shadows.

The bench shattered when it hit a wall shrouded in darkness and it almost appeared to have crumbled, rather than shattered.

"From that sudden display of brute strength," Kathleen boomed through the quietness, "I assume that you are now ready to face the light of day, figuratively speaking of course."

"You *bitch*," I hissed, making no attempt to conceal the abhorrence I felt towards my malevolent "friend".

I saw Kathleen blink her eyes and flutter her eyelids for a twinkle before she spoke up again. "And I would also assume that you have all your memories back," she uttered.

"Only the ones that involve a *mutt* with brown eyes who claims to be my friend and then betrays me by killing me and then damning me to eternity as a demonic creature who preys on the weak," I countered in one breath, by way of explanation only.

"I'll take that as a yes."

My eyes narrowed. "What do you want, Kathleen?"

"I only want to help you, Sophia," she replied, sounding like a kindred spirit rather than an evil beast. I knew better by then.

"Don't call me that," I seethed. "My name is Catherine, Catherine Diana Opaque."

Kathleen smirked at me. I could not tell if whether she was taunting me or sympathizing me for my foolishness. "Catherine Opaque is *dead*," she confirmed. "You are no longer Catherine, you never really were to begin with. You are now Sophia."

"I am *not* Sophia," I protested, but already I felt that my conviction was disintegrating. Her words were believable and my faith now was frail against the fiery truth behind her voice.

"If you are not Sophia, then go home to your family and see if they will accept you into their house and home after the hell you have put them through over the last week," Kathleen challenged.

"Week?" I reiterated in disbelief. "No, that's not possible. I've been here for only three days."

Kathleen cackled. She tilted her head back and roared hideously. "You've been here for seven days," she averred. "It may have only felt like three to you, but it's been a week."

The thought that this "friend" could have murdered my family instantly entered my mind.

"What have you done to my family?" I questioned her.

Her face was modest. "Nothing," she assured me innocently, though I was not convinced.

I stomped my feet on the ground as I went for the door. I recalled and listened to the sound of the door in my mind and traced for it that way, not even aware of what I was doing.

Before I reached the door, Kathleen's voice called me back.

"That's not such a smart idea, Sophia."

I opened the door while I muttered under my breath, "My name is

Cath—"

I was stopped mid-sentence when an abrupt ray of light flooded through the doorway. I did not shut the door. I did not have time. I felt the sunlight singe my flesh, burn through me as if my arm had been shoved into a fire and I lunged to the right, off to the side.

"I told you," Kathleen mocked.

I shielded my eyes from the light with my forearms. "What in the name of God is going on?" I sought furiously.

"Do you not realize what has happened?" she flung back at me. "You are a vampire, a child of darkness, and ultimately, sensitive to the light." She reconsidered her choice of words. "Well, actually, it's just not good advice to go out into the blazing heat of the afternoon sun so early after you've been changed. You'll be obliterated into black cinders. You have to wait at least seven days after your turning, which is basically today. Once the sun sets, you are free to walk in the night and the next morning, if you wish."

"What about you?" I queried.

"I'm older than you," she said. "The light of the sun does not harm me any longer since I was brought across, although I do find the afternoon sun quite irritable. You probably will, too. You should stay away during the midday, just for your safety. We can be somewhat vulnerable during that time."

I heard her footsteps cross in front of me and then to the door. She stood in front of the lit doorway for ten seconds before she decided to shut the door.

Kathleen slowly turned to face me.

I could still see her clearly even in the lightlessness.

"What do you want with me?" I questioned her.

With my heightened vision, I could see Kathleen put out her wan hand towards me.

She smiled wickedly at me.

"I want to show you the world," she declared.

CHAPTER THREE

εφ

THE WORLD IS A VAMPIRE.

It's cruel and savage and monstrous. It drains the blood of the people. And if it's one thing I learned from Kathleen, it's that blood is life. Blood is everything in this world. It makes you warm, or keeps you cold. Blood is the vital fluid of life. All life exists on blood.

We go right to the source of life itself: blood.

It's easy to see why vampires drink blood to sustain life.

Blood is more than a liquid. It's almost like a drug, if one could call it that. Blood becomes an addiction for vampires, a necessity.

I've attempted to swear off blood, but it's unthinkable for me to do so.

I have failed to keep my oath, just as I have failed to keep every other oath I have made in my life.

Yet there is one oath that I have vowed to keep.

THERE WAS LIFE INSIDE THE mansion. The wealthiest man in town, Harris Gibson, was throwing a bash for no particular reason except to show off his fortune. It was not necessary for him to throw together a superb soiree for others to understand that his riches were abundant. It was evident in the well-tailored and expensive suits he wore and the diamond cuffs around his wrists.

My family and I had spent time with him in his majestic mansion. Of course, he owned more than one mansion in more than one country.

From what I remember, Harris Gibson made his riches off of slaves that labored tirelessly in his diamond mine. He had his own boutique named Gibson Diamonds. He owned several boutiques in France, Germany, and Madrid. The Gibson Diamond business was something that had been passed down from father to son for generations. Harris's father, Demetrius Gibson, left the company to his oldest son in his will. Harris then inherited the company and spent more time flaunting his precious stones rather than running the business his father entrusted him with.

Kathleen had brought me here.

For what reason, I was unsure of.

It was the first time that I had gotten outside since I had been *changed* and she brought me to a place where hundreds of humans were alive with energy and joy.

I could sense it from the outside.

I could sense the happiness from all the attendees and I understood it. To be in the presence of someone as wealthy as Harris Gibson and to be allowed entrance to mingle inside his estate was an offer that rivaled immortality, eternal youth and beauty.

I looked at the latter offer as a curse.

I did not ask to take it.

I was simply given it.

I hid underneath the shades of the thick evergreen trees that stood a few yards away from the entrance to the lively and bright mansion. I knew that Kathleen was inside somewhere, in full party mode. Festivities and celebrations were Kathleen's specialty, no matter what the occasion.

I did not want to be seen. I wanted to be out of view, to fade away forever into the darkness of the shade and become a shadow.

Amazingly enough, that's exactly what happened in my later years.

"What's a lovely young lady like you doing out here all alone and by yourself?"

I darted around.

Though I had slightly sensed the arrival of this individual, I had not been prepared by the suddenness of his approach.

He was a handsome young man, though not my preference.

His age bracket appeared to be somewhere in between mid-twenties to early thirties.

He had dark hair tied back in a ponytail with a ribbon. His lower lip was slightly bigger and fuller than his top lip. His eyes were brown and huge. And in his hands were two glasses of crimson wine.

I was hesitant to reply, but I did.

"Just lurking around," I asserted with a seductive grin.

He gestured with the glasses in his hands. "You should be inside, enjoying the food and entertainment Sir Gibson has provided us with," he offered and then glanced at me from top to bottom and reconsidered his words. "Or is it that you don't eat?"

I was thin. I've always been thin. My mother was thin herself and her waist was tiny. I suppose it was something I had inherited from my mother's side of the family. I could eat like an African elephant and not gain a single pound.

It was at the end of the man's comment that my hunger suddenly struck me. My stomach was full of emptiness and yet there was a vast void unfulfilled.

The stranger put out his hand. "My name is Leander Lloyd," he introduced. "What's your name, lass?"

I always hated being called lass.

I hesitated momentarily. I was going to tell him my full name, the one that I had been given at birth, but I thought better of it.

"Sophia," I answered, putting my hand in his.

After all, was I not Sophia?

Leander's eyes brightened. "Lovely name," he complimented before he planted a gentle kiss on the back of my hand.

To my surprise, I found that I could read his mind. It was an accident. His thoughts suddenly intruded mine and it was as if he had spoken; yet he had not opened his mouth to produce a syllable.

I knew what his intentions were, the same as every scoundrel who passed himself as a man.

He wanted to make love to me.

He found that I was attractive and alone, the perfect combination for him.

I smiled at him. "Have you come to flirt with me or do you plan on something bigger?" I asked him.

My words were unexpected, direct, and not to mention correct. My words were so frank and undiluted that it caught him off guard. I could tell, not only from the bewildered expression on his face, but from his thoughts.

Leander's smile was enigmatic, full of many secrets and desires. He said nothing in response. He simply offered his hand again and I took it.

THE MARBLE STATUE MY BACK was pressed against was cold to the touch, colder than my own skin. I sometimes worried that I would become as cold as the marble statue. The statue was in Harris Gibson's private garden. It appeared that Leander somehow gained access to it.

There were many statues in Gibson's Greek-flavored garden. It just so happened that the marble statue I leaned against was a female angel with outstretched wings and arms wide open, ready to accept anyone who came into her arms.

Leander covered my neck with sloppy kisses.

The kisses I returned were just as passionate, if not, more than his were.

But it wasn't quite passion that I felt.

I cared nothing for this mortal.

He was just a man willing to do anything to get what he wanted.

I made it easy for him.

But I did not want his body or anything else that he wanted to offer me.

I wanted something that was strictly off-limits by God's principles.

I wanted his life.

I wanted his blood.

As his desire to have me grew, my craving became unbearable to the point that I could not stand it any longer.

"Ravage me," I whispered into his ears.

He had enough time to retort. "I thought young ladies don't like to be ravaged," he breathed onto my neck.

I clutched a handful of his dark hair and I suddenly felt my face change as I announced, "I'm not a lady."

At those words, Leander looked up at me and his eyes froze open when he saw the demonic entity that had fallen upon him.

He was about to yelp like a ten-year-old girl when I covered his mouth with my hand, muffling his scream as I lowered my head and pierced his rough skin with my fangs.

Instantly, I felt his blood pour into my mouth.

It was a warm, relaxing elixir for me.

It was a mixture of sweet honey and rich chocolate.

I wondered if I had been human, would I still have thought the same way of the taste of his blood? Would it still have tasted candy-coated and honeyed? Would it still hold its forbidden appeal?

But then I wondered if all humans felt this way about blood if they ever tasted it.

Perhaps you didn't have to have the taste buds of a vampire to taste the saccharine of his blood. Maybe the taste buds were the same and it was in all humans.

Leander's blood issued into my mouth like a gushing torrent and I found it hopeless to remove myself, even though my heart told me that it was wrong. It was against God's laws.

I closed my eyes and allowed the blood to flow into my mouth when suddenly, I was struck with images that caused me to open my eyes and gasp out loud.

When I opened my eyes, it was not the garden that I saw.

I saw images, excerpts almost, from Leander's incredibly boring and promiscuous life. He was nothing more than a scoundrel with the worst tastes in women ever.

After all, he had chosen me.

These images flashed before my eyes and stopped only when I yanked myself away from Leander, though I was still reeling from the odd occurrence.

Leander fell to the ground unconscious, but I knew that he would not die. I had not taken enough blood to kill him, just enough to satisfy my hunger for the time being.

I supported myself against the marble statue, unable to comprehend what I had seen or why I had seen it.

Kathleen appeared from the darkness. "It's a rush," she stated. She had seen everything.

"What *was* that?" I interrogated, baffled beyond my understanding.

Kathleen's eyes fixed on Leander's body. "Blood is life, Sophia," she educated. "You took his blood and you saw his life. Blood contains memories and now you share his. He's a part of you now and his memories will be with you for as long as you are alive."

"But how?" I glanced at her, expecting an answer. "How could I have seen what I saw?"

"I promised I would show you the world and everything in it," she began, "including life. This is only the beginning. There's more to come. Life isn't the only thing that exists in this world."

I HAVE NEVER BEEN ABLE to stop thinking about Leander. Kathleen was telling the truth. I took some of his blood and with it came some of the many memories from his life. They were now with me forever, for as long as I had his blood inside my veins. He was part of me, now. He and I were intertwined.

Kathleen had explained to me that because of this, she was always careful of who she chose to feed off of because they would be with her forever.

I once asked her how she could possibly live with something like this and she told me that it only got easier the more and more you drank. After a while, all the memories kind of blended into each other and got blurry until the point that you could not tell which one was which and who it had belonged to.

But you never forgot that they were a part of you forever.

CHAPTER FOUR .

εφ

I LAUGH TO MYSELF IN this silent prison. I've spent most of my immortality here. Life is brief compared to death. Death, on the other hand, is eternal. I am "living" proof of that.

I gaze around at the blood markings on the cold stone and I scramble to my feet and gently stroke the smooth, imperfect vertical lines on the ragged surfaces.

I sigh to myself, in awe at these fine markings.

Here is my proof, God, that at one point long ago, I attempted to hold onto my humanity and cling onto the mortal world with all my will and power.

Yet I failed.

One hundred twenty-one days went by and I renounced this daily task of recording each sun and moon that passed by.

You can hardly blame me.

It was once said that if you go one week without natural sunlight, you would go insane.

I am a vampire; should I have lost my sanity? —I doubt it. Vampires don't need natural sunlight any more than we need artificial light.

Our eyes adjust quite well to the darkness and since we tend to thrive more under the cover of darkness, our exceptional vision is a necessity.

I collapse onto my knees and bury my face onto the unclean ground.

For no reason in particular, I begin to weep.

PERHAPS I WEEP BECAUSE I continue to mourn for my soul as well as for the souls of others. So much pain. So much sorrow.

Years have passed by—I am certain of it—and still time has not allowed me a proper period of grief.

I have spent so many hours scheming my vengeance that I have not cried suffice tears to requite the loss in my soul and heart.

I thought that my grief was finished long ago, but that does not seem to be the case.

I suppose I haven't allowed myself the time.

I have spent far too much time thinking about Kathleen and Michael and Christine and all the others, who I wish not to think about, yet cannot help but to.

In my muffled sobs, I descend into an eerie reverie plagued by these innocent faces.

Oh, my dear Christine, how I miss her so much.

Her sinless features remind me of happier days when smiles were more often and laughter could be heard for hours upon end.

I can recall her face, her exquisite porcelain face with excruciating details.

How can I ever forget her? —My beloved Christine.

"ARE YOU STILL UPSET ABOUT what happened with that scoundrel you picked up at Gibson's mansion?"

We sat at a dinner table inside an estate that Kathleen had seized control of. She killed the owners and took over. It was only temporary, of course. It was just a place for her to stay until she chose to move on.

I said nothing.

That alone was enough for Kathleen.

She glanced at the silver salad fork she had been rapping against the polished table. With an aggravated sigh, Kathleen put down her pronged utensil and she interlaced her delicate, white fingers.

I sat across from her, at the far end of the table.

I did not wish to speak to her, but my own silence did not do much to silence her.

She was, of course, referring to the little "incident" I had with the Leander fellow; the things that I had seen from excerpts of Leander's life had not escaped my thoughts since.

Kathleen folded her arms on the table and rested her chin on her hands. "What can I do to make you forget about him?" She pondered her own question. She snapped her fingers suddenly. "Ah-ha! Jewels, perhaps? Emeralds, rubies, sapphires?"

Kathleen already knew me too well. She knew about my weakness towards sparkling materials.

My face remained expressionless, blank. *I will always love the glitter of multi-colored gemstones but tonight, they mean nothing to me.*

Kathleen returned to thinking. Then the realization sunk into her and lit up her facial cast. "I know!" she chirped. "You're just hungry!"

I scoffed and turned my head away.

"I know the feeling, Sophia, believe me, I do," she went on. "What would you like? —Perhaps a man better looking than Leander? I know plenty of handsome men; all you have to do is ask."

I made no motion of response.

"Ahh...I understand now. You don't want soiled blood, contaminated with age. You want pure, innocent blood. You want the blood of a chi—"

I snapped.

I slammed my fist onto the table, rattling the contents on top, and I rose from my seat as if I had never been sitting on it.

"Damn it, Kathleen!" I snarled. "Don't you understand? I don't want to *kill* anyone! I don't want to *hurt* anyone!"

Unlike me, Kathleen kept her patience in check. "You may not want to, but you don't have a choice, Sophia. It's in your nature; it's in your blood to kill people, to hurt them anyway you can. Why deny it any further? You're only prolonging the pain. You don't have to feel the sting of the bloodthirst. Quench it and let it be done with."

"It *won't* be done with!" I growled back at her. "I will drink and then tomorrow night I will have to drink again and again and again."

"Well, of course," Kathleen replied. "Of course you'll need to feed again. A human can't live off of one meal. He must eat again and again to sustain living. You expect to drink once and be full forever? You're stupider than you look, Sophia."

Through gritting teeth, I hissed, "Choose your words carefully, Kathleen."

"Or what?" the vampire mocked. "You'll *kill* me?"

She snickered in an insane laughter, the one she was always so good at.

I balled my fists. "At the moment, it's not a very bad idea," I told her.

"On the contrary, it is a very bad idea indeed," Kathleen insisted. "If you kill me now, you'll never get the answers to the questions you so sorely seek."

My ears perked up. Indeed, my curiosity was great. I had many questions, but no answers yet.

"I'm listening," I said softly.

Kathleen gestured to my chair. "Sit down and we will talk. I will tell you what you wish to know."

I sat in the chair, but I did not allow myself to relax until I got the first answer to one of my several questions.

Kathleen's nonchalant attitude unnerved me. She should be shivering like I was; she should be vibrating as if she were at an earthquake, like I was.

"What do you want to know?"

"Tell me about us, what we are, where we came from," I said. "Tell me anything about our kind."

Kathleen's brows arched. "Are you certain? Truth is often painful."

"I don't care."

Kathleen exhaled before she began telling me the "truth".

"Vampires, immortals, whatever you want to call us, we're above humans," she started. "They should be bowing at our feet and instead we move among them like silent mice, afraid of them, these lower beings. We have powers. Our powers are all the same, or at least accurately similar. Some of us are stronger than others and some of us are weaker than others. It all depends."

"On what?" I interrupted.

"On the power of their maker and on the power itself," Kathleen answered. "It also has to do with how much you feed or how much you practice your powers. If you seldom use your gifts, they will fade and though they will always be there, your power may not reach its full potential. Furthermore, you must feed in order to feed your supply of power, to make it stronger."

Instantly I brought up all the stories and legends I had heard of vampires.

"What can kill us? Can a stake through the heart kill us?" I asked, impetuously.

"*Stakes*?" she repeated, incredulously. "No, not stakes. No mallets, either. A blade will do the job."

"Why a blade?"

"Because it was a blade that was plunged through the heart of the Demon Queen, thus destroying her, making it the only weapon capable of annihilating Her beloved children. Blades are flawless and lethal, beautiful but deadly."

I pondered this. "If I were to drive a blade through my heart—"

Kathleen made a dismissive sound. "Don't be silly. You don't *drive* a blade through a vampire's heart; you stab the heart and if you can, you drive the blade all the way through. Twist it if you have to, but always be certain that the blade has punctured the heart until the blood has poured from it."

"If I was stabbed with a blade, would I turn into ashes or dust?"

"You would turn into ashes," Kathleen confirmed. "Fire can also kill you."

I urged her forward. "Anything else that I must beware of? Garlic? Holy water? Crosses? Beheadings?"

"Childish things, those," Kathleen snickered, appearing tired from the conversation already. "Garlic is never a pleasant smell for anyone. If you have the heightened senses of a vampire, you would not find garlic very pleasant. But that is not to say, of course, that it terrifies us or causes us to recoil in terror."

"What of holy water?"

"Holy, consecrated, divine, it doesn't matter what you call it. It's still water and we can drink water if we choose. And crosses, crucifixes. Tsk, tsk. For some, they are terrible things. For others, they are welcoming sights. But do not expect us to shriek if someone should happen to shove one in our face."

I continued my interrogation. "Beheadings?" I asked her.

"When done with the proper techniques and the right blade, someone could cleave our heads cleanly from our necks and cause us to turn into ashes."

"Coffins?" I prodded.

This question gave Kathleen slight grief.

"Hmm…Well, personally, I think coffins are much too confined for my liking. I prefer a room with a view. But I suppose that if you wish for the air-tightness of a room, where you can't toss or turn, you should sleep in a coffin if that's what suits you best, but it's not necessary. The first vampires used to sleep in coffins, and some still do, only as a way of maintaining tradition."

My head swirled with this new knowledge about the definition of vampirism.

"Is there any myth about vampires that's true?"

"If there were, they wouldn't be called myths, now would they?" she shot back.

I was annoyed by her response and my face mirrored that irritation. "So everything that is spoken of vampires for centuries is fiction?"

"Now, I didn't say that," Kathleen said. "Just not everything you hear is true. Some of us can fly, if our powers and strength allows us to. More often than not, the case is that we are swift creatures and if we choose, we can move too quickly for any human eyes to see. We can read minds, influence the thoughts of others. But flying and telepathy are not easily done. It often takes an absurd amount of concentration to learn these things, if you really want to be good at it. For some, it is difficult, and for others, it comes natural for them and the skill is remarkable. But that is only for the blessed few."

I thought about any other question that I wanted to ask her, about this new life, this immortality I was given.

But vampires were not immortal.

Kathleen had just explained to me the many ways that vampires could die. But what separated vampires from mortals was that mortals *will* die; vampires *can* die.

"How do I *make* a vampire?"

The question surprised me as much as it surprised Kathleen, but she had an answer to practically everything.

"Why? Do you have anyone in mind?" she questioned.

Catalina Chao

"No," I snapped. "No one. I just want to know in case there is ever a reason for me to."

Kathleen propped her elbows onto the table and rested her chin on her interlocked fingers. "It's simple to make a vampire. You simply drink their blood to the point of death—until your victim is lingering in the land of the living and the domain of the dead and then you cut yourself and give him your blood to replace what he has lost. The more blood you give your victim, the stronger he will be. It's all about the blood. It's always about the blood."

"How long before the person ..." I trailed off, uncertain of how to finish the question I had started.

"Dies?" Kathleen said for me. "The human self of the person dies the moment you give him your own blood. Your vampire blood destroys any trace of humanness and replaces it with the blood of a demon. After the blood has been exchanged, the person will fall into a black unconscious state; it is just the mortal self dying and when they wake up, they usually do not remember anything. It is usually only when they feed that they begin to remember events acutely."

"But all those memories ..." I murmured under my breath. Yes, I still breathed, though it was only about a breath per minute. It was not constant and it was not necessary, but it was natural.

"Oh, you mean those memories you saw when you fed on Leander? Yes, well, if you practice and exercise your powers enough, especially your mind-altering abilities, you can learn to shield your mind with invisible walls of magick, almost like force-fields of power. And if you can do that, you can learn to easily block the memories of others from you while you feed. You do not have to keep every gift you receive, Sophia. But I'm still very careful about who I choose to feed on. There is no need for carelessness."

I brought up another question immediately as soon as she finished her answer. "Can you read my mind?"

"You mean, can the maker read the fledgling's mind? Yes, I can. I can read your mind quite well, actually. But in time, you can learn how to shield me from your thoughts, if you are indeed that powerful."

I contemplated all this information, judging if it would be of any use for me.

But then I wondered something else. *A curious student, I am.*

"Are there any others like us?" I asked her, my maker.

"Alas, I grow tired of educating you about your own origin," Kathleen concluded. "Experience is the wisest teacher, Sophia. You must experience these things before you learn them."

"Just tell me, Kathleen, are there any other vampires?"

Kathleen met my fierce glare.

"What if there are? What should you do then? Seek them out? Invite them to our lair? Ask them to educate you?"

I did not cease my barrage of questions. They came at her, like darts on a board. "What about *your* maker?"

"What *about* her?" Kathleen echoed.

"What was her name? What was she like?"

Kathleen rose from her seat. "Her name is not important. She is none of your concern."

"But tell me, Kathleen, what was she like?"

Without warning, her temper erupted and she pounded her firm fist into the table, breaking the beautiful table into two uneven halves.

"Vampires can have strength up to a hundred men," Kathleen informed me. "Depending on the amount of power. We can crush human ears with our words, shatter glass with our screams, or break anything that can and can't be broken."

Her eyes were dangerous, warning me to back away.

"We shall speak nothing more of my maker," she declared and turned her back on me.

End of discussion.

I REMEMBER HER RAGE CLEARLY. She was vexed when I brought up the question of her maker. *What could have caused such a vexation?* I often wonder. I will never know. She never told me.

Her past was painted scarlet.

She never spoke much of how she came to be or who created her. She avoided the subject altogether, as if it would hurt her to speak of her history.

I guess I will never know why it pained her so much.

She concealed the pain under a mask of false strength but I saw past that, just as she saw past my own mask of abhorrence.

Neither one of us could hide from the other, no matter how hard we tried.

I hated the fact that she was always right about me.

She knew things about me before *I* knew them.

I loathe that.

Why does it seem as if the adversaries always know the truth, even though they lie themselves?

Hmm...This puzzles me, intrigues me beyond curiosity.

I still do not know enough about my powers, my strength.

I did not receive the opportunity to test the full potential of my powers. I don't know what I can or I can't do. I can do some things.

After I was changed, I picked up the basic skills I needed for survival.

But honestly, I would rather have died than to have survived this long.

There is no way I can die here in this stone chamber.

Kathleen explained to me the four different ways that vampires could die: blade through the heart, fire, beheading, and magick.

Yes, magick.

Even if there were people who were impervious to manmade weapons—though I doubt such an existence—magick always had a different set of rules for the same game.

I found this out early on in my vampire days.

I do not think that there are any other ways that vampires can be killed besides the above mentioned. But Kathleen was always lying to me. She could have kept secret something that she didn't want to tell me, something that might bring about my own undoing.

Kathleen cannot be trusted.

I found that out much too late.

At first, when she answered my burning questions, I was not certain that Kathleen was a reliable source of truth *or* information.

In fact, I tested my own immortality.

I drove a stake through my heart; I did not die. Even if I had, it would not have mattered. I did not burst into a cloud of ashes. I watched the sun rise—at first, it hurt my eyes like a searing cauterized blade, but I adjusted to it, though not as quickly as I could adjust to the darkness.

When Kathleen threw me into this dungeon of despair, she made certain that there would be no way that I could kill myself; no, she wouldn't make it that easy, that simple for me, to just take my own life. But to hate, that is simple, all too simple.

Perhaps there is something still that Kathleen has not told me.

Well, that's just lovely.

That brings me back to square one: Kathleen cannot be trusted.

It just occurred to me that perhaps Kathleen is already dead.

Perhaps someone has already robbed me of my justice, my glory, my vengeance. Then, if that is so, there is no reason for me to go on with my tortured existence. I might as well die.

But alas, I cannot die.

Kathleen made sure of it.

What if she is dead? Would I be free and allowed to cross over to the other side where Michael, Christine, and my family are waiting for me?

No. It cannot be.

I still feel Kathleen's presence.

Her existence is powerful.

She once told me that the maker has a connection to the one who she makes. I imagine she still has a connection to me and I, to her, though my skills are not quite as sharpened as hers are.

I learned how to block my thoughts, but Kathleen has probably forgotten about me.

And there is always the possibility that she *could* be dead. Although, she was rather cunning. It would be difficult to kill someone like her, in spite of the fact that she has come close enough for Death to kiss her and yet she has always escaped His lips.

But I am Death.

I am the Avenging Dark Angel, unforgiving, relentless, and merciless.

I will give Kathleen the final kiss.

The Black Kiss of Death.

THE NEXT FEW DAYS OVERWHELMED me. The bloodthirst intensified every morning and every night. My eyes bled into the crimson tint when the bloodthirst overcame me at times. My usually normal teeth grew into threatening canine fangs. I often ran screaming through the colossal, vacant halls of Kathleen's stolen estate. I just wanted to muster all the ache that the bloodthirst left me with in an elongated scream of frustration and anguish.

Kathleen found it amusing to watch me suffer, to watch me torment myself. But she knew that I was *so* good at it. No one could make me suffer as much as I could myself.

During my screaming spells, she perched on the railing of the staircase, watching me as I raced back and forth through the marble hallway like I was on fire, entertained by my agony.

She had a perfect seat: front row and center.

There was no one else in the estate to hear my woeful screams.

The estate itself was isolated from the rest of the town like a recluse living in perpetual solitude.

There was no life anywhere near us.

It was just the two undead immortals in the luxurious property.

It was as if I had gone on a fast; I swore off blood of any kind. Even the occasional rat that scampered across the marble floor could trigger my bloodlust, but I refused to give in.

I had convinced myself that if I yielded to draining the blood of a mouse, I could just as easily submit into the draining of an innocent human being.

Five weeks after I swore off blood—that is thirty-five days after I had been changed—I was continuing the customary routine.

I ran through the halls of the estate when the moon hit its highest hour: midnight, the Devil's Hour.

It was only then that the impulse to kill had reached its maximum pinnacle. It was at Devil's Hour precisely that my natural, instinctual craving for warm, living blood reached its zenith. It was then that I could hold off no more.

You must understand something here.

I was a young vampire, still, about a month old and I had drunk only a pint of blood from Leander. After that, there was no more blood. For vampires who have fed early on in their vampire days, it is much easier for them to keep their vow. But I was still new at all this. I had barely fed and I needed to do it. Everything in my body yearned for it; needed it, wanted it. To want is often worse than to need. For we want more than we need. And I needed blood. I did not deny it. I needed it, I just refused to want it, to have it, to give in though I already sensed that my resolve was wavering.

Kathleen took her usual seat at the stair railing and I thundered up the stairs, yanking my hair. I actually managed to pull out some clumps of it.

I raged through the estate.

I ripped my dress, exposing most of my milk-white bosom.

I felt as if my dress were confining me and that if I did not have it on, it could not suffocate me as much as it did.

But this staircase had two more that followed after it that would eventually lead me to the third floor where Kathleen would be sitting, leveled with the chandelier on the high-raised roof.

By the time I reached the second stair landing, I had already shredded the outer layer of my dress, the thinnest part.

There were two more layers separating the fabric from my sheer nakedness.

I bellowed.

I heard my bellow echo back to me in the estate.

It was the bloodthirsty scream of a maniacal, starving immortal.

Kathleen had warned me several times that a vampire was at his most murderous state when he was going through bloodthirst.

"Never approach a vampire who has yet to feed. That's when vampires are most unstable and deadly. They are risky and will do anything to anyone for no reason at all, just out of the agony the bloodthirst creates if it is not appeased."

But Kathleen was not afraid of me, not in the least.

She took undeniable pleasure and giddy in my pain.

She was like a vulture circling a wounded and dying prey. Soon it would give up and she would swoop down in merriment and grasp her prey. For one's death is another's life.

I was approaching the third stair landing at a rapid rate, faster than that of normal.

I tripped over the second to the last step and I doubled forward.

Infuriated, I tore off the second to the last layer of my dress, leaving only my thin, transparent gossamer slip, which was as white as the snow that fell in the Paris streets.

I crawled up the last stair and crawled on my hands and knees to the center of the hallway where Kathleen would be waiting for me with a kind of rapture that I would never know.

How could she watch a creature suffer?

How could anyone watch anyone suffer?

Kathleen cackled when she saw me crawling.

This was the worst night up to date.

I knelt on the ground and stared at the ceiling. I let out a savage, inhuman scream that would shatter the eardrums of any mortal—and possibly a vampire as well—who was in the appropriate vicinity. But there was an expanse of two miles between this estate and another.

Only Kathleen was there to witness my pain and my suffering, just as she had done all along.

I felt my eyes wash into the color of blood. My mouth was wide open and I knew that my full vampiric nature was revealing itself with my fangs as well as my eyes.

My stomach tightened, as if someone had tied strings to both sides and were jerking them. A bolt of lightning struck me so suddenly, caught me completely off guard, even though I had been experiencing this same pain for around thirty nights a row. It did not ease the suffering any less.

I collapsed onto the ground, burying my face on the cold floor, welcoming the rush of a winter breeze on my scorching face.

I heard Kathleen laugh again, though her voice sounded so far away to me, as if she had been buried underneath the thickest fabrics.

"It would be much easier if you just gave into it, instead of fighting it," Kathleen persisted. "I admire your fortitude, Sophia, but even that can dissolve and fade away. It has been quite a fulfilling experience to watch you suffer as you do and to witness your courage in your perseverance, but surely you do not believe that you can keep this up forever."

I chuckled painfully as I muttered as clearly as I could: "Forever is exactly how long I've got."

CHAPTER FIVE

εφ

KATHLEEN LOOKED LIKE SHE WAS ready to burst. She had held onto her tolerance the same way I had held onto my resolution, but she teetered where I was solid.

It was not an easy thing to do.

It was like a ferocious battle taking place underneath the surface of my skin. It was like all wars: brutal and unending, no hope for peace even if it was declared.

True, I held on as long as I could, but I felt as if this would be my last night, the last night that I would be able to handle this starvation.

Kathleen was ready to give up, as I was.

But she snapped a moment before I did, a split second before I caved in she did. Nevertheless, one moment—a split second—can make all the difference in the world.

Kathleen hopped down from her precious railing and seized me by the hair, grabbing a handful of it and pulling it along as she ruthlessly dragged me down the stairs behind her.

My spirit died out.

I remained lifeless and conforming. It was no use to struggle, to fight anymore.

I felt nothing as my back hit step after step, as my head did.

If I were human, I would have either developed several bruises on my body, or I would have died from the head injury.

But I am not human, I reminded myself. I had rapid healing powers. As bruises were being created, they were also being healed.

I closed my eyes. I could barely see where Kathleen was taking me. But it wasn't long before I felt the cool breeze of the night air caress my hot skin. I felt the grass on my legs and then I felt the smooth hair of a fine mare.

Kathleen flung me over the mare, half of my body dangling on one side and the other half flopping lifelessly on the other side.

Kathleen sat in front of me and she clutched the reins and then slapped them onto the mare's neck, riding him forward.

I opened my eyes occasionally only to see the gravel road underneath me. I felt nauseated and weak.

Wherever Kathleen was taking me, it was a long, rocky road.

SHE DRAGGED ME TO THE front steps of a place I had never dared to set foot in since I had been reborn into the realm of eternal night. But she had brought me here for some reason or another. She had brought me to the Opaque Household for some malevolent purpose. That much I knew.

"Get on your feet," she demanded harshly, helping me to stand on my own legs, though she did it with no sense of compassion or affection in any of her rough movements.

My eyelids slowly lifted themselves and I found myself staring at the entrance door to my home, the one I had had when I was still Catherine Diana Opaque.

But it seemed like an eternity had divided my days as Catherine Opaque from my days as Sophia.

I was so weak. So tired. So helpless. So will-less.

I felt Kathleen breathing down my neck.

"They're inside. All of them. They're all sleeping inside that cozy home, forgotten all about you. Make them remember again," she pressed. "Take them. Take them all."

My eyes widened at the prospect of slaughtering my whole entire family as well as the one servant who used to wait on me hand-in-foot. I missed them all.

A great sadness tore at me.

Kathleen sensed it and she would have none of it.

"Kill them, Sophia. You feel it. You need to feed. You need to enjoy your immortality. I didn't make you a vampire so you could suffer for all of your eternity."

"That's *exactly* what you did!" I snapped at her, remembering, with hatred, back to the day when she had changed me in the cemetery. "You damned me to hell!"

I sank to my knees.

"I gave you what you wanted!" Kathleen hurled back at me.

"I didn't want any of this! I didn't ask for this! You gave me a one way ticket to hell!"

"You don't have to go anytime soon!" Kathleen shouted at me, matching my voice level.

I was amazed that no one had opened their windows to look outside at the barking voices.

"You've sent me to hell!" I roared.

"Then we shall keep each other company in the fiery pits of Mephistopheles' domain!"

I sobbed. "I don't want to go to hell!" I confessed.

Kathleen's voice calmed, as if she was soothing a restless child. "It's too late. Come now, Sophia. You're hungry. You're lusting for the finest of blood. What is better than taking the lives of your family?"

I glared at the house.

My eyes became tinged with red again and my incisors were sharp against my tongue.

"Good ..." Kathleen whispered. "Do it. It'll be easy. No regret. No sorrow. No more pain. And no more suffering, Sophia."

Gradually, I stood up—my legs heavy like lead—and with a gentle push from Kathleen, I stalked towards the front door.

I GRABBED THE DOOR KNOCKER and slammed it against the door, curbing my strength so that I would not accidentally destroy the door. Two knocks later, a servant came to the door.

It was Hosanna. Good old Hosanna.

She had taken care of me very well when I was younger, when my mother was much too busy looking pretty than being a mother.

Hosanna was in her mid-forties and her hair was graying. She had black warts on her light brown-skinned face and pale pink lips with her honey brown eyes. Recognition instantly lit up her face.

"Catherine?" she asked in that thick Spanish accent I loved so much.

Before she could say another word, I reached for her and drew her in. It wasn't long before I pierced her dark skin with my fangs and I let the satisfaction the blood gave me fill the bloodthirst. I held her greedily, keeping her on her feet when her knees gave out. I saw an image.

I was a child again and running through a field of wildflowers. I was six years old and I was carefree and young at heart forever. Hosanna came to fetch me. Her voice called out my name: "Catherine! Little Catherine? Where are you? Are you playing in the fields again? You know that they make you sneeze!"

The image came to an abrupt halt when I released Hosanna and she sunk onto the ground.

I was awash in the blood. I allowed it to soak me as if it were some kind of lethargic drug.

I entered through the open door and the homeliness and recognition that this place had been my home for almost twenty years instantly welcomed me.

"Hosanna? Who was that at the door?"

A familiar voice.

I was in joy when I saw my father come out of his room. He was in his nightwear with a sleeping cap on. His black beard had grown almost out of control. For just a second—*just* a second—I wondered what it would be like to curl the ends of his beard and pretend it was a fuzzy curtain as I had done when I was younger.

My father's cobalt blue eyes brightened just as Hosanna's had, except that the brightness in my father's eyes was almost blinding.

"Catherine?" he whispered, stunned to see me yet experiencing an inexplicable happiness.

"Get away from me!" I howled at him, recoiling for my father's protection, knowing that I aroused the rest of the family.

In his foolishness, my father reached out for me with his hands, with wide open arms ready to welcome me back in spite of all I had done since I had left.

"I knew that I would see you again. Catherine—"

"Father, *no!*" I roared.

He came closer and out of pure instincts, I lashed out at him.

I dug my nails into his shoulders as I pulled him towards me and my fangs broke his gentle skin before he could murmur another word.

I closed my eyes.

How could I bear to see my own father die at my hands?

But my eyes popped open suddenly when an image like a shock of lightning struck me in my heart.

Sir Wesley Opaque searched the living room with a playful grin on his face. "Catty? Where are you, Catty?"

He looked behind his favorite armchair and there he lifted her up into his arms and kissed her on her cheek.

"There you are!" he declared with profound happiness at having found his five-year-old daughter, Catherine Opaque, whom I was no more.

"How come you can find me, Daddy?"

Such an innocent face and smile.

A strange thing occurred then. One of my own memories intertwined with my father's, interrupting my father's recollection.

Christine.

There she was, a face that flashed in front of my eyes and disappeared as quickly as it had come.

It was just the father and daughter now.

"It's magick," he said, laughing at such insidious things. "I can do magick."

He set her down on his lap after he sat on his armchair.

"Magick like witches?" she asked him.

"No, no. Witches aren't real. Magick like love. Love Magick."

The girl was confused. "What's Love Magick?"

"Hmm...How do I define Love Magick? It's the most powerful magick on Earth, stronger than you and I. Stronger than life and death itself. Stronger than hate and vengeance."

The little daughter was baffled again by her father's choice of words. "What's vengeance?" she asked him.

She curled the tips of her father's beard.

Her father thought about the question. He repeated it to himself before answering it. "Vengeance is something that I hope you will never know."

Before I knew it, I dropped my father and he fell lifeless on the carpet. I was disturbed by my father's memories. Such strange things that he had told me in my childhood.

I was in a fit of rage.

I did not know what I was doing.

I did not know how to stop drinking before the point of death.

It was not long before the rest of my family lay dead on the Persian rug before me: my mother—Lady Opaque—and my brothers, Peter and Jacob.

My mother had come out to inspect the noises she heard. She screamed when she saw her husband lying dead on the floor and I had no choice but to cover her mouth to muffle her scream, and in the process, I saw her tender neck and I bit down on it before I could get self-control.

But my innocent brothers.

They shouldn't have waken up either, but after hearing my mother's ear-splitting scream they woke from their dreams only to be killed by their sister.

When I drained the blood of each and every one of them, I saw moving pictures, memories of my childhood with them.

Strange, it was, that they would remember such things.

I stood in front of the hearth, holding my hands to the light from the burning fire.

So much blood.

There was so much blood on my hands.

I turned my hands, examining them, displaying them for all the world to see, but everyone refused to look upon them.

Only then did the full events of tonight hit me.

Dazed, I stumbled out of the house that had once been mine and I stalked the streets, uncertain of both my journey and my destination.

All around me, the buildings faltered in my vision and I found it impossible to stand on my legs. I slumped against the back of a tavern.

I was not sure how far away I was from the death scene, but I was glad that I put distance between that horrid house and me.

Never do I want to return there.

Oddly, I was weak, even though I had just fed.

I couldn't believe how exhausted I was.

Because I was so exhausted, I was caught completely off guard when someone launched a dagger at me, embedding itself in my right shoulder.

I instantly snapped myself back to reality.

The force of the dagger was so powerful that not only did it drive through my shoulder, but it also punctured the stone wall behind me.

The pain was brief.

I turned my eyes to the direction that the dagger had come from.

My vision was still hazy, but I managed to make out the figure of a slender young woman. She stepped closer, allowing me to get a better look at her. The light from the street-lamp shone on her feminine features and I memorized every detail.

She was a pretty, young thing, no more than twenty years old. She had passionate ruby lips, ocean blue eyes, and thin cheeks. She wore a black leather skirt and short-sleeved matching shirt.

I looked into her eyes and saw something fatal in them, something beautiful, yet deadly.

Die, leech, I heard her hiss into my ears.

I gasped, startled at the invasion of my mind.

Was it possible that perhaps she was another vampire, like me? She could read my thoughts, couldn't she?

I'm not a leech like you are, she informed me, reading my thoughts once again.

I pulled out the dagger and held it as a weapon as I struggled to rise on my feet.

She drew a sword from a sheath on her back. The light gleamed on it, making the blade of the sword appear more menacing. This sword was powerful. I could tell from just looking at it. The hilt of the sword was silver with an intricately carved design. With my preternatural eyes, I saw that the design was of a fierce dragon with ruby spheres for eyes.

In all its fatality, the sword was a remarkable thing.

She lunged for me.

I held out my dagger and slashed through the air, hoping to slice her stomach. But she was agile. She sucked in her stomach and bounced back on her feet to avoid the blade of her dagger.

She can't be human, I told myself. *I've never seen anything human move as fast as her.*

She came at me again, this time with her astonishing sword.

Remembering what Kathleen told me about the blade, I avoided it with all my strength.

She circled me and I followed her, not daring to turn my back on her. Any moment now I expected to feel the pang of her blade through my heart.

Foolishly, I attacked first, hoping to get a blow in before she could.

But she met my tiny dagger with her awesome sword and she kicked me in the stomach, almost knocking me back.

I recovered my ground, but not in enough time.

For she was on me already, cutting my arm with her blade.

Her blade seared my skin. It was unlike any other pain I had ever experienced; in my life or in my death. It felt like fire that had crawled underneath the surface of my skin. I am not certain how I knew, and I do not have an explanation for my knowledge—except to say that I just *knew*—but there was some kind of magick on that blade. Magick that intensified the ache of the wound on my arm.

She hissed at me and I stabbed the air as if I were a blind man, unaware of where to plunge the dagger to put in a final blow.

I realized only then that the bleeding from the cut did not cease flow.

Can vampires scar?

Only if there's magick involved.

I recognized instantly that this voice was not my own; but the other, the threatening individual.

I attempted to do what Kathleen had told me about— to close my mind, to block my thoughts with a wall of magick. But I had not exercised this power yet, so this intruder was allowed into the most private parts of my mind.

Without warning, she struck me with an invisible whip.

I felt it across my abdomen and I fell against the ground.

She raised her sword and I knew what she wanted to do. I knew that she wanted to cleave my head from my neck.

But it was foolish of her to think that I was unconscious, because surely she did believe it.

Lashing out at her with all the power I could muster, I attacked her twice.

First, I sent my own unique wave of magick that thrashed her and fried her thoughts for half a second before she brought herself back to her sharp senses.

An amazing feat for her to have done it so quickly, I noted before I sent out my second attack: I gutted her with her own dagger, hoping that it would do enough damage to either kill her or send her fleeing.

Indeed, she fled.

I breathed out loudly and it seemed that I could not stop panting. I looked at the wound on my arm and saw that the blood did not stop. And I did not know how to stop it myself.

The blade she had used must have been blessed with some kind of magick to have caused me so much agony with a simple cut.

Eventually, I passed out into the sweet oblivion of unconsciousness.

But I remember thinking one last thought before I blacked out, sincerely believing that the mere cut caused by some storming stranger capable of inhuman strength would bring about the death of me.

Can vampires bleed to death?

AND HERE BEGINS THE TALE of my sweet, beloved Michael. I shall never forget him. Somehow, he has found his passage to my cold heart and found some way to warm it with a peace unknown to all of humankind. And for as long as I shall live, he will remain within my deepest memories of hope and compassion. He taught me these things, hope and compassion, these beautiful things that cannot be learned by any other than the one who showed it to you; than the one who loved you.

I THOUGHT I HAD FINALLY reached Death's Big Black Door, but I was nowhere near it. The key was thrown out of my reach and the door itself was much too distant. And for one brief moment, I was certain that I would never reach this door that holds for many, serenity unknown to them by any other means. I wished for it; I longed for the beauty and sweet release of Death. I wanted it so badly; I wanted it more than I had ever wanted blood.

When I awoke, I felt the faint warmth of fire against the frostiness of my cheeks. And the pang in my arm had decreased to a pleasant numbness.

It was only then that I realized how sharp my olfactory sense had become since I had been changed into the damnable creature that I am today.

I smelled the charred kindling in the fireplace. I smelled human hands full of tenderness and love. I smelled water. I even smelled the fire. It was a bitter aroma, caustic and somewhat revolting. But most of all, I smelled blood. It wasn't mine. It was coming from the human hands and the human body.

Gradually—because I was terrified of what I would see in the instant that I opened my eyes—I unsealed my eyelids.

My vision was nebulous and blurry. And even *with* my magnified vision, the figure looming in front of me could have been mistaken for Death Himself.

"Where am I?" I mumbled, my words sounding as slurred as the words coming from an intoxicated man.

"You're safe," he told me, his voice gentle and gracious.

In that moment, the whole entire world became as clear as diamonds to me. The recollection of the recent events collided into me in a rushing torrent of agonizing image after image.

I saw my father, my mother, two brothers, and even Hosanna, not to mention that baffling encounter with that young woman who attacked and nearly killed me as well.

But all that seemed so far away now. It was as if the past few weeks had never happened and resting there was the only thing that was real.

No Kathleen. No vampires. No hell waiting for me on the other side.

It felt like all that was in the past, locked away in a vast box of oblivion where nothing was what it seemed.

Sadly, however, I knew the truth.

There was Kathleen. There were vampires. There was hell waiting for me on the other side.

But it didn't seem to matter anymore.

"Who are you?" I asked him.

"Michael."

I gazed at him, into his penetrating eyes of cerulean and I found myself fixed on every single detail of him. I read him as I would a book. He had the palest pink lips, so beautiful in their simplicity. His skin was near white, but there was a rosy tint to his cheeks that made him appear as if he was forever blushing. Glittering gold shimmered on the top of his head. Looking into his eyes was the equivalent of staring into the boundless sky where heaven was said to dwell.

I could tell, even though he was sitting down, that he was tall, about six feet and he had a muscular build though it was hardly noticeable because of the fine fabric he wore. His apparel made him appear scrawnier than he actually was. I could also see that he was a modest man who practiced humility. He could boast his body—because indeed, it was manly and beautiful—but he chose to conceal it instead.

"Do you have a last name?" I continued.

"Vandalius," he replied. "Michael Vandalius."

I smiled weakly at him, because it was the best smile that I could do, even though I knew that he deserved more better. "Lovely name," I complimented, knowing that the name "Michael" meant: one who is like God.

Michael smiled back at me; his smile was radiant and as bright as the sun that lights up every morning. He practically beamed. "Thank you." His fingers reached out for my face and he delicately brushed a few strands of my crow black hair from my eyes. "Now ..." he started with a sigh. "What's your name?"

"Sophia," I answered. In that second that I told him my name, I realized that I had not hesitated in stating it. It was clear to me now that I had finally accepted who I was. Not Catherine Opaque. But Sophia, a fledgling of Kathleen's.

"Do you have a last name?"

I detected the slightest trace of a French accent. It was not thick; in fact, it was near imperceptibility.

"Smith," I said. It was the quickest name I could think of—tells a lot about myself, my difficulty working under quick-paced pressure. But I handled it well, by my standards. "So, where am I?"

He rose from his chair and turned his back to me. He strolled to the window gravely. "You're at my estate: the

Vandalius Manor. I found you on the street. You looked like you were hurt. I thought that I would take you here and make sure that you wouldn't die tomorrow morning."

I examined my right arm, where that swift young woman had cut me earlier. The pain was no longer there at all, almost as if it had never been there to begin with. "What did you do to that wound on my arm?"

Michael slightly turned towards me, causing him to face sideways. The light from the street-lamp outside highlighted his aureate blond hair. "It's a secret. My mother taught me how to nurse people. She used to be a nurse, before she met my father." He pivoted all the way to face the window, as if drawn to it by some dark force.

"Where is your family?" I knew that I should not have asked the question, because the moment that I did, flashing pictures of my own murdered family invaded my mind. *Slaughtered by their own daughter*, I remembered.

"They're dead," Michael said, solidly as if he were attempting to set in stone the truth.

I caught the hidden sorrow in his voice as he said these two words, something that no other human could have noticed. Similar to his accent, a mortal's human ears would have never caught that either.

"Vampires killed them," he added softly, with a tinge of rancor.

"I'm sorry," I said, and I meant it. I felt compelled to say it; to apologize. *One of my own kind killed his family*, I thought.

Michael gazed at the exotic rug underneath his feet. "There's no need for you to apologize," he told me. "It wasn't your fault."

But it was, I countered. Some part of me wanted to believe it, that it was truly my fault that his family was murdered, but it could not be true. The only people who I had killed were my own family.

Michael finally turned himself away from the window, as if he had severed the cord that had yanked him there. He sat down on the chair in front of me, while I sat on a comfortable couch. His eyes locked with mine. "Are you hungry?"

The question was out of the Great Beyond. I had never expected such a question. Of course I was hungry. I was starving. In spite of the fact that I had just fed, I was still ravenous because I had not fed enough to sate my hunger pains. After all, I had been on a fast for a month.

"I should really be going now," I insisted, throwing off the blanket that he had placed on me and beginning to sit up.

But Michael did not allow me to leave.

"No, please, stay," he asserted. "It's rude to decline an invitation of hospitality."

"I feel like I've overstepped my bounds," I informed him, rising from the couch. But Michael put his hand up to stop me and I sat back down.

"Please, you look like you could collapse again," Michael declared unexpectedly.

I grinned wryly at him. "You sure know how to compliment a lady," I returned.

"I'm sorry, that's not what I meant. It's just that...you look hungry, is all."

Silence followed after that. Ironically, his truthfulness seized and held me captive. His honesty was what made

94

me want to stay. Plus, there was that sad puppy look in his eyes, as if he was going to pout because he had just lost his favorite chew toy.

"I'll stay," I announced. "If you really want me to."

Michael jumped from his seat. "That's great!" he exclaimed. "I'll go make us something to eat." He practically *leapt* into the kitchen.

A FEW MINUTES LATER, HE poked his head out eagerly, prodding me on into the kitchen room that led into the dining room. Smiling to myself, I entered the kitchen and walked through to the dining room where an elaborate table was set for the two of us.

The table itself was a symbol of grandeur and I felt as if I could not eat on this elegant piece of furniture. But it was something more than a piece of furniture; it was a work of art.

There were four white candlesticks in diamond candleholders. Silver utensils sparkled under the light of the crystal and gold chandelier suspended above the center of the table. Four small bouquets of full-bloom yellow roses were placed throughout the length of the immaculate dining table. And the floral centerpiece was a marvel, even to vampire eyes. The flowers in the centerpiece had been arranged to look like a one-foot model of the most heavenly angel that I had ever laid eyes on. She was exquisite, in a pale blue dress with overflowing curls of sunlight- drenched blond hair. Pure white blossoms designed her broad angelic wings. They were outstretched beyond her reach.

Michael gestured to an empty chair. "You don't have to stand up, you know," he pointed out to me.

Sheepishly, I perched on the chair that he had gestured to me. Michael sat across from me.

"I hope you like it," Michael affirmed. "I made it myself."

"Don't you have servants to do things like this for you?"

"I do, but when it comes to the small things like preparing food for a guest, I take on the task," he responded. "You can't rely on servants. They're people too and even they need a break sometimes."

I gazed at the brilliant wineglass to the side of my plate. The wineglass was filled all the way to the top with a deep indigo liquor. I was not fond of wine. But it didn't matter now because my vampire taste buds cannot taste wine or any food for that matter, other than blood. The food I put into my mouth, including wine, would taste like a parchment: no taste at all and no flavor to it.

But Michael gave me back the flavor of wine and the taste of food.

He had prepared *escargot*, a delicacy in France.

I was never fond of it, but I supposed that for Michael's sake, I should try it. Like he said, it was rude to decline an invitation of hospitality and he was being quite the gentleman.

MICHAEL INVITED ME TO STAY over and I was glad that he did, because I truly had no place where I belonged. I could never return to see my family. They were dead now. And as for Kathleen...I never wanted to see her face again, but something—call it what you will: intuition or instinct—inside of my gut always reminded me that I would see her again. I had yet to leave

Kathleen. She would never release me. I understood that early on.

I sat on the bed in the guestroom. I gently pushed down on the bed, testing its bouncing capabilities. It had been a long time since I had slept on a bed with a mattress and pillows. It felt good just to sit on a mattress. My eyes scanned the room, and I paid close attention to the various oil paintings on the walls.

My attention wandered off until Michael entered through the opened doorway, holding a neatly folded nightgown in his hands.

"Here, you can take these to wear for the night," he said, handing the nightgown over to me. "They were my sister's. She's not your size exactly, but I hoped you could make do with what I have."

I touched the white nightgown made out of satin and traced down the trail of lace on the bodice. There were crystal beads at the bottom hem of the dress. How could I wear such a thing to sleep? I would surely mess the loveliness of the dress with my constant tossing and turning. I would only ruin this thing of such splendor and grace with my monstrosity.

"It's beautiful," I whispered under my breath, sounding more feminine than I had ever wanted to sound. But I could not help it.

Michael turned his back and began to walk out of the room.

"I'll be two rooms away," he intoned. "Call me if you need anything."

Before he could exit, my voice beckoned him to stop when he reached the middle of the opened doorway.

"Michael?" My voice was smooth and soft. The intimacy of a bedroom always called for one's voice to be softer than usual.

He did not turn around; he kept his back faced to me like he usually did, but I knew that he heard me when I saw him stop.

"Why are you doing this for me?" I asked him, my tone sounding as if I were pleading for my life.

With his back turned to me, he returned, "What do you mean?"

"*This*," I said, although it did not clarify anything for him. "You took me into your home, treated my wound, made me dinner, and now you're letting me spend the night wearing your sister's nightgown? I just want to know why you're being so kind to me. I'm just a stranger. How do you even know that I deserve all this kindness?"

Michael's voice was clear and his words could not be misunderstood by anyone. It was also somber, which I did not quite understand.

"Everyone deserves kindness."

And he reached for the doorknob.

"Good night, Sophia."

And he closed the door.

CHAPTER SIX

εφ

My family hounded me in my dreams, making them my worst of nightmares. They pointed their fingers at me, accusing me of the worst crime imaginable: killing someone of your own blood.

I woke with a start, gasping for air as if I had been plunged into the icy river of the Seine on a cold, brisk morning.

The beams of the morning sun painted my room with a majestic light that could only be created by the daystar.

The mild heat of the light warmed my frigid skin and I felt cheery inside, in spite of the hellish nightmare.

There were two windows in my room and they were both opened and the cool gentle morning breeze blew the flimsy curtains. I sat up on my bed.

One of the servants must have come into my room this morning to open the windows, I concluded.

From outside of the windows, I heard the cacophony of swords being clashed.

My first thought was that perhaps that woman had followed me here and now she was sword fighting everyone in Vandalius Manor to get to me. But I could hear that there *two* swords, not one, in play. Whoever was fighting was putting up a good battle.

I rose from my bed, throwing the covers from my body, and I stood over by the window and at first, the brightness of the morning stung my eyes so much that I almost cried, but I adjusted to it.

On the emerald grass below, Michael and another man were dueling with swords.

I saw the way Michael handled himself. He was swift with the sword. He allowed it to guide him, to lead him, to show him the way. Michael was not the hand that held the sword; he was the blade on the sword itself. He had become "one with the blade", though it sounded hokey.

I sensed that there was no danger in the man that he was fencing with. This other man had wheat-yellow hair that was tied back with a black ribbon. He was somewhere in his mid-thirties, much older than Michael, who was twenty-seven. He had large hazel eyes and his nose was pointed at the tip.

Excited, I rushed out of the room and pounded the staircase of the Manor as I hurried outside to watch the sword fray. I stood at the opened French doors, my naked feet slightly touching the lush grass, which was chilly from the morning dew. It felt so wonderful to have nature underneath my feet.

Michael was rapidly moving backwards, fending off the other man's attack. Suddenly, Michael fired back, causing his opponent to rush backwards as Michael had done. They clashed swords up and down, sideways and in the center. It was intense and so quick that if I had not the preternatural sight I had now, I would not have been able to see the sword cutting through the air.

I closed my eyes and I concentrated, focusing my mind on that of Michael's opponent. I wanted to exercise my telepathic powers. In a few seconds, I felt my mind lock into Michael's companion and I searched mentally for what I wanted to know. I was swimming in a sea of knowledge. Various words, phrases and sentences passed through my mind, things that I did not understand. Images of numerous individuals flashed in my mind and then suddenly I found what I was looking for.

His name was Preston Bennington. He was an old family friend of the Vandalius'. He had been there for Michael when Michael had lost his family a year ago. He was thirty-three, doomed to become thirty-four in a matter of two months. He was married to a noblewoman at one time, but she passed away from syphilis six months ago. His main goal in his life was to marry again before the age of forty and to have one son.

I was stunned at my success. I felt like I needed to celebrate it somehow. It was the first time that I had flexed my power since I had become a vampire.

Unexpectedly, Michael put an end to the fight when he punched Preston, kicked him in the stomach, causing him to double back, and then he thrust the sword at him, an inch away from his chest. Preston had fallen onto the wet grass while attempting to escape Michael's fleet sword.

"I win again, Bennington," Michael declared, smiling the same smile that I had loved from the beginning.

Preston grinned. "Yes, it seems you have."

Michael removed the sword from his friend and put out a hand for him. Preston graciously took his hand and

Michael pulled him up. Preston wiped the back of his white shirt and black tights. Michael handed his sword over to one of his servants, and Preston did the same.

"You've been practicing," Preston noted briefly.

"Always," Michael confirmed. "You used to beat me all the time; now, it seems I have the upper hand."

Another servant approached the pair with a silver tray where two glasses of orange juice waited them. Each of them took one.

Preston sipped from his glass and then placed it back on the tray, dismissing the servant. "Ah, my friend, I'm growing old," Preston argued. "I'm losing my speed."

"Perhaps you just choose not to admit to my improved skills," Michael countered.

"I'll see you here next Thursday morning," Preston declared. "And just to let you know, I am winning this next game."

"We shall see about that, Bennington."

"We shall, soon enough, Vandalius."

They patted each other's back in a friendly manner and finally, Michael took notice of me for the first time, standing in his sister's nightgown at the doors.

Preston's eyes shimmered when he followed his friend's gaze. "Who is your lovely guest?" he asked, approaching me.

"Sophia Smith," Michael introduced, also following his friend and taking another sip of the delicious juice.

Indeed, when I was human, I loved the flavor of orange juice. It was tangy; sour, but sweet.

Preston took my hand and kissed the back of it. "Madame," he greeted.

"Monsieur," I returned.

Preston turned his attention over to Michael. "Why didn't you tell me that you had such a pretty visitor over at your house?" His attention averted to me. "I would have come here sooner."

His flirting did not amuse me, but I was nevertheless complimented by it.

"Did you sleep well?" Michael asked, ignoring Preston's ambitious comment.

"Like a baby," I replied.

"Good," Michael affirmed. "Sophia, this is an old friend of mine, Preston—"

I cut him off, eager to show off what I already knew because of the usage of my powers. "—Bennington."

Michael shot me an odd look, his brows knitted. "How did you know his last name?"

"I know his family, of course," I answered, covering up the less obvious one. "I'm terribly sorry about your loss," I added, even though I shouldn't have, referring to his late wife.

Preston seemed to believe me, but Michael still had the look of curiosity in his eyes.

"Thank you," Preston said.

Shrugging it off, Michael turned to me and asked, "Sophia, would you like to join us for breakfast?"

"I'd be pleased to," I responded and then looked down at the nightgown. "Allow me to go change first."

THE TALE OF MICHAEL DOES not end here, I just felt as if I should interrupt it for a moment to put in a word or two. (Of course, it always ends up being longer than a word or two.) One must understand how much Michael meant to me in order to understand my grief.

Michael was the embodiment of humanity. His words about everyone needing kindness have embedded itself into me and remained in this silent resting-place.

It is rare to meet someone with the finest qualities of humanity. In fact, people like that are few and far in between. But I am glad that I got to meet Michael, even though I honestly believe that his life would have ended more happily if I had never entered it.

But perhaps it was destined to be the way it was.

Perhaps I was meant to kill my family that night and encounter that strange woman with the painful sword. Perhaps meeting Michael and all the events that followed were all meant to be, fated, destined.

That is, if you *believe* in destiny.

THREE WEEKS HAD PASSED SINCE I had come into Vandalius Manor. I was no longer a guest; I was practically living there. I had my breakfast and dinner there and I also slept in the guestroom, changing it to fit my needs, for instance, I needed thicker drapes. It wasn't that the sunlight hurt my eyes, but I did not want gauzy shades. I knew the servants well and it was as if I had become a member of the family at the Manor. But I was always careful never to overstep my boundaries. The Manor did not belong to me and I altered a few things here and there, but I never did it without Michael's permission.

I also began to learn how to fight. Michael taught me how to use a sword and I was a quick learner. I learned well in the first few lessons and even Michael was astonished at my rapid progress. He once commented that I was perhaps born with these skills, since I seemed like a natural.

But something more drastic than altering the fabric in a room and learning how to sword fight had occurred since I started "living" with Michael.

I had begun to drink blood, not the blood of living humans, but animal blood. Every night, we usually had some kind of poultry or perhaps a pig for the main course and when the cooks were preparing the food, I would ask them to save the blood that they extracted from the animals. They never questioned what I asked of them, so I was not worried. And if they ever did, I would just tell them that it was customary in my family for the daughters to save the blood of an animal that you would eat for dinner in order to pay homage to the animal that was slaughtered in order so that others could live.

Strange family traditions …

But it was enough. I began to accept my vampiric nature. I had no other choice. I could no longer deny it. But I did not just drink blood in order to sustain living; the last time that I stopped drinking *any* blood ended in tragedy when I murdered my family.

I never wanted that to happen to Michael.

I loved him too much to hurt him, but in some ways, it felt like just being in his presence hurt him because he didn't know what I was: a vampire, the same thing that killed his family.

It was because of Michael that I finally accepted my vampiric nature. He once told me that we are who we are and sometimes we just cannot change it.

It was still early in the evening, ten minutes till nine. I sat in silence in my room but I could not bear it any longer so I came out to Michael's room. He had a grand, master bedroom. He sat at his desk, scribbling madly at the papers in front of him.

I wondered what he was doing, but after catching a glimpse of his mind, he was preoccupied with studying vampires and the witch vampire-hunters who were said to pursue the vampires in a never-ending struggle to destroy them and make the world safer for the greater good.

Vampire hunters…I had never heard of them. I tried to think that perhaps Kathleen had told me but I was not paying attention. I replayed all our conversations and never once did she ever mention that there were such things as vampire hunters.

I should have known better, however. It was an ancient law of the world: for as long as evil shall exist, so shall good.

I approached him at his desk and perched myself confidently on the corner.

"You could not sleep, I presume," Michael intoned.

I grinned at him and sincerely returned, "Is there anything that you're not right about?"

Michael placed his ink quill in the round crystalline bottle where it rightfully belonged and he turned to me. His eyes dazzled, even in the darkness.

"What are you doing?" I asked, although I already knew the answer.

"I'm researching," he replied. "On vampires and vampire hunters."

I lowered my gaze, saddened at his quest for knowledge about the vampire realm. *It would be much better if he didn't know about us, but his family was killed by my kind. He has every right to learn what he can to stop us from hurting any more innocent people.* "What have you learned?" I asked, curious at his discoveries.

"I've learned about the vampire hunters," Michael answered. "They're powerful hunters, witches possessing painful magick. The most powerful line of witches is the Rath line. Ever heard of them?"

I shook my head.

"It seems there's a Rath in our midst here in France," Michael added. "She's quite the gallant girl."

"You've met her?" I asked in disbelief, my brows raised.

Michael nodded. "I met her shortly after my family was killed. She taught me a few things."

I pondered something then. Could it have been possible that the woman who attacked me was the same woman that Michael was talking about?

"You never speak of your family," I pointed out, softly, hoping to encourage him to speak more about them.

He closed the book on his desk. "No, I don't."

There was something utterly cold in his voice. It chilled my spine. There was some kind of hatred inside of him that surfaced when talk of his family emerged. This frightened me. If Michael—the most beautiful human being that I have ever met—were capable of such great hatred, I would be capable of even more malice.

The silence must have pestered Michael because the next thing he said was something about his family.

"I was married once, you know," he commenced. "She was beautiful, like you." His eyes met mine and I saw the sorrow behind them under the façade of brilliance. "Her name was Morgan. She was pregnant with my child."

I braced myself. I knew that the next words that were going to come out of his mouth were going to end in tragedy.

"She was killed, along with the rest of my family, along with my unborn child," Michael concluded.

I could not bear to meet his eyes. I cast them down. I was much too ashamed. Michael cupped my chin with his hand and gently lifted it up so that I met his alluring gaze.

"I love you, Sophia," Michael said. "I've loved you for so long, but I've been afraid to tell you because so many people that I love are dead. I only hurt the people I love, Sophia. I don't want you to love me if it will cost you your life."

If I had not been so saddened, I would have laughed. *How ironic. He thinks that if he loves me, he will hurt me. Most likely, I will be the one who will hurt him because I love him.*

Silence ensued and Michael, finding it unbearable, rose from his chair, turned his back to me, and stalked towards his bed, muttering: "I should not have said that."

I caught up with him and put a hand on his shoulder and forced him to turn around and look at me. I wanted him to know that I felt the same way. In that one instant, I wanted to tell him everything about me; I wanted to tell him the truth. Consequences didn't matter. I just wanted him to know so badly. But there were no words to express the joy in my heart upon his confession of his love to me. There was only love.

It was perhaps the most beautiful thing that anyone had ever said to me. Michael was willing to sacrifice his love for me in order to protect my life, a noble purpose indeed.

"I'm afraid to love you," Michael confessed and I truly did see the fear shine through in his ethereal eyes.

I put my finger to his lip to silence him, to hush his fear and calm his storm inside of him. "Don't be afraid," I breathed into his ear.

Then I wrapped my arms around his neck and my lips touched his before I had even considered my actions.

The warmth of his mouth, responding to mine, heated the coldness of my dead, frigid lips.

He wrapped his arms around my waist and pulled me in closer, as if he never wanted to release me—and I, myself, did not want to be released from the captivity of his graceful love.

Michael's love and passion devoured me whole.

He had been so lonely for so long after the tragedy of losing his whole entire family, including his wife and his unborn child.

And I, like him, had been so lonely for so long...too long.

He embraced me, crushing his strong body to mine, our lips never leaving each other's for more than one second.

I fell back down on his feather bed, and he on top of me, bowing his head to plant lovely kisses on my neck. I loved his scent. As a vampire, I could smell the unique and natural fragrant from his body. And because I was a vampire, I could not taste anything but blood. Yet I could taste Michael. I could taste him in every bit of my immortal soul.

My slender fingers lightly caressed his fair skin and his touch brought me ecstasy beyond my imagination. To be so near him, so close to him, and to not *have* him—*all* of him—would have been hell for me.

Our clothing decorated the air in its final descent to the floor. We melted into each other as we crawled underneath the velvet covers. My heart exploded from the full capacity of my content.

Every time he whispered his love for me, I shuddered with the feel of his breath. But I loved it. I loved every moment I spent with him, either pleasantly numb or passionately charged.

He held me close to him all throughout the night, and there was nowhere else that I would rather want to be. This place, freely captured in the circle of his arms, was the perfect place.

A sudden sleepiness overcame me, but I fought it. There was no way that I would want to fall asleep, not after this beautiful lovemaking. I had to stay awake. I *fought* to stay awake.

I never knew that I was capable of loving someone as much as I loved Michael. I thought that when I had become a vampire, I had forsaken all feelings of love and I would never be able to love again. But that was not the case.

I embraced Michael, the same way that he embraced me, but the fierce and raw intensity of his touch and embrace overwhelmed me. I had never known someone with as much emotion as Michael; he was truly incredible, in more ways than one.

Could it have been that Michael was an angel? —A perfect being sent by God as a sign that I had been forgiven for my past deeds?

I wanted to believe it, even if it wasn't true, and for just one night, Michael *was* my angel: courageous, hopeful, compassionate, and loving.

OUR FINGERS WERE AS INTERTWINED as the thread of our life and fate together. I rested my head on his naked chest and he stroked the hair on the crown of my head, tenderly planting a kiss there as well. I observed our fingers, the way they seemed so perfect as they were interlaced, as if our hands had been made for each other. It was near perfection. I was finally *with* Michael, with the man that I loved. And everything would have been perfect if my mind had not been plagued with the face of Kathleen.

This troubled me. I could not stop thinking about her. All I could do was worry that she would strike out and hurt Michael as a way to hurt me and truly, if she had done so, it would wound me eternally. I could not imagine life without Michael. I could not even understand how I was able to live without him for so long. I was concerned for his safety, as well as mine, and though I attempted to not allow it to hinder our passionate night together, I could not help it either.

Michael sensed this worry from me. He and I had a deep spiritual connection rooted in our love for each other and in the fact that we had found our missing halves.

"What are you thinking about?" he asked me, his tone mild and soft.

111

"Someone," I told him. "She's not important though."

His curiosity was aroused and he was not the kind to silence when you told him to. "Who?"

"No one important," I said again.

"She must be important if you're thinking about her so much," Michael noted.

I could not deny this fact. Kathleen was an important figure and I could not stop thinking about her, for some vexing reason.

I resolved to tell him part of the truth—it was the least that I could do for him. "She was my friend ..."

"And ...?" Michael prodded.

"And she hurt me," I finished for him. That was all there really was to tell. In eight words, I had summed up my past with Kathleen. She had truly hurt me, in several different ways.

"And you're still hurting," Michael declared firmly. He knew me too well.

I nodded my head against his chest and I felt him begin to sit up on the bed just slightly. I conformed to him, sitting up just a bit so that I would not be in an uncomfortable position.

Michael stared into my eyes. "What did she do to you?" he queried.

I did not know how to reply, because I did not know where to begin. Kathleen had done so many things to me: she had brought me across the river of never-ending blood against my will to make me into a damnable creature and she forced me to kill my own family, taking advantage of me while I was in such a vulnerable state. "A lot of things," I answered.

"And you hate her for it," Michael intoned.

"With a burning in my soul," I added, making no attempt whatsoever to mask the revulsion I felt towards Kathleen.

"They say that only fools hold grudges," Michael reminded me.

"Then I must be a fool," I answered him.

"You would probably feel much better if you forgave her for whatever it was that she did to you," Michael offered.

Usually, an idea as ludicrous as forgiving Kathleen would have been easily dismissed by me, but it was Michael proposing this notion...It could not just be shrugged off.

Michael always knew what he was talking about.

I sat up and listened tentatively.

"To err is human; to forgive, divine, Sophia," he quoted, wisely.

"I am not divine," I whispered almost inaudibly. *Quite the opposite.*

He caught my gaze and held it, something he was undoubtedly skilled at. "When I say that you're divine, don't argue with me. You know that I'm right."

I smiled at him, in spite of the serious tone he had set.

He went on. "Forgive her, in spite of your past differences, and you both will benefit from it, for the greater good."

"She doesn't deserve it," I seethed under my breath.

"Forgiveness isn't done because someone deserves it," Michael told me. "It's done because a person needs it. Forgiveness is an act of mercy, Sophia. Be the bigger person here. Show this person, whoever she is, *what*ever she is, whatever she's done, mercy even though she showed you none."

I could not turn away from his potent gaze. He held my attention as if he were Homer, the Epic Bard.

And perhaps he was right.

Perhaps I should show Kathleen the mercy that she never showed me, in hopes that possibly she will learn it and show it to others.

CHAPTER SEVEN

εφ

ORGIVENESS IS AN EASY CONCEPT to grasp, but it is difficult to do. Forgiveness is a rare act for vampires, who show little or no mercy. But Michael made it sound possible; he made it sound so simple. Forgive Kathleen and all will be fine. Michael made forgiveness appear as uncomplicated as hatred, but it is not. Forgiveness is hard. To forgive someone for what he or she has done means burying what has happened and to leave the past behind is never an easy task. Forgiveness, much like the Road to Redemption, is marked by jagged stones and seemingly insurmountable barriers. But Michael made me believe that forgiveness can be done, even by a vampire. When he spoke of this concept, he did not speak about humankind specifically; he spoke universally, of all creatures on the earth, not just one particular kind. He believed that forgiveness could be done by all and every one. Perhaps it was this very idea that led our love to loss and forced me to bury any hope of forgiveness under cold stone, forgotten and forlorn.

IT TOOK ME A LONG time before I was able to even *consider* the idea of seeing Kathleen again, of confronting her. But I had to, for Michael's sake and mine, I had to forgive her.

I found her at the mansion where I had once roomed with her. She was sitting alone in the colossal dining room and I let myself in, seeing no need to knock on the door or wait for someone to open it.

I advanced upon her, discreetly, even though I knew that it would be no use. She was incredibly perceptive and could probably have sensed me from a mile away.

A bond between the maker and the made is strong.

Before I could even part my lips to say a word, Kathleen was already ahead of me.

"Ah, Sophia...Come to grace me with your presence?"

My face was solemn and my tone matched it with exactness. "I've come to speak with you," I announced.

Kathleen was sitting sideways on the table, but she spun around so that her front would face me. Instantly, her eyes caught sight of something about me. "You've been feeding," she declared. "I can tell."

There was no use in denying the truth. "Yes,...I have."

She seemed smugly pleased by this. "Then you've accepted your true nature?"

I retorted instead, "I've come to terms with it, yes."

"Then what is it that you would like to say to me?" she prodded.

I took a breath and paused, thinking about what Michael had told me about forgiveness being an act of mercy upon the merciless. "I forgive you, Kathleen," I said, spitting out the words as quickly as I could in order to avoid having to prolong it any longer.

Kathleen's ears perked up. "*You* forgive *me*?" she spat, as if it was the most ridiculous thing she had ever heard with her immortal ears.

"Yes," I said, ignoring the flippancy in her tone, "for doing what you did to Catherine Opaque."

"The question *is*, Sophia, not if you forgive me, but if you forgive yourself," Kathleen countered.

In that moment, I saw that there was no way that peace could ever be made with her—in this life or the next.

"I mean, you killed your own family," Kathleen continued, wounding me even deeper with every word she spoke of my family. "There's no greater crime than that." She crossed her arms.

"I still forgive you," I said again, my words hurried and quick as if there was a certain falseness behind it that I could no longer conceal.

"Oh really? And is that all that brought you here? — Forgiveness?"

"Yes, because someone taught me something that you could never teach me: humanity," I informed her, coldly.

I turned my back on her and I was about to walk out on her forever, but she said something that caused the gently trembling nerves of mine to quake.

"Oh, you mean that blond fellow of yours?"

I stopped as if I had just been frozen in a tomb still standing upright. The hairs on my neck raised as I gradually turned to face her. "I never told you anything about him," I pointed out.

Smugly, Kathleen affirmed: "You didn't have to tell me. That Michael friend of yours, he's cute. Hang onto him."

"How do you know about him?" I interrogated, now fearing for his safety more than ever.

Kathleen pointed to her temple and tapped it twice.

"If you so much as harm one little golden hair on his head, I'll come to you personally and cleave your head from your neck myself," I threatened, straining my voice when I tried to make it sound dangerously low.

Kathleen jumped onto her feet on the top of the table. Enthusiastically, she exclaimed, "See, that's why I chose you! You have so much anger and passion! No one else could have what you have."

I brushed off that last comment and found my way out the door, praying that I would never again have to look into Kathleen's vampiric eyes.

THE COOL NIGHT AIR CARESSED my fair skin as I pushed open Michael's balcony door and I stood outside, viewing the world with my vampiric eyes. Michael was laying in bed, sleeping. I could not rest. I stirred, then tossed and turned, and finally forced myself to rise and seek the darkness that I never wanted to be a part of.

It was not that hard to wake in the night as it was to wake in the morning.

The full moon shone in all its brightness; lighting a path of ribbon for many nighttime travelers. I was enchanted by the awesome magnificence of the pure moon, white and chaste, untainted by humankind.

I wished silently that the moon would never be touched by any man or woman. It was bad enough that humankind had ruined most of the earth, it did not need to ruin the moon's virginal soil as well.

I felt Michael approach me. He put his hands on my bare shoulders and stared at the moon with me.

There were so many little twinkling stars, glittering in a pool of bluish-blackness. I feared that perhaps all these stars would soon vanish from the sky when humankind begins to contaminate it with their macabre inventions.

But that was the last thing on my mind. I had something else to think about.

It was one week after I had visited Kathleen and even though it did not seem as if she accepted my forgiveness, it still gave me a peace of mind that I had yet to know of until then. I hadn't thought about her for seven days. I was much too troubled with this new thought.

"What are you thinking about?" Michael asked. He was perhaps the most perceptive of all humans that I had ever known.

I turned to him and he embraced me lightly, like he was trying to protect me because I was a fragile child. But I wasn't. I had already *been* broken.

"I'm going to ask you something—but I don't want you to say anything until after I'm done talking. Just hear me out." I inhaled a big breath, though I probably did not need it. "Will you marry me?" I quickly followed the question. "I know that we've just met and we've only known each other for about three months, but I feel like I've known you forever. And I would understand if you say no, but I just want you to know that—"

"—Yes."

I hushed. There really was nothing more to say. But I was still stunned by his reply. It was brief, but in one word, in one breath, he said all that was needed to be said. He said all that I wanted to hear. *"Yes"*, an angelic chiming in my ears.

"Yes?" I repeated, uncertainly. Could it have been that I just heard him say it?

"Yes," Michael confirmed, solidly, immovably.

"Yes?" I echoed once more and Michael nodded his head. "You said yes!" I hollered and I hugged him and I kissed him. Then I turned to the night, the world, and all the darkness and I scoffed at it: *Never again will you claim me*, I swore. *I've pledged my life to love, to Michael!*

I HAD FOUND MY SALVATION, but not in a faith, a god or a devil, but in love. I had found it in Michael. He was everything to me. He was the brightest light at the end of the darkest tunnel; he was the shoulder I cried on and the one person that I could always turn to. I would lie awake at night, not because I was restless, but because my pure happiness kept me awake every night, blending into my natural instinct to stay up at night.

Michael was a beautiful creature. He was full of such grace and when I lost my peace, he gave me his. Michael was probably the closest thing to an angel that I had ever known. Never had such divinity been on earth before, until he was brought into the world.

I felt as if darkness could never claim me again. I was once their child and I still am, but I would never submit to it. I thought that my darkness had finally left me for good and I was allowed to live in peace with Michael, but then something happened with Preston Bennington that made me think twice about the ending of my life in darkness.

I WAS IN THE VANDALIUS Manor, surrounded by seamstresses who Michael had hired to make my wedding dress the way I wanted it to be. The women encircled me, measuring things, putting pins in, and taking them out just as much.

My darkest secret that I was a vampire remained a secret and I had no intention of telling Michael. I did feel guilty, however, for not telling him this. But sooner or later he was going to figure it out, and I was always the kind of person who would rather do things later than sooner. I suppose that it was wrong of me to think that way, but I was a vampire in love.

I sent away the seamstresses. I told them that I was weary and hungry and that the dress would still be able to be fixed in the morning. They were reluctant to leave me until they had finished the dress entirely, but they caved in before I did and went away.

I was alone again, but I relished this kind of solitude. Michael was out doing more paperwork and though he invited me to the "rigorously boring" meeting, I declined his invitation.

I stood in the living room, standing in front of the long mirror, gazing into my reflection. Yes, *I* had a reflection, though I doubted that some of the older vampires had reflections.

There I was.

I was around five feet, four inches and I had elbow-length ebony hair, dark rich chocolate eyes, and thin dark pink lips with a hint of light crimson.

And I was in my wedding gown.

It was certainly beautiful, although it was unfinished. It was tight around my slender body; a pure white gown mostly made of lace and a floor-length hem with crystal beads covering my bodice and a thin trail around my bottom hem. I almost laughed when I realized that I was almost as white as my wedding dress.

"You look ravishing."

I thought that it was Michael, but I sensed the odd aura and replayed the voice and I verified that it wasn't Michael before I even turned around.

Preston Bennington was standing at the arch into the living room, holding two glasses of wine.

"Thank you," I said and then pivoted to look at myself in the mirror again. It wasn't that I was conceited; it was that I was astonished at the figure standing in the mirror. I hardly believed that it was me. She looked so different. It was like I hadn't seen her in such a long time. *Where have you been?* I asked myself. The person in the mirror reminded me of happier days full of sunshine and smiles, days that became gloomy after Kathleen entered. But these days were returned to me when I met Michael.

"Michael is a very lucky man," Preston went on. "If I had seen you first, I would've proposed to you right on the spot."

I forced a sincere laughter and thought back to the night that Michael had found me. I was wounded and possibly near death. Needless to say, I probably wasn't the prettiest sight on earth that night. It was a marvel that Michael welcomed me into his home at all.

"I was not at my best the night that Michael first met me," I informed him. "I could have been better."

"Oh, I'm sure that's not true," Preston argued and then moved from the archway towards me. He raised the wineglasses. "A toast," he suggested.

I did not sense any immediate danger in having a drink and besides, Preston was a very good friend of Michael's. I took one of the two wineglasses and we clinked them together.

"To love and all that other stuff," Preston intoned, already sounding somewhat drunk. He tilted his glass to his lips and sipped from it.

"To love," I repeated and took a tiny sip from my wineglass.

All of a sudden, Preston threw his wineglass onto the floor, shattering it into dozens of pieces washed in a sea of liquor. His hands reached out for me and I dropped my glass and I heard the distinct sound of it against the stillness in the air.

Preston grabbed me by the waist and drew me into him before I even realized exactly what was going on. He forced his lips on mine and I struggled against him.

I did not want to hurt him, but I saw no other way.

I had not exercised my powers of late—I had been more preoccupied with making wedding plans—but I hoped to pull off the same stunt that I had done on the vampire hunter who had confronted me after I had slaughtered my family.

Gathering all my powers into a tight mental bundle, I lashed out at Preston, striking his mind with my own and I sent him flying back, hitting the top of the archway.

I recovered my wits and watched him cautiously as he struggled to rise on his feet without any equilibrium.

"What the hell did you do to me?" Preston muttered, his mind foggy.

I did not reply to his question, instead I sent a threat. "If you ever try to touch me again, I will do more than what I just did to you," I growled.

Preston's eyes widened and he pointed his finger at me. "You're a witch!" he accused. "In league with Satan!"

"Just because I am in league with Satan, it does not mean that I am a witch," I snarled.

"Wait till Michael hears this," he said and started heading towards the door.

I could let him do no such thing, so I naturally gave chase. I pursued him, and before he could ever even come within a yard of the door, I was standing in front of him, my eyes dark and menacing.

"You will do no such thing," I told him.

"And who will stop me?" he challenged.

I growled again, "I will."

And there was no falseness in my voice. I meant what I said. In order to protect my secret from Michael, I would go to the greatest lengths, even to go as far as to …

"Kill me?" Preston questioned. "Is that what you will do if I tell him? Or perhaps you will cast a spell on me. Give me leprosy or curse me with seven years of bad luck."

"Worse," I promised him, darkly.

Preston saw the murderous gleam in my eyes and though he did not know me well, he knew me well enough that he understood that I kept my word on everything.

He darted around me for the door, but once again, I was on him like a laughing hyena to a carcass. I seized him from behind and when he attempted to yell, I muffled his yelp by covering his mouth with my hand.

But then I saw it.

His adrenaline was pumping and his heart was racing. I could clearly see the plump veins on his exposed neck. I attempted to fight it off, to resist it. I licked my lips and turned my head away, but when I shook my head, I felt myself *change*. I became a primitive savage, ruled purely by instincts.

I was aware that my eyes had become blood red and my teeth had become fangs. But mostly, I was aware of Preston's juicy veins, inviting me to drink from this fountain of life.

Before I could gain enough control, I lowered my head and punctured through his clean skin with my sharp fangs.

His blood poured into my mouth like a sweet and hot elixir. I remembered that I had once called it a "devil elixir" and perhaps it was.

I pulled up my walls of magick to halt Preston's memories from entering into my mind as I fed. This was the first time that I had ever done so and I did it with success.

I held Preston's limping body with my strong hands and I drained his blood until there was no more in his body.

Then I released his corpse and it fell to the ground as if it had never even once stood.

I backed away and leaned against the wall for support, otherwise I would have fallen down.

I was shocked by this.

I had taken another human life without displaying the mercy that Michael had preached.

I touched my fangs and I felt them and my eyes retreat to their prior normality. But I could still taste the blood in my mouth.

Only one thought raced in my mind. *What do I tell Michael?*

I DIDN'T TELL HIM ANYTHING.

In fact, after I killed Preston and after I finally came to terms with the shock, I carried Preston's body out and dumped it into the murky night waters. If his body were to be found and recovered, I could never be placed with the crime. And if his body were never found nor recovered, it would be as if he had gone missing and no one would have to know, especially Michael, that he was dead.

But a week and a half later, the body of Preston Bennington was found and Michael was anguished by this, especially when he discovered that Preston had two puncture wounds on his neck. That made Michael beyond furious. But he had a self-control that I had never possessed and he concealed his fury, but I sensed it every time I got close enough to, or when I put in enough effort.

Preston was supposed to be Michael's best man, but now that would never be. And I thought that perhaps since Preston was dead, Michael would cancel the wedding—which was scheduled for the month of May, two months from now—but instead the exact opposite happened and even I could have never predicted it.

I was resting in bed by him, resting my head against his chest as I had done that very night when I had lost my innocence to him. He was restless tonight; he had been so since Preston's body had been found. I could hardly blame him.

I gazed at the engagement ring on my finger. It was a slender silver band with a gigantic rectangle sapphire stone in the center, surrounded by tiny squares of diamonds. The sapphire stone in the center was a brilliant and deep blue, as deep as the ocean, not faded or washed out at all, but pure instead. When I looked at the sapphire, I felt as if I was staring into the eyes of Michael.

In an attempt to break the silence, I announced something that I thought he was thinking about for the past few days. "We can cancel the wedding, if you want to," I intoned softly.

Upon hearing this, Michael sat up and I with him. His majestic blue eyes stared into my eyes. He gave me a look that I could not read.

"What makes you think that I wish to cancel our wedding?" Michael asked me.

I explained, "Preston was your friend and he was supposed to be your best man, I understand that. And since he's gone, I assumed that you might want to cancel the wedding and wait a little bit, and I would understand that, that you need your time to mourn and grieve. And I will be with you every step."

Michael smiled at me and caressed my cheek. His hand felt almost as cold as mine was. "Don't you understand, Sophia, what all this means?"

I shook my head; I truly did not understand what light he could see in the midst of all this darkness. But Michael had a gift, a true and rare talent to see the candlelight among the darkness.

"When I found out that Preston was dead, it made me appreciate life more, and it made me appreciate the precious things in life, like you." Michael had a way with words. "Preston made me realize that we can't wait around for a long time for opportunities to pass us by; we have to take what we can get right here and right now. I don't want to postpone the wedding any longer."

My eyes sparkled at the implication behind his words. To verify, I asked, "So, what do you mean? Do you want the wedding to be sooner than May?"

"Well, how soon can your wedding dress be finished?"

"Tomorrow," I answered.

"Good then," he said. "We can have the wedding the day after tomorrow."

I repeated incredulously, "The day after *tomorrow*? Are you certain?"

"Yes," Michael chirped. "The preparations have been made and everything is ready, all we have to do is move up the date."

"By two months?" I returned.

Michael took my hands and held them. "I love you, Sophia. I don't want to lose you. I want us to be bound together in marriage so even if something happens to one of us, we'll be together forever."

Forever was such a big word. I never knew that a mortal would be able to commit to it. But Michael was like no other mortal that I had ever known. He seemed like a heavenly being to me, someone from out of this world.

"I can imagine our lives right now," Michael began. "We're going to have seven kids: four boys and three girls."

I had yet to tell him that I could not have children, that I was a vampire. But I played the part of a mortal for him, for my sweet Michael. "*Seven* kids! That's seven too many." I laughed with him at the preposterousness of the idea. Even if I had been human, I would not want seven kids. One would be enough.

"Oh, come on, Sophia. Just think about it." His voice sounded childish and innocent.

"I *have* thought about it," I informed him.

"No, *really* think about it," Michael insisted, his tone sounding low and serious. "Our house will be filled with the innocent laughter and tender smiles of children, *our* children. And then when they all grow up, they'll go and have families of their own and leave us to grow old in peace and see our gray hair together."

This was Michael's dream. I could tell that he dreamt this very same thing with his previous wife. He loved children. He was a good man; faithful, kind, and loving.

These were the times when I felt guilty for not telling him the truth. The truth about what I really was, about Preston's death, and even the truth that Preston tried to rape me before his life was cut short. I wanted to protect Michael from the same truth that he wanted to protect me from. I wanted him to remember Preston only as his best friend who would never betray him in any way, but I knew different. I knew the truth.

I sat next to Michael placidly, envisioning the same thing he was: a house full of children and their tender laughter, us aging and growing gray hair. I thought that perhaps I would be able to have children. A lot of the vampire folklore proved to be nothing more than myths anyway. Maybe it was possible that I could bear children, even though it was a long shot. Michael had taught me how to hope and it was a hope. And sometimes, hope was enough.

IT WAS THE HAPPIEST DAY of my life. But my happiness ended soon after.

CHAPTER EIGHT

εφ

HOPE AND HAPPINESS, THESE THINGS that we are told to keep when the light has grown dimmer and the tunnel has become darker. But what happens when this, this hope and happiness, is lost as easily as everything else in life is? I know the answer to this question. Without even asking, I was answered.

I WAS RETURNING HOME FROM a boutique where I had picked up the completed wedding gown that was prepared for me without my assistance. It seemed that the seamstresses had all the measurements they needed and they finished my gown at their little boutique. The gown was folded neatly so that it would not wrinkle in a big box that I was carrying in my hands as I opened the door to the Vandalius Manor.

Michael had asked to accompany me to the boutique to pick up my dress, but I told him that it was bad luck to see the bride's gown before the wedding.

I closed the door behind me and set the box down on a table in front of me, by the staircase.

"Michael?" I called out.

The house appeared vacant.

I glanced at the table upon which I had put the box. There was a lush bouquet of long-stemmed white roses in a matching ivory white vase. There was also a smooth white rectangle card propped against the bottom of the vase. My name was written there in beautiful black ink cursive. I also gathered up the wedding ring, mine, which was sitting next to the card. I opened the card first and there was a simple message written in the same beautiful cursive in black ink: *Come upstairs.*

I smiled to myself and I put down the card and held up the wedding ring. The wedding ring was less complicated and less dazzling than the engagement ring, which was fine with me. Though it was a simple design, it had a large impact on me. The wedding bands were silver, Michael's and mine, and while Michael's ring were tiny silver crosses around the whole band, mine was little silver hearts around the band. On the inside of my band, there was a brief inscription: "Love is immortal." *How ironic,* was what I thought whenever I read it. On the inside of Michael's ring, the inscription was: "Love never dies."

I slid my wedding ring on top of my engagement ring and, finding it uncomfortable, I removed my engagement ring so that I only had my silver wedding ring on my finger. In spite of my vulnerability to sparkling material, I adored the simplicity of the silver ring more than I adored the shimmering of the sapphire and diamonds.

I grabbed the vase with all the splendid white flowers inside. I thought that they would look much better in my bedroom than in the living room.

I stepped towards the staircase and I noticed that there were short, fat white-lit candles on every step, leading up to Michael and my room upstairs. There were also deep blood red petals scattered on every step of the staircase as well and I followed these, grinning at myself. I felt an unconfined happiness spreading inside of my heart like a wildfire.

I held the vase in my left hand as I advanced to my room.

I finally got up there and I quietly opened the door, wanting my appearance to be a surprise.

The door opened halfway and I stepped through.

And then, what I saw next, I have never been able to forget.

The room was beautiful, lit only by the same white candles found on the staircase. There were crimson rose petals everywhere and then, on the bed, there was Michael.

Michael lying on the bed, his arms stretched outward as if waiting for someone to come down and take him away from all this pain and death. His eyes were still open, staring expressionless into the ceiling, hoping no more.

I dropped the fragile vase and it shattered, an ear-splitting commotion in the center of the dead silence.

The water spilled out and the delicate white roses fell apart, and I, I fell apart.

I came towards him and I looked into his eyes and I no longer saw the sky in them; I saw the death. So hollow. Lifeless. Empty. *Dead.*

I could say nothing. I thought nothing. My mind was literally blank.

I approached Michael and I took a closer look at him, hoping against hope, praying to God, that it wasn't true, that it couldn't be. But it was true. There it was. Two puncture wounds on the side of his neck.

My hand reached out for him, as if my touch would somehow resurrect him.

I felt a clear layer of tears cover my eyes, blurring and stinging them as I had never been stung before.

My heart, though it had never truly been still, froze as if I had actually died and my heart, like the vase, cracked at first and then shattered into sharp fragments.

I felt a tear roll down my cheek and without even thinking, I brought my left hand up and wiped it away. Then I gazed at my hand and realized that I was not crying just tears, I was crying blood.

Blood tears.

I had never known that vampires could cry blood tears. I thought that that had been a myth as well.

But here I was, crying this blood from my eyes, streaking my face in sanguine.

A blood tear accidentally stained my silver wedding ring and I stared at it, transfixed. Now some of the silver hearts were drying with blood.

I looked at Michael's eyes again and saw that there was no more compassion in him, no more hope, no more love. He had been full of life and now he was death. I saw a single tear formed at his eye fall down. It chilled every part of me, even the coldest part of me. This tear had fallen after Michael had died. He was not supposed to be able to cry.

I saw his hand, he was also wearing his silver wedding ring.

I covered my mouth with my hand. In horror, I slowly retreated against the corner of the room, in the hellish pit from whence I had come.

I could not stop crying, could not stop shedding this blood.

I stayed there and sobbed until I felt the sun rise. The light betrayed me. It brought with it a brand new day, full of new hopes and promises, but a new day did not erase the old one.

Michael was still dead.

Michael was still crying.

AND MY HEART BREAKS EVEN now as I remember this night, the eve of my wedding. Michael's lifeless face is etched in my mind forever. I cannot even begin to describe the pain I felt when I saw him. Misery unlike anything I had ever known before swallowed me whole. What part of me did not break when I discovered his bloodless body? What part of me did not die and surrender all hope when my source of hope perished?

Happiness is often so brief. It lasts for a moment and then the next it is gone as quickly as that. So why must we experience happiness when we will be robbed of it the very next moment?

A man once said that it was better to have loved and lost then to have never loved at all. He was wrong.

When you love and then lose, the loss is only sharpened by the memory of love. To never love and then lose is not as bad as it could be. There is nothing to be sad over because you have never loved. Nothing to miss if you never knew it.

I have given up on love and on salvation. I have forsaken hope and compassion. Why? Because none of these things matter. Not even hatred and vengeance matter, really. What mattered to me the most was cruelly taken from me and now life is nothing. Death is nothing. To be honest, if I died, it would not matter because there is nothing in life that I want. And in death, I pray for the hellish fires to preoccupy my mourning. I cannot suffer if I cannot feel pain and indeed, I cannot feel pain. I can *feel* no longer.

When I was reborn into the realm of eternal night, I thought that I had lost all my feeling, but then I met Michael and he reconnected me to what I thought I had lost. And after he died, I lost it again and the only thing that kept me going was my hatred for Kathleen.

Michael was dead and I knew who killed him.

How did I know? Well, let's just say that I know Kathleen's handy-work anywhere. Michael smelled of Kathleen. His death reeked of Kathleen's evildoing.

I cannot change the fact that Michael is dead. I realized this from the moment that I saw him. And I cannot change the fact that Kathleen was the one who killed him. This I realized from the very beginning. I learned to accept, long ago, the things that I cannot change. But it doesn't make anything easier.

I loved Michael. That will never change. I hate Kathleen. That will never change.

ON THE DAY OF MY wedding, I did not marry the man I loved. I did not marry Michael…I buried him. But after the funeral, I could not just stay inside the Manor and grieve for him, though I suppose it would have been the proper thing to do.

No, my broken heart called for something more than endless shedding of blood tears. My broken heart needed healing and restoration, and this would never happen because there would never be another Michael, but his death would be avenged.

I packed certain things in a bag and against the wishes of the kind servants who were concerned for me, I went outside, took one of the horses, saddled him up, and I rode off into the night.

I WAS HELL-BENT.

I rode my horse to the yard of the estate where I had last visited Kathleen. I stopped and removed the bag from the bridle and then tied the reins of the horse to a sickly nursling cherry tree and in the shadows of the night, I stalked up to the estate.

I could feel nothing more than my rage and my pure anger and fury. Nothing and no one could have stopped me. God would have had to send a thousand plagues just to slow me down, but it would not have been enough to fully stop me from executing justice in the name of the man that I loved.

I entered the estate and vivid recollections of me screaming throughout the colossal halls and Kathleen watching me flooded back to me. I wanted to shudder, but I did not allow myself to.

My skills had sharpened as of late and I could sense Kathleen in the enormous marble dining room.

Catalina Chao*

I entered through the dining room and there was Kathleen with her back turned to me, facing the flames from the fireplace.

I smelled the fire and I ignored the bitter scent.

I would allow myself to show no emotion to Kathleen.

So far, every emotion that I had shown my maker, she had skillfully used it against me, even hate. Hate was not supposed to hurt you, not as much as love could.

I approached the dining room, passing the high-raised archway, in a stealth that I had never known I possessed.

"You know what Michael's last and final thought was?...Of you."

Kathleen's voice seemed to boom throughout the empty estate.

I did not reply. I left my facial features hard, impassive. Even when Kathleen answered and my heartstrings were tugged with, I did not show any emotion.

She darted around and she saw the raw savageness that had entered my eyes.

I knew what she saw because I saw it as well: a young woman who was betrayed by someone she thought she could trust. A young woman full of a ruthless fury that could no longer be suppressed or imprisoned behind bars of morality.

I saw myself in a new light. I had never known that I was capable of such animosity and for a brief second, I was terrified of myself and my own capacity for hatred.

But I quickly tucked that fear away under the thick layers of spite.

138

"What do you say now, Sophia? Do you still forgive me?" Kathleen slowly came around the table. "Are you still willing to show me that great compassion and mercy that Michael taught you? Or have you lost it in the moment that you lost Michael?"

Without answering, because she already knew what my answer was, I withdrew a sword from the bag and dropped the bag onto the marble floor. This sword was the last that Michael had touched. It had been blessed by a saint for me, a devil, to use in destroying Kathleen once and for all.

Kathleen gave me a ridiculous look. "Are you kidding me?" she asked. "You're way out of your league, Sophia."

I felt my fury blind me, but I did not allow it to take control over me. I would use it as a valuable asset, but I would fight with it. I would not allow it to fight for me against my immortal enemy. This I would do myself.

Kathleen had truly turned me into a monster, but it was not just her doing. I had a part to play in it as well. Michael had attempted to revert me, without even realizing what he was doing, and he had succeeded, but Kathleen had turned me back to the way of darkness.

Kathleen stopped when she saw that I was not bluffing. Indeed, I was not. I was prepared. I was ready to use this sword.

"You think you're scaring me, Sophia? You're really not," Kathleen insisted. "I'd beat you in a second."

Still, I said nothing.

Kathleen was standing against a wall where there were two swords clashing. She could easily take out one of the swords and use it against me. But I was ready for her. "You've come to kill me, I understand that. But what happened to all those things that Michael taught you? Mercy? Forgiveness? Compassion."

I snapped. *How dare she mention Michael's name again? Once was enough.* "Michael's dead," I hissed under my breath, my blood boiling every second. "And I'm here to avenge him!"

I charged at her with my sword.

Kathleen pulled out one of the swords from the wall, like I knew she would, and held hers at ready.

I roared, "And you *killed him!*"

I ran to her in a breakneck speed that I had never used before. Up until this point, I had not a reason to use it. I raised my sword to bring it down upon her head and split her skull open, but she prevented it by clashing her blade against mine.

I retreated my blade and kicked her in the stomach. *Michael has taught me well*, I remember thinking.

Kathleen returned it and kicked me in the stomach as well, but then I brought my sword in a cut from left to right, but Kathleen hopped back to avoid it and I missed. Then her sword ran into mine and our swords were touching together. My elbow collided with her face and Kathleen withdrew her sword. Then I kicked her in the left shin, forcing her to kneel down on her bended right knee. My sword came down at her head again and she prevented my attack once more.

Then I opened my mouth and my voice was inhuman. Even I did not recognize it. It was full of pure, savage rage.

"You showed him no mercy!" I howled, pulling back my sword, pivoting and then swinging at her again from behind. "You showed him no compassion!" I punched her in the face and then yanked her by the hair and drove her face into the ground. "*Why? Why? Tell me why!*" I bellowed, ramming her head repeatedly into the ground until I saw her dark blood—the same blood that ran through my veins since the night I was reborn into this damned world—form a puddle on the marble floor.

I released her, spun, and kicked her with enough force that I sent her flying to the other side of the room. She slammed against the wall and slid down, seeming unconscious, but I knew that she heard every agonizing word I spoke.

Kathleen chuckled softly, almost as if it hurt her to do it and I was glad. I was glad if I could hurt her in any way.

"You wanna know why? Because he deserved to die," Kathleen laughed, once again amused by my pain.

I unleashed an evil scream, bloodcurdling to anyone, unlike anything I had done before. It was different from the scream that I had let out when I roamed through these halls, suffering from the lack of blood. This scream, it was as if the gates to hell had just opened and I was seeing all the suffering and wrath of hell for the first time. There was an anger and misery in this scream that could have never been voiced in any other way.

I charged at Kathleen again, but this time, she was the one who was ready. She rose and kicked me in the abdomen before I could even put in the first blow. Then she kicked my hand and I dropped my sword. She docked me in the face, left and right, as I began to walk backwards, senselessly.

Then, dazed, I fell onto the ground and Kathleen was looming over me. She raised her sword. She was ready to kill me. It did not matter to her whether I lived or died, but she knew that if I lived, I would go after her again and again until I would finally prevail. She would not allow that to happen.

I looked over to my left and saw the opened bag and then averted my eyes to Kathleen.

"Well, looks like there's no hope for you, Sophia," Kathleen intoned, almost sounding sympathetic for me. *I'd rather be hated than pitied*, I thought. "You could have been great, if you had just done what I told you to do. But that little nagging voice of humanity kept you from glory and greatness. That's just too bad. I *will* miss you, Sophia. Who am I going to torture without you?" She smirked at me.

My fingers reached out for the bag as stealthily as I could so that she would not notice.

"Tell the devil Kathleen says hi," Kathleen finished and then began to swing her sword down.

I removed a small barrel of gasoline from the bag and declared clearly: "Tell him yourself."

I threw the wooden barrel at her with all my vampiric strength and it actually cracked open when it hit Kathleen's body. The liquid spilled from the barrel and drenched Kathleen's dress and body.

I grabbed a candle from a small table next to me by the wall and hurled it at her, the tiny flame igniting Kathleen onto fire from bottom to top.

Kathleen screamed and stumbled through the dining room, now engulfed in flames. The brightness of the orange almost hurt my eyes. Kathleen got too close to the fireplace and some of the fire from there caught onto her flammable fabric. She bellowed, horrifyingly.

I picked myself up and turned the other direction, scurrying underneath the archway and running out of the opened entrance. I untied my horse's reins from the cherry tree and mounted on the saddle. I sat on the horse, still, for a long while, watching as the estate was devoured into flames.

Then I turned the horse around and commanded him to leave, only when I was certain that Kathleen was dead.

My stallion and I galloped through the shadows of the night and all its darkness and I was finally free.

I knew that I would be meeting the devil sooner or later, but he would just have to do with Kathleen for now.

CHAPTER NINE

εφ

WITH KATHLEEN FINALLY OUT OF the picture, I had felt a freedom that I had never known. Perhaps it was because I felt like the ties that had bound me to her had finally been severed and I was now delivered from her, not from the devil and the crimes I had committed, but right now, that was all that mattered. Salvation was not important anymore, not that it ever really was. My beliefs of good and evil no longer held a place for me. All that was extinguished when Michael had breathed his final breath. I fed on human beings whenever I needed to, but I did not drink to the point of death. I left them alive. But that is not to say that I still had an issue with taking human life. No. I was fine with killing. I was a vampire. I could not change that.

After I torched Kathleen and her beloved estate, I returned back to Vandalius Manor to take a few things and then I went on the ship that was going to take me to the New World.

Kathleen told me about the New World. A man named Christopher Columbus, in 1492, had discovered it, and it was populated with Indians for a while before the Spaniards came. She said that perhaps she would take me there one day. *Liar.*

One and a half years had passed since I had first become a vampire. It was the year 1604 when I was moving away from France to a new colony in the new country.

I have never taken off my wedding ring. I have always worn it, never even removed it once since Michael died. I would not allow myself to do so. This wedding ring was perhaps the only tangible object I had of him still.

He was no longer alive and his soul had probably forgotten about me, too busy with the bliss of the heavenly afterlife. I once believed in a heaven and I still do, but I knew that I would never see this heaven, never be accepted in it.

But that was fine with me.

Never being accepted in heaven probably meant that I would never be reunited with Michael as I had hoped, but that no longer bothered me as much as it had the first few days after his death. What happened to me in the afterlife no longer mattered; it was what I did now, in my life, that really held an importance to me.

If my soul was to suffer in death, then so be it.

Nothing in my life or my afterlife really mattered to me anymore. But there was one thing in my life that still meant something to me, that still kept me connected to the mortal world, otherwise I would have given up long ago and killed myself.

It was my dear, innocent little Christine.

I came to the New World in loneliness, in despair.

I had lost the only man that I had ever really loved; I had moved away from my home and I no longer had a family. Even the loneliness hurt my soul. It reached to

145

the point where I could bear it no longer and I adopted a daughter, Christine.

Christine was only six-years-old when I had found her on the streets. She had no family. Her parents had died from an unknown illness and since they were poor, they left Christine poor as well, a tiny creature left to defend for herself.

I sympathized with her. I saw my reflection in her face. I was a tiny creature left to defend for myself. I was an orphan of great loss and sadness, as was she.

So I brought her into my new home and I cleaned, clothed, and cared for her. In this New World, I was rather wealthy, since I had taken some of my riches from the Vandalius Manor. I had to survive somehow.

And I was living in a peaceful home with my Christine.

I hired the best tutors to educate her in all areas of life. I told her stories every night, especially her favorite story which she always wanted me to tell over and over again—you know, the story about the evil vampire queen who made a good vampire who didn't want to hurt anyone. And then the good vampire ran away and fell in love with a handsome prince. When the prince kissed the good vampire after telling her that he loved her, she became human and they lived happily ever after in a castle of sparkling jewels, surrounded by seven beautiful children, four boys and three girls. And never did the evil vampire queen hurt the princess ever again.

Christine was my life. I looked to her for inspiration, for strength to carry on. I went on living for her. Christine was full of an innocence that I had once known but since then, long forgotten. Her hair was full of soft gold curls and she had lovely blue eyes that reminded me so much of Michael. Her skin was like a porcelain doll. She was, in essence, beautiful.

We lived together in peace for six years. Everyday, she grew more beautiful. And I saw a vision of hope in her.

When Christine was ten, I resolved to tell her what I really was. I told her I was a vampire and then I told her the true ending to her favorite "fairy tale". —The one where the good vampire fell in love with a handsome prince, but then the evil vampire killed him and then the good vampire killed the evil vampire, but had lost the only thing in her life that mattered.

Amazingly, Christine understood my sorrow and we comforted each other. I loved my Christine. She was the light at the end of my tunnel, just as Michael had been. They were both the lights at the end of my tunnel, but Michael had darkened before I reached my journey's end. Christine, however, renewed this lost light and gave it back to me.

CHRISTINE WAS TWELVE WHEN IT happened. I had gone out to feed. I was hungry and Christine knew about my bloodthirst, my need for blood. But I promised her that I would never hurt anyone who didn't deserve to die in the first place. She believed me.

I opened the door and the hair on the back of my neck immediately stood on ends. Every bone in my body quivered and my skin crawled up and down.

"Hello, Sophia."

I would know that voice anywhere.

I slowly turned around, terrified at what I would see when I peered out into the family room.

There she was, as if she had never left me.

She looked a little different. Her hair had gotten shorter and I could see a few scars on her face and neck—though they appeared to be gradually healing—but other than that, she was still her. She was still Kathleen.

And she was sitting on my cherished rocking chair, cradling a frightened and trembling Christine in her arms.

Kathleen saw the look on my face. "You thought I was dead, didn't you?"

I inched closer to the family room. Christine's eyes revealed a genuine terror and she implored with me silently to save her.

"Well, I almost did die," Kathleen informed me. "But remember that pond I had out in the back?"

I cursed in my mind. I had forgotten about that pond behind the estate. I remember that I went out once during a sunrise and I observed the reflection of the daystar against the calm water.

"Yeah, it definitely hurt like hell," Kathleen went on. "I got over the pain and then I thought, 'She tried to kill me. My own fledgling tried to burn me to ashes'." Kathleen nodded her head and glanced at Christine. "Do you know about her? She tried to kill me." Kathleen stroked Christine's cheek and I saw my adopted daughter cringe at Kathleen's touch, just as I had.

Kathleen turned her attention to me. "She's cute, Sophia. I do have to admit that you have excellent taste."

"Let her go, Kathleen," I ordered her.

"Or what? You'll burn me to ashes? Oh wait, you tried that, it didn't work now did it?"

I met Christine's innocent eyes and I knew that I could not just wait to reason with Kathleen. If I were Kathleen, I would not reason with anyone either. As much as I hated to admit it, Kathleen had all the rights in the world to be angered with me, as much as I had all the rights in the universe when I did what I did.

But that was a feeble excuse to use with Kathleen. She never saw me as her equal. I never had the same rights she had. The rules were always different for me.

Kathleen bared her gleaming fangs and her eyes changed colors.

Then I made a move.

Without hesitating, I lunged for her.

All of a sudden, a momentous weight pulled me back and restrained me from making my attack.

Christine cried out for me. "Mother!"

I turned to see vampire captors at my side. There were four of them, two at each side of me. They were more powerful than I. Their combined strength was beyond mine.

I watched helplessly, struggling with all my power, as Kathleen brushed away some of Christine's golden curls from her neck. Kathleen caught a glimpse of my devastated face before she pierced Christine's skin with her fangs.

I felt my face break. I fell apart inside again, just as I had done when I saw Michael. But somehow, this was worse. I had not been around to see Michael die; this time around, Kathleen was forcing me to watch every excruciating and painful moment. I crumbled as if I was made of ashes and a wind had just blown in. Blood tears rolled down my cheeks as I watched Christine wince in indescribable pain. Ah, but I remembered this pain. I still vividly remembered when Kathleen had killed Catherine Opaque and created Sophia.

I only prayed that she would not do to Christine what she had done to Catherine Opaque.

Christine's face became wan as all the blood dried from her and for a bit, I was glad that Christine died and that she was not damned to rise from the grave and walk in the darkness as I had.

Christine's tiny and lifeless body slumped into Kathleen's arms and then Kathleen rose, allowing Christine's body to hit the ground in a gruesome, rude manner.

"No," I sobbed. "Christine."

Kathleen advanced upon me and I stared into her eyes with no fire inside of me. I was truly dead.

Kathleen had destroyed the remnants of my life.

"Tsk, tsk, Sophia," she intoned. "You've been a very naughty girl."

A blood tear fell from the corner of my eye as I looked up into Kathleen's face—as if I was searching for some sign of sympathy or compassion or even understanding, though I was not—right before she punched me and the welcomed black oblivion of unconsciousness overcame me.

I SURRENDERED ALL HOPE THEN.

When I met Christine and adopted her, she had given me back a piece of hope and showed me how to live again, but when Kathleen killed her, I lost all of myself forever.

I kept the name Sophia, but I was no longer Sophia. I was not Catherine Opaque. I was not Kathleen's fledgling. I was not Michael's fiancée. I was not Christine's mother.

I was a vampire, alone in my despair, misery, and pain.

I WOKE TO BLACKNESS, JUST as I had done when I first became a vampire. But I knew that this time it was different. My chained hands reached out and hit wooden walls.

"Awake, I see," Kathleen observed. "You're probably wondering what's going on. Well, you see, you're now in a box. I'm going to take you somewhere, Sophia. I think you'll like it. It's as gloomy as you are. There's no point in fighting anymore."

I agreed with her. There was no point to anything anymore. There was no point to life, in living. No point to death, in dying. No point to love, in loving. No point to hope, in hoping.

I could only pray that my death would be quick, painless and easy. Simple. Over and done with, just like that.

I had no idea that it would be like this.

THAT I WOULD BE TRAPPED HERE, damned here in the confines of stone. I remember when Kathleen first threw me in here. She and my vampire captors shoved the box—with me in it—into the stone room while they hurriedly sealed it up before I could escape. I still remember the way Kathleen sounded when she spoke her final words to me. I still remember those final words as well: "We will meet again," she promised me.

I finally managed to break free of my chains and then I broke out of my box. I gazed at my new surroundings, wondering: "What kind of hell is this?"

This is hell.

I have learned that there is no real devil. The devil is whatever we fear. There are no real fires in an abyss of suffering souls. There is just this: a void of emptiness and loneliness, a place where hope no longer exists.

This is hell.

I bled myself the first day. I punctured my point finger with one of my fangs and I drew a tally mark for day one. I kept this up for—oh, you know already.

But that is the first part of my story.

I know that this is just the beginning. There is still more to tell; I just have yet to know *what* to tell. But this tale has not ended, this tale of immortal bloodlust and retribution.

PART TWO

THE CITY 2002

CHAPTER TEN

εφ

A LIGHT! GOOD GOD, I see a light! It is coming from the west wall, where Kathleen and my vampire captors had sealed it up after they threw me in here. I sense a presence. It is female. It is human. At the same time, it is not very strong, so I doubt that it is Kathleen. Nevertheless, I steel myself for whatever danger awaits me on the other side. Who knows what humans have evolved to in the past years that I have been incarcerated here, accompanied only by my dismal recollection of my past?

For the first time since I have been locked up in here, I hear a voice, other than my own, other than the voices of my memories.

Her voice is spirited, lively, zesty, and full of exuberance and a sense of energy and life that I have never known.

"Damn it! These are new shoes!"

At the same time, I sense that this person is going to be irritating.

The stones are beginning to crumble and I back farther away into the room, hugging my knees.

I see a head, along with the new light. She has light brown hair tied in a ponytail and honey dewdrops for eyes. She is young, nineteen. Her eyes meet mine and she is in shock for a moment before she recollects herself and continues to remove the weakened barrier.

"Hold on, I'm coming," she tells me, struggling to free herself as well as me.

More stones are removed and finally, the hole is large enough for me to step out. She prods me, making a ridiculous gesticulation with her hand. "Come on!" she urges me. "Hurry! This building's probably going to collapse!"

Hesitating only briefly, I rise to my feet—something I have not done in years—and I follow her out the crumbly-shaped hole.

She waits for me on the other side, prompting me to bend forward and pull myself out of the hole.

I finally get out and I take a quick sweep of my surroundings. There are long wooden beams and poles everywhere and it is dusky, dim, and I can tell that it has been uninhabited for decades.

The young girl guides me to the exit and I follow her, my violet Parisian dress flowing behind me.

The world that I enter is darkness, and yet there are billions of tiny resplendent lights that flare in kaleidoscopic hues. The brilliance of this beauty hurts my eyes and I rub them in an attempt to soothe the breathtaking sight.

"Where am I?" I question the one who freed me. She appears to be an angel, even among the thousands of tiny lights, which could also resemble angels as radiant as she is.

Hands on her hips, she sniffs the air and inhales. "You're in New York," she informs me. "Times Square, a mile away from Courier where I happen to be staying."

I spin in a circle, staring at everything because it is the first time that I have seen any of these wonders. There are machines with round lights on the front and back that speed off into the distance, leaving a cloud of black smoke. *What kind of devil has invented this monstrous-looking mechanism?* But there are still more things that I have never seen before, like the enormous boxes and moving pictures on them. I can see people through it and they appear so huge that they must be some kind of giants! There are horribly dressed women standing at the road. They have—what appears to be—a slender, narrower version of the cigars I often saw my father smoke. These monstrous mechanisms that spew smoke from a pipe in the back stop at the corners and they roll down a window—what marvelous things! Never have I seen a window move in such a mysterious, magickal way!—and they speak to the women. They seem to strike some kind of deal and the women enter the mechanism by opening some kind of small rectangular door.

Good God! What brave new world have I entered?

There are red, green, and yellow lights on black rectangular boxes that come on or off. It is difficult to tell which light will come on—it is almost like a guessing game! Which light will come on next? —Red, green, or yellow? And those moving mechanisms seem to stop, slow down, or go when a certain light comes on.

I am utterly overwhelmed!

"How long have you been in that place?"

I turn my attention to the young girl who freed me.

"What year is it today?" I return, instead of replying.

She looks at me and then turns her attention onto the overflowing of moving mechanisms. "It's the year 2002," she tells me.

Two thousand two? I answer, "I've been there since 1610."

Her eyes turn to me and we lock gazes.

"1610?" she repeats, incredulously. I cannot blame her.

"Yes, it's been three hundred, ninety-two years," I confirm. "Almost four centuries."

Her eyes widen. "You're a vampire!"

It is not even a question. She knows and she has strength in her belief. She is human; how can she know of vampires? A terrifying thought occurs to me now. What if vampires run the world today? What if this brave new world is over-swarming with tyrannical vampires that threaten the safety of humankind? But this cannot be. Standing here, among all the chaos, I sense only a hint of vampires here and there. Everyone else is human or some kind of demon unbeknownst to me. I think that I sense even a werewolf in my midst.

"How do you know?" I ask her, not even attempting to deny it. If need be—God forbid it—I could kill her to protect my identity, if she threatens to expose it in order to harm me. But I sense that she is human, capable of understanding and compassion, capable of everything that I have forgotten how to show.

"If you've been there since 1610 and haven't aged—or *died* for that case—I think it becomes obvious that you're not exactly on the 'most human' list," she says.

I cast my gaze downwards. "I wasn't always like this," I whispered, almost beyond audibility. "I was human, once."

"I figured that," she intones. "I mean, all vampires were at least human at one point in their immortal lives, right?"

My curiosity peaks. How can she, this insignificant little mortal, know so much about my kind when *I* know next to nothing?

"Why don't you come over to my apartment and we'll talk over coffee?" She leads me over to her own moving mechanism—it's shiny violet and the shape of a chest!—and I approach the door and I gawk at it, uncertain of what to make of it. I search for the doorknob, but I cannot find one. Instead, I find an oddly shaped silver thing that resembles a tiger's fang. I pull on it and the peculiar door opens for me.

"Hop inside," she tells me and I do as she says: I hop into the moving mechanism. "Let's get some coffee."

"What's coffee?"

AMAZINGLY ENOUGH, THIS CUSHIONED CHAIR is quite comfortable. I gaze out the window in front of me, and then I hear her spirited voice take on a form of mock authority.

"Put on your seatbelt," she orders of me.

I glance inside the moving mechanism. *What's a seatbelt?* I wonder. As if she read my mind, she points to a belt hanging to the door side of my seat. I grab it and begin to pull on it, astounded by how far it stretches out, as if it would never end.

"Plug it into that thing on your left until you hear it click," she tells me.

I search around for that "thing" and find a small square where I see a slot that the belt—though it is strangely shaped like a flattened cork—would fit in. I jam the belt into the slot until I hear a click.

"Good job!" she compliments me. "Next thing, I'll teach you how to use the radio."

I think about this one. *What on earth is a radio and how do you "use" one?* But my attention is focused on something else. Before me, there lay a black panel. Above the black panel, there is another window, exhibiting the business of the outside world. I never knew that the world could be so busy. Paris was, indeed, busy, but not in the same sense. I stare blankly at the various knobs and I feel a sudden urge to fidget with these sensational little things!

I pull out a black stick that has a small white picture of a slender cigar on the top. There is a light at the bottom of the stick and I am careful not to touch it, though I have never seen such a thing before.

"What is this?" I ask her, holding it up.

Her attention suddenly turns on me and she picks it up and pushes it inside the hole. "That, should not be touched," she informs me. "It's a cigarette lighter."

"What's a cigarette?"

"It's something that stupid people smoke that fries their brain cells," she answers me, matter-of-factly.

Brain cells?

I press a button and suddenly, a caterwauling voice splits my eardrums. Never have I heard such music come out in such a way, and never have I heard such a dreadful, thick voice! I cover my ears with my hands and make an expression of distaste.

She notices this and she presses another button, shutting off whatever that horrible yowling was.

"What *was* that?" I question her.

She waves her hand. "Ah, it's just Britney Spears," she tells me. "I know, she's pretty nasal. Not to mention, all around sucks. That's why you turn to a different station." The moving mechanism stops and she reaches over, presses a button, and twists a silver circular knob and loud music—the sound of catastrophic discord— blasts through my ears.

She begins to bob her head up and down, a ridiculous motion that makes her look like an uneducated baboon. "Rock music," she declares, while she continues to make that insidious and appalling movement. "It's the music of the twenty-first century. It's made a comeback. And it's the best kind of music."

I hear a male voice come onto the "radio"—his voice is soft and gentle as he sings the first of a line with a tender melody in the background. He says that he is seeing red.

I hear the girl beside me squeal. I look at her, curiously, for an explanation.

"I love this song!" she cries out." 'Seeing Red' by Unwritten Law."

She speaks to me as if I understand what she is saying, which I do not.

I gesture to the interior of this rather fascinating moving mechanism. "What is this?" I ask her.

"It's called a car," she answers. "I rented it. Like it?"

I nod my head eagerly. "It is nice ..."

She shakes her head in an obvious sign of disapproval. "No, you're going to have to learn slang or you won't fit into this century and people will look at you like you're a freak."

"What's slang?"

"It's a type of jargon spoken by most teenagers of today," she replies. "Okay, instead of saying 'nice' or 'wonderful' "—Amazing how her eyes never leave the road as she speaks—"You have to say 'cool' or 'tight'."

I question her "slang". "Why do I want to say 'cool' or 'tight' if none of what I have experienced is neither cold nor firm?"

"That's beside the point," she says instead. "Of course something really isn't '*cool*' or '*tight*', but we use it as our way of saying that something is really great or nice."

I nod, comprehending the point she is trying to get across. "I like your car—It is *tight*," I say, showing off my knowledge of slang.

She puts a quirky smile on her mask and nods. "Okay...Pretty good, but just don't try to sharply pronounce any words," she advises.

I nod again and put my gaze to the window. So many iridescent lights. I have never seen such a thing. I open my mind for a moment and allow the thoughts of the people of New York to enter my mind—and I am nearly deafened by it. Such commotion. I seal my mind just in time to hear her speak again.

"My name's Brielle April," she introduces. "I'm from Sundry, California—although I don't suppose you know where that is."

I shake my head and she elaborates: "It's on the other side of the country."

"Of the New World?"

Brielle shakes her head and I see the darkness play inane shadows on her youthful face. "It's called America now," she corrects me, adding, "North America. There's a South America below us."

"You are a long way from home," I tell her. "You must be if Sundry, California is on the other side of North America."

She shakes her head. "Nah. Just a couple thousand miles...no biggie," she shrugs it off. "Get familiar with that term, too: 'no biggie'. It means that it's no problem or it's not important."

Such a strange language these people of America have.

"What's your name?" Brielle asks me, as she sharply turns the wheel in front of her, and I feel myself being yanked over to her side.

Thank God for seat belts, I think. "My name is Sophia."

"Is that it?"

"I do not understand."

Brielle speaks again. "That's it? No last name?"

I lower my gaze to the floor underneath my feet and I shake my head. "No," I whisper under my breath. A sadness strikes me then. I was once an Opaque, but I am no longer. I came close to being a Vandalius—oh, how I would have loved that—but I was prevented from the happiness it would have given me.

Brielle caught a glimpse of my sadness. I can tell that she did. She averted her gaze before I could look up at her again.

"Where are we going?" I ask her.

"To my apartment in Courier, the quieter side of town," Brielle responds. "I think you'll like it, Sophia."

Brielle smiles at me and I smile back at her, in spite of myself. Could it be possible that, after all these cruel and lonely years, I have finally found a true friend?

CHAPTER ELEVEN

εφ

BRIELLE ENTERS HER APARTMENT AND I follow silently behind her. Even though she was first through the door, Brielle turns around and closes it behind her. Even in the darkness, my eyes adjust quicker than they do in the light. I can see everything in the apartment—my visibility no doubt keen. Being a vampire enhances almost everything—my hearing, my speed—and magnifies every other emotion left untouched by vampiric improvement: pain, loneliness, misery.

There is a kitchen, but there is no fireplace to warm your food. There are a few plates in a square white box divided into two sections. There are two knobs and an arching silver bar that lunges over the square white box with the unclean plates, dishes, and various utensils.

I look over from the kitchen to a small table by the door. It has a painting on it. I am still observing all this in pure darkness, but I can see the painting as if I am looking at it in daylight. It has color to it, lifelike colors that could not be portrayed realistically with the many tones on an artist's canvas. Not even Michelangelo himself could have painted this tiny picture covered in a transparent glass. There is a man on this painting and I can tell that it is Brielle behind him, with her arms wrapped around his neck in a playful, loving manner. The man is merely a man; he appears the age of seventeen. He has dark brown hair, skin, and eyes with a squared off nose and a short-sleeved shirt—as bright as an orange—conceals his lean, yet somewhat muscled, body. A necklace made out of puny shells hangs around his fine neck.

All of a sudden, the whole room is illuminated and I stare up into the ceiling where I see a light fixture—nothing at all like the crystal chandeliers often found in Paris, my home. The light fixture is more of a round white ball. Strings of crystal are not suspending from it at all and I see no candles.

"Electricity," Brielle announces to me, as if she sees my bewildered expression. "Thank God and Ben Franklin for it."

"God?" I repeat. "Do you still worship God in this time?" I turn to look at Brielle as she replies.

"Of course we do," she says. "Christianity is the number one religion in this country, probably in this world."

I declare solidly, "Christianity is not a religion; it is a faith."

Brielle shoots me a stunned look of hers. "You believe in God?" she asks, her voice quivering as if I would rip out her throat at the mere mention of such a ludicrous question.

"I *believed* in God," I amend for her.

"It's okay," she confirms. "I'm an atheist myself."

Brielle saunters over to the kitchen and glances at the dirty dishes. She moans. "I don't remember eating all this food."

My eyes scan the room once more. I see a couch, similar to Michael's, in the room and in my mind's eye, I see a flash of that couch in the Vandalius Manor that I left behind nearly four centuries ago.

Brielle gives up on the dishes and she removes her coat and throws it recklessly onto the floor and sits down on a chair at a circular wooden table. I follow her.

I take a seat across from her and I interlock my hands and I look at them for a twinkle, realizing how pale they have gotten under the light fixture.

"So…what's your story?" Brielle questions.

"Beg your pardon?"

Brielle rephrases the question without hesitation. "How did you get here? Why did you come here? Where did you live before? Background info stuff."

"I suppose I should start at the beginning," I say and then clear my throat. "I was born in the year 1586, to an aristocratic family. I had two younger brothers, Peter and Jacob. I lived in a small village outside of Paris, France and I enjoyed going to theatrical plays."

"Okay, we've gotten past the exposition," Brielle urges me. *Obviously patience is not practiced in this century.* "Now, let's get to the complications and then the rising action."

I regret telling her what I have already told her and I instantly try to make the subject appear unexciting. "My story is long; it could take the whole entire night and it is not riveting or full of happiness."

"Those are the best kind," Brielle goads me on. "There are no real happy endings in reality, Sophia. Life is a game of chance and we're merely the players of the cards that we're dealt."

"You don't believe in destiny?" I ask her.

Brielle shakes her head and almost laughs out loud at the preposterousness of it. "Life is about a journey, not a destination," she says to me, wisely. "It's full of crossroads and I don't want a map giving me directions for it."

"Why do you want to help me?" I question her, her and all her motives.

She is taken aback by my question, but she has a reply. "Because I've never known a vampire and I want to help with whatever quest you might have now that you've been freed."

"The quest for vengeance is done alone," I tell her.

But this does not silence her. As a matter of fact, Brielle becomes more thrilled than before. "Ooo!" she squeals with unconfined delight. "Vengeance! I *like* the sound of that!" *Zesty little creature*.

"Perhaps you should listen to other sounds," I return. My next comment does not lighten the seriousness I display. "Possibly from that nasal Britney Spears you speak so negatively of."

"I just want to help," Brielle repeats with less words than before. And her tone is sincere and I can tell that she is benevolent—a rare quality, I thought, to find in such a new time.

I attempt to stray her away from the subject of my past again. My past is too painful and even I cringe at the thought of it. I rise from the chair and swipe the marvelous picture of Brielle and the seventeen-year-old man with the shell necklace. "Is this your—"

"—Boyfriend," Brielle finishes, sheepishly. "He's all the way in California. His name's Andrew Kaleiho."

Her gaze seems as if it could pierce through the glass. "I hate that photo. It was taken three years ago when I was seventeen and so was Andrew."

I further study the image through the glass screen. "Why is he in California and why are you in New York?"

Brielle rises from her chair and strolls over to me, sighing. "I ran away from home."

I look up at her, curiously.

Brielle fixes her attention on the glass picture. "My parents were so strict and they suffocated me. I wasn't allowed to do anything I wanted to do. I wanted to study vampires, to learn more about the mythology surrounding them and my main goal was to meet a vampire—a *real* one—not some drugged gothic who dresses in black and cuts himself to drink his own blood.

"And then I started dating Andrew during my senior year at Sundry High School and at first, everything was cool, and then I realized that Andrew was suffocating me too. He was kind and sweet, but he told me not to do certain things if I asked for his opinions, and he never asked for my opinion on where we wanted to go and what we wanted to do on a date. He just never listened to me. So, to escape the confines of my parental censorship and Andrew's ignorance, I ran away—about ten thousand miles into New York.

"I thought that I'd find a lot of vampires here. I thought that New York would be a vampiric city—an enormous one, probably the hotspot for all vampiric activity. I sought out the vampires and found none. Then I went to a building that was going to be finished, but they decided not to do it because the construction workers would sometimes hear voices there—screaming, laughter, and insane cackling." Brielle's eyes meet mine. "I guess it was you who was scaring them."

I have never thought about it before. I never realized that there could be people around me. I had assumed that I was so isolated no one would ever find me again.

Brielle went on. "The workers went on a strike and they refused to finish the building and since none of them would work on it, everyone gave up and left it there. They're supposed to demolish it, but they haven't gotten around to it. No one here really does get around to anything."

"How do you know that there weren't any vampires in Sundry, California, where you lived?" I question her.

"First of all, you can stop saying Sundry and California together," Brielle points out. "Sundry is the city in California, which is the state. I lived in Sundry, which is in California. Second of all, I doubt that there was any vampires in Sundry. Sundry was such a boring town. There were the occasional murders, but nothing vampire-related. Nope, Sundry was an all around normal town."

I put the picture back onto the table. "Sometimes things are more than what meets the eye," I utter, directing my statement to Brielle.

"What about you?" Brielle asks again. "Tell me how you got into that little room. And what's with the box and chains?"

"Are you certain?" I ask her.

Brielle nods her head. She stands still while I move away towards the thick curtains that cover most of the window, leaving only a small slit revealing the darkness of the outside city. I stand alone in front of the window, observing all the activities that go on below us, with my back turned to the human girl. Brielle stands by the door as I continue my incredibly long story.

"To reiterate, I went to theatrical plays often. It was a pastime for me. There was little else I could do, little else I *wanted* to do. And it was at this new play in Paris called *Immortal* that I met Kathleen, my friend, my maker, my eternal enemy ..."

I told Brielle the vivid accounts of everything that had happened to me from the year 1603 all the way to the year 1610, when I was incarcerated in my custom-made cell. Though the first part of the story spanned for only seven years, it felt like an eternity. I vividly recalled the moment when Kathleen destroyed what was left of Catherine Opaque—I would have gladly died instead of being accursed—and created this damnable beast, Sophia. For Kathleen is not the only vampire that I have spent my years loathing. I was forced to relive the moment when I entered the bedroom, finding Michael's bloodless corpse on the bed. I experienced the sorrow and frustration of seeing Christine killed right in front of my eyes again.

When I was finished, it was morning.

RADIANT SUNLIGHT SPILLED THROUGH THE slit created by the heavy curtains, which reminded me of the curtains I had selected for my bedroom when I lived at the Vandalius Manor. I still had my back turned to Brielle. I did not even want to imagine what expressions her face made at the shocking points of the story—when I took my first drop of blood from a scoundrel named Leander. When I slaughtered my family and my servant, Hosanna. When that vampire hunter attacked me. When Michael was murdered—and I foolishly attempted to avenge his death—and when Christine also suffered the same fate.

Brielle is speechless. I understand this. She never spoke once throughout my whole entire story. She never interrupted me and she kept quiet, allowing me to finally perform the same story that I have been rehearsing over and over again the past three hundred, ninety-two years.

I ended the first part of my tale with: "And then I was thrown into that room, with no hope of ever being found."

I focus on the cars that seem to jam the roads. Hundreds of people engrossed with their personal matters stalk the streets of New York, but not quite in the same numbers as people had done in Paris. These New York folks double the amount of Parisians on the streets back in the sixteenth century.

I kept my back to Brielle for the duration of the time because I could not face another person while I wove these threads of history. I could not bear to see my pain reflected in another person's eyes.

"Wow," Brielle finally speaks. "That was pretty incredible. And again I say wow."

I finally turn around and look at her, my eyes dry when I can see that Brielle has obviously shed tears during the length of my seemingly never ending tale. I have not cried for a long time—unless one would count that sudden burst of weeping I succumbed to when I thought again of Christine. Now you know who these people are: Michael and Christine. Never do I have to mention them again without you understanding what roles they have played in this tragic drama.

"I can't believe all that stuff happened to you," Brielle utters, folding her arms across her chest and rubbing her sleeveless skin. She had sat down sometime while I told the story and now she had risen.

"Yes," I agree. "Tragic and...painful."

"More like...sucks like hell!" Brielle shouts. I am astounded by her choice of words. "I mean, you were a good person and then you meet some treacherous bitch who corrupts you slightly and then makes you a vampire to corrupt you completely. And then she makes you turn on your own family and then she kills your fiancé and then you go off to kill her, and just when you think she's dead, she comes back and kills your daughter."

I am nearly stunned into silence. Though her words are rough and brash, she speaks the truth and summarizes all that I have gone through in seven years, explained in hours, in just a matter of seconds. *Wow*, I think.

Brielle is fiery. She has yet to finish stating her emotions on this subject. "Who does she think she is? — Some kind of god? This is completely outrageous! What a *bitch*," she huffs again.

"The vampiric world is not so glamorous after all," I utter, directing my comment to Brielle.

But Brielle shakes her head. "No. The vampire world has become *more* than glamorous. There's depth and meaning behind it, now. It's not just some shallow obsession of mine, anymore. It's real and it's cool and it's beautiful and heartbreaking."

"All these words and yet it is still not enough to epitomize all that I have experienced," I tell Brielle and turn to the side, staring at the kitchen.

I see Brielle's face out of the corner of my eye. She is unexpectedly angry and she stomps up to me and grabs me by the shoulders, violently shaking me to the best of her *human* abilities.

I am forced to look into Brielle's profound brown eyes. She is full of purpose—though her purpose is still unclear to me.

"What are you going to do now?" she interrogates me. "The story just doesn't end with 'unhappily ever after'."

"I thought you said that most stories do." I see my own ghostly reflection in Brielle's passionate eyes.

"*No*," Brielle protests, contradicting everything she told me prior to the commencing of my story. "I mean, yes, that's true, but some stories have openings to the brighter end. Your story isn't finished Sophia, it's just begun. Now you're free. Now you can finally take your vengeance on Kathleen!"

Brielle's eyes search my face for some kind of response, but I give her none, facially.

"I realized something as I retold the story for the last time in that little prison," I begin, my voice strong and firm, and my ears are amazed to hear such solidity behind my tone. "Vengeance will not bring back anyone that I have lost—my family, Michael, Christine. They're all dead. They are but ashes now in a cemetery and perhaps it is time for me to join them. I have no real purpose here anymore, but to suffer Kathleen's wrath. I had forsaken everything in there when I was replaying the story one last time. I finally realized that nothing matters anymore. I should just die because there is nothing left for me here in this world. Kathleen will just come back and hurt me again—she can do it, Brielle, she's fiercely capable of it. But at least in hell, I cannot be tormented by her anymore."

"No, you'll only be tormented by Satan," Brielle counters bitterly to me. I sense no fear in this girl, whatsoever.

"Maybe there's more than one," I return, "and Kathleen is one of them. Maybe the one in hell will be better than the one on earth."

Brielle scoffs at me. "Don't you understand, Sophia? Of course vengeance will never bring any of your family members back or Michael or Christine, but you can't go down without a fight. So far, you've only battled Kathleen once and you were foolish to think that she was dead when she wasn't. But now you're smarter than that and you can *beat* her, Sophia. You can *win*."

I remember that when I began the story, I was full of a fiery hatred for Kathleen—and do not underestimate me, I still have that—but I was also full of a wicked vengeance that no longer seems to matter.

It was like I had an epiphany while I told the story for my last time. I realized that there is nothing left for me here on earth and now it's time to take my proper place in the next world.

"I appreciate what you're trying to do for me, Brielle," I console her, "but some stories don't have endings at all unless the hero dies. This story needs an ending. It has to stop, somewhere, this cycle of violence."

"The only way that violence and hatred can be stopped is with forgiveness," Brielle intones, almost echoing what Michael once told me. "And you tried forgiveness, Sophia, and it didn't work. Sometimes the only way to *beat* violence and hatred is to end it with your own."

I could only stare at her. Brielle, in some ways, reminds me of Michael. She has the same intense and raw passion that he had. It chills me.

"Maybe you should get some sleep," Brielle suggests. "I'll get you a pillow and a blanket and you can stretch out on the couch."

Brielle went into her own room and retrieved for me one of her own pillows. She handed me a blanket, though I did not need it but I knew it was rude to refuse such hospitality, and I "stretched out on the couch".

My sleep was plagued with dreams, mysterious dreams for which they had no meaning that *I* could understand. In my dream, I saw Christine being cradled in the arms of Michael. They both still had their puncture wounds on their necks and they were looking at each other fondly, as if they knew each other.

"Do you remember the scarf?" Christine asks Michael.

Michael nods his head, cradling Christine the way Kathleen had done right before she killed her. Michael is sitting on my rocking chair. "I remember the scarf," he answers. "It was like silk."

"Do you remember how it fell to the ground?"

"I remember."

A flash of a silent Kathleen set ablaze running around the estate interrupted the placidity of Michael and Christine. Now Michael was sitting on a rocking chair, cradling Christine, behind a roaring fire. Its shadows leapt out from the raging fire and touched Michael's face.

"Did you see the glint of silver?" Christine queries him again.

"I saw a light," Michael offers instead. "And for a moment there, I was blinded."

"We walk this world blind," Christine says and then her gaze connects with mine. "But you see everything...even the things that can't be seen. Like Death."

Michael nods gravely. "Ssh...It's a secret, little one. She mustn't know. The silent mice are dead ones."

The bloodless carcasses of my family litter the carpet beneath Michael and Christine. They look as if they are sleeping— "silent mice"*—but they are dead—*"are dead ones".

I shake my head, hoping to get out of this warped dimension. I know that it's all a dream, but for some reason, I cannot bring myself out of it. It's like I have no control over anything—and perhaps that is what dreams are: you don't have any control except to follow the guidance given to you by higher or spiritual beings.

"Vengeance is the Way," Michael informs me, looking straight at me, boring through my soul with his dagger-eyes. "From the Seed of Hatred, a Mournful Warrior shall be born. Stray not from your path, Mournful Warrior, and you will find the Way of Forgiveness. Look to the glint of silver and you shall find salvation. Study the face of innocence and you shall find compassion. Walk the path of the dead one before you with strength and you shall live. Follow the footsteps of loyalty and you will not fail. But Vengeance is the Way."

I wake, gently stirring to the mild heat of the sunlight on my fair skin. The blanket is pulled up to my neck and I am curled comfortably on the couch. I glance around at my surroundings and I see Brielle standing in front of the dishes in the kitchen.

"Good afternoon," Brielle greets me. "You're a late sleeper, or is it just that you prefer a more nocturnal schedule rather than a diurnal one?"

I smile tautly, unable to find humor in her comment. It does not appear to me that she takes vampirism seriously enough. When I had been brought across—or *cursed* as I often look at it—it seemed that I had taken it much graver than any before me.

"I don't suppose you're hungry," she says.

Food…What a pleasant thought. But food is nothing to me. I have long forgotten the taste of poultry or the flavor of wine. Yet somehow, Michael was able to give me back that which I had lost.

"Do you want blood?" Brielle asks this question with a humble meekness; I detect mild fear in her tone for the first time. She is scared about my vampiric menu.

"Would you happen to have any blood from animals?" I ask. "A chicken or a pig?"

Brielle turns around and swings open a white door with several transparent shelves and a bright light. She explained to me earlier that this was a refrigerator— humans used it to preserve food and drinks.

"I'm not sure if I have any pig's blood …" she mumbles, lowering to the bottom shelves. "Or chicken's blood for that case." She closes the door and turns around to meet my eyes. "I know! We can go buy some blood from the butcher! It'll be a cool experience! You'll get a chance to be outside and I can show you the world."

Catalina Chao

I freeze and I feel my spine shudder. Kathleen once whispered the same exact words to me: *"I can show you the world,"* she whispers to me again, chilling every bone in my slender body. I shrug off my discomfort and reply to Brielle in the most uplifting voice I can muster, "That sounds nice."

4444444

CHAPTER TWELVE

εφ

DAYLIGHT IN THIS WORLD SEEMS different from daylight in the sixteenth century. I gaze out the window at the throngs of people all rushing to go about their daily lives and I wonder what would be so important as to not allow them one single moment to stop and smell the roses? The red, green, and yellow lights come on and off and the sky no longer seems to be endless. Since humankind has advanced so much in their technology, it appears as if one day the sky will become an actual limit and they will one day reach it and perhaps colonize it—as they have colonized practically everything else. Brielle teaches me how to "roll down" my window and when I do, I put my face through it and feel the rush of the breeze against my wan skin. Rock music explodes from the radio in the car. Then I see Brielle press a simple button that causes the roof of the car to disappear and now I am a part of the outside world. I stretch my arms out to my sides as if I am flying. I lift my face to the sunlight and I appreciate this gift of light from God. For I have not seen it in nearly four centuries. Brielle laughs at me. For I resemble a naïve child who is experiencing everything for the very first time and indeed, I am.

THE BUTCHER SHOP IS SO white that the blood on even the butcher's apron is a disturbing and stark contrast. I stand in front of a spotless counter—though I can smell the blood that has been on this counter and washed off throughout the years—and fold my arms on it. Brielle stands to my side, conversing with the butcher who is a balding fifty-one year-old Filipino who has been running the butcher shop for at least thirty years. I receive all this information from probing his mind. This is something that I have not done in a long while and so I am still a bit, as humans say, *rusty*.

The butcher goes into a back room which is tainted with the blood of animals, creating an eerie red hue, and returns with a small white container of, no doubt, pig's blood, which is finer than any other animal blood. For pigs, in spite of their insulting reputations, are intelligent animals.

Brielle gives the butcher a few American dollars and he thanks her. Brielle pivots with the container now in a bag with the butcher shop's trademark in red on it—how suitable.

As soon as Brielle and I are both seated comfortably in her car, she takes the container from the bag and hands it to me.

"Take off the plastic lid first," Brielle instructs me.

I gaze at the container and I see the slightly transparent lid. I remove it by applying pressure from under it with my fingers and the lid pops off. I examine the pig's blood before I drink it—an old habit of mine. Ah, what is that human saying? —Old habits die hard? Indeed they do.

It is convenient of humans to put animal blood in a container to be bought for a measly amount. How I wish I could have been born and live in this time rather than the sixteenth century.

I put the container to my lips and I sip a small amount and then my insatiable blood craving overwhelms me and I find myself taking large gulps at a time. In a matter of three seconds, I have finished all that was in the container. I wipe my mouth with my bare arm. Brielle is looking at me; I can tell. I can sense her eyes watching me.

"I guess you were thirsty," she comments. "We can get some more blood later, but I think we need to buy you some new clothes to make sure that you blend in with the rest of New York."

I study my clothes. I am in a purple gown, the color that denoted wealth in my time—it was what I wore the night that Christine died. *Killed is more like it*, I think to myself bitterly.

THERE IS UNIQUE APPAREL OF every kind and color on racks about the shop. Brielle guides me to one rack after another, attempting to find something that suits me and will allow me to "blend in with the rest of New York". I touch the cotton fabric of the shirts and my eyes nearly bulge from my sockets when I see tight black pants made out of cowhide, as Brielle explained it to me earlier, before we entered the shop. It was degrading in my time to wear something as sluttish as that.

"Leather," Brielle declares to me, putting her arm around the back of my neck. "It's fashion."

"It's slaughter," I argue.

"True, but I bet you'll look sexy in that with this." She holds up a black piece of cloth that looks so tight and impossible to fit in. There are no straps to it; instead, it becomes a triangular shape at the bottom and I am supposed to tie it in a large knot in the back to hold it up and in place.

I shoot Brielle a skeptical look. "You are not going to put me in that," I state clearly.

"You wanna bet?"

I STARE AT MY REFLECTION in the several mirrors decorating the confined square room that reminds me so much of my past confinement. I still have a reflection, although I doubt that in a few more years it will be gone from me completely. I think I remember Kathleen once mentioning to me that once a vampire reaches one millenium, their reflection will vanish forever. Thankfully, I have not reached my first millennia. I gawk at my figure. I am stunned by the gracefulness that it presents, yet I lack. My black hair has grown over the years. It goes below my hip and it is wild, untamed, and in need of a serious brushing. It is full and as black as the night that often shrouds me. I cannot believe that this is actually Sophia. This is who and *what* I have become over the centuries. I hardly recognize myself anymore. I have truly abandoned Catherine Opaque in the years of yore.

SHEEPISHLY, I CONCEAL MY NEW attire with my arms as I open the lock and step out from the mirrored dressing room. Brielle is sitting down on a bench in front of me, waiting for me to make my entrance. But my entrance is nowhere near grand. Brielle hops from the bench when she sees me emerge like a butterfly out of its cocoon for the first time after a long metamorphosis.

"No one will be able to see how good you look if you're constantly covering up with your arms," Brielle informs me, annoyed by my lack of audacity with my twenty-first century garb.

"What if I wish for no one to see how good I look?" I return.

"Come on, Sophia," she prods me on. "I bet you have a great body underneath. You just have to flaunt it."

I shake my head. "I do not wish to flaunt."

Exasperated, Brielle stomps her feet over to me and takes my wrist, gently pulling them down to my side, revealing my feminine figure.

"Wow," Brielle notes. She spins my body to face the dressing room that I had come out of. The door is open and I can see my reflection in the mirror. "See, you're beautiful, Sophia. What do you have to be ashamed of?"

I narrow my eyes to take a closer look at this womanly figure. I am beautiful—not to be full of myself. But I was blessed with an alluring body. My face, save for the lack of color, is slender and there are curves throughout my body. I have a trim stomach and slim fingers. My nails, despite the lack of care, are still in a rather good condition. My lips, however, are a much paler shade of pink than they were before and my brown eyes are almost a reflection of the coffee Brielle had made the night before but never got around to drinking.

"Now, just a few more changes here and there and you'll be a modern-day, twenty-first century woman," Brielle promises me.

HOURS LATER, I AM STRUTTING through the streets with a new and easy sexy walk that I picked up instantly after being reborn centuries ago. I am moving among the mortals as if I am one of them—and they would hardly be able to suspect that I am not one of them. Brielle is strolling beside me, wearing darkly shaded sunglasses.

Brielle took me to a hairstyling salon and they evenly trimmed off my hair so that it now reaches down to my elbow. They straightened my hair and "tamed" it, so to speak.

Afterwards, Brielle brought me to a manicurist and they filed my nails, coated them with a translucent glossy liquid and then painted over the gloss with black, making the blackness appear shiny.

About two shops away from the manicurist was a make-up shop where Brielle sought the aid of a highly-trained make-up artist to deepen my lips with a rose red tint and curl my eyelashes with a frightening-looking device.

On the way out, however, I saw a shade of black that I liked much better than the crimson. Brielle bought the black lipstick for me and helped me to apply it on.

Then, she decided, I was ready to show the world exactly who I had become: a seductive creature who thrived much on darkness.

When I first became a vampire, this was not what I wanted to become, but in the end fate was inevitable.

As I stroll on the street next to Brielle among the flurry of the lively, from the corner of my eye I can see heads turn as I walk by. Brielle explained to me earlier how seldom it was that someone would stop and gawk at another, especially since several civilians walked by everyday and it would be a difficult task for one to grab the attention of so many of them all at once.

But most of the civilians that took the time to stop what they were doing and ogle at me were men.

I grin to myself, thinking. *Men still have not changed over the years.*

I SIT DOWN ON THE couch in the center of Brielle's apartment, where I was now to sleep if I chose to. I clasped my hands together and closed my eyes, focusing, concentrating, and pouring all my thought into finding another's.

Of course, I am searching for Kathleen. I feel as if I have had enough time to adjust to this new world and now it is time to show Kathleen exactly what kind of individual she has taken part in creating.

Brielle stands behind the couch, behind me, silent. I explained to her that this takes an enormous amount of concentration on my part and I cannot have anything interrupt this or I will lose my train of thought.

I have not done this in so long, unless you count the butcher. But this time it is different. I am extending throughout a vast amount of space, traveling beyond the minds of thousands in a different location than mine. The butcher had been standing right in front of me. Kathleen, wherever she is, can be several states away.

For now, I have to believe that she is still in New York somewhere to be found.

I let out a small breath and in my mind's eye, I begin to travel through the city with the speed of light.

Several things flash through my mind. I see the jumbo-sized televisions and billions of gleaming lights in the sky and on the streets. The cars are moving fast-paced on the street, causing what Brielle deemed as "traffic". There are sleazily dressed prostitutes at the corners of these streets, vying for attention from the male population in the cars. But beyond all this, I begin to see past the people with an accelerated speed and I feel as if I am actually there, moving swiftly past these unsuspecting humans.

All of a sudden, it hits me, like a lightning bolt to a tree branch.

I see a brown-haired woman turn around and it becomes clear to me that this is Kathleen.

Kathleen's eyes sweep her surroundings, as if sensing that someone has just connected with her mind in an attempt to invade it. Then her eyes stare at me, as if she can see me though I am not really there, and she laughs.

I open my eyes, bringing myself out of the mind-connection with Kathleen.

Brielle comes around the couch and sits to my right. "Did it work?" she interrogates.

I nod my head. "It worked," I confirm.

"What happened?" she prompts me.

"I saw her," I tell her. "I saw her and I think she saw me."

"Who? Kathleen?"

I nod my head again in reply. "She's here, Brielle," I add. "She's here and she knows that I'm alive."

"Is that a bad thing?" Brielle hesitantly asks.

"I don't know yet."

I HAVE NEVER BEEN TO a carnival before, but Brielle insisted that it is full of fun and merry pleasure. She says that there is an amusement park in Courier, New York and it opens only one week out of each month. She dragged me here, but I truly am amused with the clowns dancing around with their overly exaggerated faces and painted tears. I am as entertained as Kathleen was when I used to scream through the halls of the estate. But this is not a twisted entertainment. It is intended to be jovial and indeed, I sense the convivial atmosphere all around me.

Brielle skips to me and holds up a white stick with pink cotton hanging unstably from it. Brielle picks out a clump of pink cotton and throws it into her mouth. I never knew that cotton could be edible.

"Cotton candy," Brielle says to me, as if reading my mind. "It looks like cotton and tastes like bubble gum. Wanna try some?"

I am not certain of this as I reach out and take a small portion of the cotton candy. I am amazed by how soft and fragile it is. I put it into my mouth and I begin to wonder, as I chew this malleable substance, what am I supposed to be able to taste?

"Isn't it good?" Brielle asks me.

I swallow what is left of the cotton candy in my mouth. It is so flimsy that it almost immediately dissolved in my mouth upon contact with my tongue. "I cannot taste anything," I answer. "Only blood."

Brielle continues to eat the cotton candy, seemingly ignorant of my desire to taste food as humans do. But anything that is not blood is tasteless to me. There is no flavor, no spice, no sugar, no bitterness and no tartness. It is the little things that humans take for granted. To be able to taste food as they do is a miracle beyond God.

"Man, that's lousy," Brielle speaks, finishing up her stick of cotton candy. "Do you want to go on any rides?" She removes a string of paper tickets from her back pocket and holds it in front of me. "I've got plenty of tickets. We can go on the Hurl Whirl ten times if you want."

Brielle brought me out to the amusement park in an attempt to assuage my concern over Kathleen from the previous night. But when surrounded by thousands, it is all that I can think of. This is the extent of loneliness; not to be solely imprisoned in an isolated room, but rather to be surrounded by thousands of people and yet not able to belong to any one of them. This is solitariness, to be alone among many.

"Okay, I'll tell you what." Brielle's clear words snap me out of my solitude and back to this bright carnival. "I'm going to go on the Merry Go Round and when you choose to, you can join me." She rips off two tickets from her string of thirty and places them in the palm of my hand and curls up my fingers. She smiles tenderly at me. "Try not to worry about anything, Sophia."

Without uttering a single syllable, I nod and watch Brielle stroll to the entrance. She hands a man two tickets and, in a way, I feel like I am looking at Christine when I see Brielle climb onto a fancy and creatively decorated horse that looks like it could have ridden out of some magical fantasy fairy tale.

Before they start the Merry Go Round, Brielle waves to me from her perch and she flashes the widest smile that I have ever seen.

I wave back to her and manage a half-smile as Brielle disappears from my sight when the carousal begins to move in a counter-clockwise direction.

Brielle turns away on her fantasy horse in the darkness and I see others riding behind her on a horse, or a lion, or a love-boat. They are all leaping away from this reality and into the next, where they are carefree and not haunted by their past as I am. Thus, I remain here, watching them, watching this opportunity for escape pass me by. Even if the release is only momentary, it might just be enough.

As I look on, I see someone on a lion. Someone that I know. Someone that I would recognize anywhere. Hair the color of sunshine. Eyes the mirror image of the cobalt blue sky. *Michael.*

No, this cannot be him. But it is. It is my Michael, the one that I lost nearly four hundred years ago. It is he, and yet, it is not. But I sense nothing different.

Michael sits atop a ferocious lion and he waves to me as Brielle had done, but his wave is slow and solemn. This frightens me. Michael has never been able to frighten me. He is not the kind of man who does.

No, Sophia, this is not him, I think to myself. *He is dead. You saw him dead, remember?* Oh, I remember. How could I ever forget? I remember him laying on the bed ever so lifelessly. But some part of me is hoping against hope, praying against all odds, that it is somehow Michael. That the pure power of my one true love was so strong that it survived the cold centuries to find the other half of his heart and soul.

Michael.

I reach out my hand to him, in desperate hope that he will take it and we will be together forever and the happy ending that I often spoke of to Christine will finally come true.

But Michael only smiles at me and he disappears at the turn and Brielle emerges from the other turn.

Brielle leaps off her horse and jumps over the puny gate surrounding the Merry Go Round. She scurries towards me.

"Sophia? What's wrong?" she queries, her tone a genuine combination of worry and fear.

When the lion returns again, its seat is empty and Michael is gone, as if he was never there in the first place.

BUT THAT IS IMPOSSIBLE, I think to myself. Michael was there. I felt him. In that one single moment that I saw him, everything from my past with him rushed back at me in a turbulent flood. All the passion, all the pain, all the pleasure slapped my face all at once and I was overwhelmed with joy to feel all that I had once felt with Michael. I had never known life until I knew him; therefore, I had never known death until he died. Michael left deep footprints in my heart—could it be possible that he has returned to walk the set of prints he left behind so many years ago?

I twirl the wedding ring on my finger, pondering the irony of the inscription on the inside of the band: *Love is immortal*. It truly is. It cannot die because it is immortal.

Brielle approaches me with a sapphire mug of coffee, hands it to me, and then sits down to my right. "Careful," she advises me. "It's hot."

I wrap my slender fingers around the mug with ease. I feel the heat, but it does not bother me. I sip from it without needing to blow the steam from it like Brielle.

"Are you sure you saw him?" Brielle blurts out. She is not the kind to hold back her words or emotions. She is quite brash and it could very well end up getting her killed.

"Yes." My voice displays no emotion whatsoever. It is firm and solid, however, and slightly on edge, sharp. Wouldn't you be a little on edge if you saw someone you thought was dead ride on a Merry Go Round? Especially if that someone was supposed to marry you three hundred years ago?

"Maybe it was a lookalike," Brielle offers.

I shake my head. "No," I tell her. "I know my own soulmate when I see him. It was Michael, not some imposter." I sip some more of my coffee. It does not ease any of my tensions because I cannot taste it, but I enjoy the simple motion of sipping.

"But I thought you said that Michael was dead," Brielle reminds me.

I do not argue with her. I thought he was too. "I did," I confirm. "But apparently, he's not."

"Maybe you were just seeing things," Brielle suggests.

My gaze locks with hers. "You believe in vampires, but you cannot bring yourself to believe in people coming back from the dead?"

Brielle says nothing in reply to my question. Instead, she turns the question on me. "But what if he wasn't dead?" she hints. "What if, when you found him, he looked dead but he wasn't? There are drugs that can paralyze your whole entire body, making it seem as if you're dead, but you're not and it's only temporary."

"It still doesn't explain his remarkable *non*-aging," I say, avoiding the only possible answer that I know of. *But he can't be...He just can't. No, there must be some other way, some other answer that I do not know yet, that Brielle and I have yet to find. I refuse to allow him to be, to be—*

"What if he's a vampire?"

My eyes dart up at the mention of the word. I glance up at Brielle.

"What if, instead of killing him, Kathleen turned him into a vampire in order to torment you?"

This is a likely answer. In fact, it is probably the only answer that makes sense, in spite of the lack of sense and reason and logic. But love is not logic. You can't take it, dissect it, and run experiments and record down your results. Or perhaps they can in this time. They seem to be able to do everything else.

"I didn't sense anything vampiric about him," I tell her.

"What if he blocked anything vampiric from you so that you would think exactly that? I mean, you said it yourself, Sophia. Vampires can put up shields of magick that act as walls for their minds so that other vampires can't sense it."

Brielle is correct. It is possible for a vampire to do so, but I am still hoping against all odds that it is not true, that my sweet Michael cannot be a...I can hardly utter the word in the same sentence with his name. It would be like defiling his whole entire soul and everything he stood for if I were to utter his name and the word "vampire" in the same breath.

I say nothing. For there are no words to describe anything that is racing on in my mind, heart, and soul as of right now. It pains me to think of Michael as a...He just can't be. His soul was so good, so pure that he could not be a demonic entity that lives off the blood of others. He was so full of light that I refuse to allow him to be like me, a world wrapped in a never-ending blanket of darkness.

"...What did you feel when you saw him?" Brielle quietly asks me.

I contemplate my answer. "What did I feel?" I felt that I needed to repeat the question before I could properly answer it. "I felt lost. I felt so lost, every part of me. I felt like how I did that night, just moments before Michael found me, and I mean in more ways than one." I turn to look at Brielle directly in her spirited eyes. "Before I met Michael, I was nothing. I was a savage attempting to live off morals, but I could not succeed. I failed in doing so. And then I met him and he was my salvation. He was my world...And so, when he died, my world died with him. And now I find that he is back. What is my world now?"

"You can't depend on others to be your world because that's exactly what happens," Brielle intones with wisdom beyond her youth. "You say that your whole universe revolves around one solitary person and then something happens and then your universe is thrown off-balance and destroyed because now it has nothing to revolve around. You have to find independence so when you fall in love with someone and then maybe you break up, you'll still have your independence to turn to."

"I was weak…and young, Brielle," I tell her. "What could I have known about love?"

"A lot," Brielle answers without even needing a second to think it over. "You obviously knew enough to recognize your soulmate. Love isn't an easy thing to find or to feel or to know. It's incredible for anyone to be able to see love in someone so quickly and not have it be some kind of disastrous mistake."

I argue. "But it was a mistake. I should not have fallen in love with him. I shouldn't have asked him to marry me because otherwise, he might not have had to die so early."

"You can't help who you love, Sophia," Brielle consoles me. "Anymore than you can know the future. What happened was meant to be, no matter what you say. And no matter how many times you wish it was different or how many times you rewrite the script with an alternate ending, it will always come out the same. That's fate, Sophia. That's life. That's what it means to be human."

"If being human means loving someone for one moment and then losing them the next,…I could never survive in this world." I turn away from Brielle because I do not wish for her to see my tears as they form over my eyes. They slide down my cheek and they are the same color as the blood tears that I shed for Michael. They are not at all like human tears, salty and crystalline. I know that human tears are salty because I was once human, even though that seems like an eternity ago.

"Being human means more than just living and dying," Brielle explains to me. "It's also about experiencing all that life has to offer you, the happiness, hope, pain, love, hate, success and failure. Life is about more than just a destination; it's about the journey."

I look at Brielle. She is certain of the words that she has just told me. She finds no uncertainty in what she has said and the solidity that she possesses convinces me that what she says is true. Life is not always just about living and then dying, although that seems to be the whole of my existence. "Perhaps you're right," I incline.

"And if life means experiencing one brief moment of happiness rather than living an eternity without it," Brielle continues, "then that's better to have loved and lost then to never have loved at all."

I nod my head without saying a word. Silence ensues and I allow Brielle to plunge through the ice.

"I'm going to bed," she says. "I've got work tomorrow morning." She rises from the couch and cordially pats me on the shoulder before she crosses in front of me to her bedroom.

I lay down on the couch, contemplating every word that has just been shared between the two of us. My eyes are open, staring at everything before me, yet seeing nothing. No direction. No destination. No journey lies ahead of me. I sigh and close my eyes, hoping for the black oblivion of sleep to whisk me away for just one night before I know that I shall never have it again.

CHAPTER THIRTEEN

εφ

I FIND MYSELF RESTLESS. THE nirvana of sleep did not come as I had hoped. Instead my mind ran with fleeting and endless thoughts of Michael. How can it be? My Michael cannot be a vampire. It is not right. It is not fair. He does not deserve the same wretched curse that I was given. To be a vampire is to be condemned to walk in the realm of eternal darkness. Michael should have never known that. He should know only sunshine and light. The dark shadows that afflict my life should never cloud Michael's or touch him. He was innocent, as I was when I was first changed. But then there is always the simple possibility that he was never there at all. Perhaps that truth is better than the possibility that he is a vampire. Maybe I was just seeing things—maybe I had wished so hard for Michael to be here that I was convinced I saw him. After all, no one else saw him.

With my preternatural vision, I have counted the various dots on the ceiling nearly one hundred times. There are three thousand, forty-eight hundred and nine dots on the ceiling and here I am, beginning my count again.

Unexpectedly, a sharp pang rips at my heart and though my eyes are open, staring at the darkness enveloping me, another image hits me like a spiked minesweeper to my head.

My sweet and beloved Michael is awaiting me at the lavish lion on the Merry Go Round. *"Come, Sophia, come to me. I have been searching for you across time and centuries,"* Michael presses on. *"Will you not come to greet your soulmate? Will you not come to receive the comfort you so often sought?"*

I bolt out of the couch as soon as the image of Michael vanishes out of my mind as mysteriously as it had come. I am in red shorts and a red shirt that Brielle loaned for me as my "pajamas"—as she deems them—but what I wear does not matter to me.

I turn around and I see the large window before me that I looked at when I told Brielle my tale. The door is behind me. Since I cannot see any possible way of opening the window, I simply move towards the door and like the furtive feline I am, I escape Brielle's apartment without causing the slightest disturbance.

THE AMUSEMENT PARK IS DESOLATE at this time of night. The merry lights that once glistened deeply in the darkness are all gone now and there is only the occasional rustle of leaves scampering across the grass or the chilling sound of voices long gone.

Even with the glorious reputation of fun and entertainment, the amusement park is a place to be avoided at night, when the hours are at its darkest.

I approach the locked metal gates to the park—an effortless obstacle I overcome with a simple inhuman leap over the gates. I land with slight pressure to my feet and I rise, scanning the shaded park. Copses of trees cast ghostly shadows on the rides that have been taken apart here and there. I stalk towards the Merry Go Round, which seems to move gently—a soft rotation as if the wind had blown it. But a mere breeze cannot cause this colossal child's toy to move. No, someone turned this Merry Go Round. Someone exceptionally strong. Someone inhuman. Someone like a vampire.

"You've come," he says and I dart around, tracing the direction from where that voice had come.

There is Michael, appearing around the turn of the Merry Go Round, just as he had earlier tonight. He is gracefully perched on a chaste swan and this simple image of him before me reminds me of his innocence.

"I knew you would come," he speaks again and yet I am speechless, breathless almost.

He has not changed at all. The ocean is in his eyes and gold in his hair. This is my Michael. This is the man that I love more than any other living person on this earth.

Michael moves from the exquisite swan towards me. I sense nothing wrong with him. He is as human as Brielle is. He is within a foot of me and coming closer every second.

"I *dreamed* that you would come," he continues. "You were standing in the Manor, looking beautiful in your wedding dress—although I've never seen it. But you were like an immortal goddess."

Save for the immortal part, you are not even close to the truth, I think to myself as Michael continues speaking.

"When you first came to me, Sophia, you were a goddess on some cloud in the heavens that floated down to me," Michael utters. "You were a vision from God."

"You do not know how far you are from the truth when you saw that, Michael," I counter.

Michael is standing at arm's length from me. *So close, yet so far away*, I contemplate.

"Why? Is it because you are a vampire?"

These words stun me as if the venomous needles of the thousand bees that work for love and truth itself have stung me.

I say nothing. How should I react, none the less *reply*, to such an inquiry? But I need not say anything. Michael speaks for me, voicing thoughts that I never could have assumed he had.

"You have fallen from grace in the eyes of humankind," he tells me, "but not from the Eyes of God. You can still redeem yourself, Sophia. You are still forgiven in God's eyes because even the most darkest of vampires are still His children and if we give our soul and heart to Him, He will protect us and lead us to the Gates of Heaven."

I am taken aback. Michael has never been religious. His words came from the purity of his heart and soul; not from a chapter that sounds like it could have been in the Holy Scripture. I have never heard him speak like this before, yet I sense the same authenticity in his voice as if he was speaking about the human forgiveness and not the Lord's.

Michael comes towards me and I allow him to take my hands in his. I shudder with his touch. I have not felt it in centuries. I want to tell him so badly. I want to confess all my sins and announce all my experiences to Michael right here and now. I want to tell him of all I have gone through and witnessed and been a part of. *Oh,*

Michael, you could never understand how lonely I have been without you. All those long, harsh, cold nights that I yearned for the fire of your embrace and the passion in your kiss and the desire in your touch...I have been without for an eternity and now that you are here, so close to me, I must have you now. You must ravage me with your calenture and devour me in your unquenchable craving. You must hold me and never let me go again.

Yet I keep silent. I say nothing to him. I do not express my carnal hunger to him. He would never be able to understand what I had to endure without him. He does not need me as desperately and fiercely as I need him.

He raises his left hand and the moonlight reflects on the silver band on his ring finger. The gleam of the silver is so bright that in one instant, I was nearly blinded by it.

"I have never taken off my wedding ring," he informs me with sincerity. "I could never even imagine going one second without it."

I think back to Michael's funeral. He was wearing the wedding ring. I had asked the mortician to allow me to put his wedding ring on his finger—the tiny crosses carved out of the silver band in a never-ending circle. I vividly remember sliding the wedding ring down Michael's finger just like how I would do if we had gotten married that day. I thought, childishly, that if Michael wore his wedding ring now, when he crossed over to heaven, he could show God that he loved someone he had left behind on earth—someone who was cursed to spend eternity on that earth. But Michael had not known that I was a vampire.

Michael is behind me now, his arms wrapping around mine with the same feverish passion that I can so distinctly recall from nights abandoned long ago.

"Love cannot die ..." Michael whispers sensually in my ear.

"Because love is immortal," I whisper back to him, in the same amorous tone he used with me.

I turn around, still captured in his embrace, and face him. I put my cold hand to his cheek and caress it, the way that he often caressed my skin in those forsaken days.

I look into Michael's merciful eyes and tears begin to form in mine. I am seeing red now. For the first time, I see the blood tears. My blood tear is a scarlet screen over my eyes.

"Michael, I've missed you so much," I begin to sob. "I thought I'd never see you again, but some part of me hoped that we would be reunited in God's Grace, even though I knew that it was impossible." I begin to weep and I rest my head against Michael's chest, taking in the same warm comfort I took in a lifetime ago. I have never known solace until I knew Michael. No man nor woman nor living creature—undead or otherwise—on this earth has ever known solace until Michael has delivered it to them.

Michael puts his hand behind my hair and smoothes the tangles caused by laying on the couch too long.

"Ssh ..." Michael calms me. It was as if it was in his nature to pacify the tempest.

I permit him to hold me, to embrace me the way that I have never been embraced before and would never allow another to.

I gaze up into his eyes. The blood tears have rolled onto my cheeks by now and I wonder if Michael is at all terrified at this woeful sight. I can taste my own blood on my lips.

I can only watch as Michael nears towards me and presses his lips against mine. Only now do I realize how cold he actually is. His hands tighten around my back and though this would usually be an encouraging thing, something in the back of my mind goes off. Something is very *wrong*.

INSTANTLY, I REMOVE MYSELF FROM Michael's embrace and I take a step back. The blood tears on my face have begun to dry now. There is no use in crying, in shedding these macabre tears. I should know that by now.

Michael looks as if he is fearful of my sudden withdrawal, but there are no words for which I can use to explain to him what I felt the moment that he kissed me.

"What's wrong, Sophia?"

"Who in God's name are you?" I interrogate.

Michael stretches his arms out and his palms are open, still ready to take me back into his grasp if I wish it to be so. *That will always be my Michael*, I declare. *He will always be ready to take me back when I need him. But this man, this man before me is not my Michael. He is a figure of light concealed in shadow. He is but a carapace of what he used to be.*

Michael looks at me with shock. "What do you mean?" he asks me, his voice innocent as it always was.

"I don't know who you are or what you are trying to pull off, but you are *not* Michael," I say to him.

"Of course I am, Sophia," he returns.

"No," I hiss at him with more firmness than I could have ever dreamed of. "Drop the charade. Tell me who you *really* are."

Michael's face is a mystery to me for a few seconds. I cannot read his expression or his mind. But then, he bursts into a fit of high-pitched laughter and he cannot contain himself from squealing in pleasure. *One moment he is as enigmatic as the ancient pyramids and the next…he is laughing as if we were best friends*, I think pessimistically.

"It took you a *kiss* to figure it out, Sophia?" he asks me incredulously. "My God, what does that tell you about our relationship?"

He grins at me, just as he has done before, but the expression behind the smile is different from what it used to be. His smile used to be full of amiability and now it seemed full of devilishness.

"It's true what I said before," he continues. "I *have* been looking for you since…well, since you left France. Hell, I've checked in every cave from Asia to Jerusalem and, what do I find? Nothing."

"Why have you been looking for me?" I ask him.

He turns his eyes from me to his hands and the ring on his finger. "You think Kathleen is good company?"

My eyes widen in bewilderment. *Michael knows Kathleen?*

"I admit, she can be fun when the moon is full," he says, slicing into my heart with every word he utters. "But other nights, *God*, it's like she's having her menstrual cycle or somethin'. You get what I mean? She's not even human; why in hell would she act like it?"

I try not to display my hurt, but it is impossible for me to do so. I admit, I am an emotional being. I have always been so. But I suppose you already know that.

"And she *never* shuts up about you," Michael adds. "It's always, 'Sophia, this, Sophia, that'. My *God*, the woman knows no boundaries!"

Michael catches a glimpse of my betrayed face. It is the first time that he has noticed it since he began his monologue about Kathleen. He approaches me, slowly.

"You shouldn't look so surprised, Sophia," Michael says. "I *have* been looking for you. Kathleen and I, we want you into our family. We are ready to accept you and forget all that has happened and bury those days in the long-forgotten past. We want you back, Sophia."

I finally speak. "This cannot be possible, Michael." It is brief, but it is all that I can say at the moment.

"It *is* possible, Sophia, anything is. I see it now."

"You're dead," I declare, yet my quivering voice shakes my solidity. "I saw you dead, laying on the bed." For just a blink of an eye, I am brought back to the Vandalius Manor, in the bedroom where I see Michael's lifeless corpse on the bed. He did die.

"You saw me dead," he corrects me. "But you missed something, Sophia, you overlooked one, *tiny*, little thing."

I am still in that room. I am standing next to Michael's body, examining it for what I overlooked.

"You were so busy with your blood tears that you didn't see the other blood," he persists. "*There was blood on my lips.*"

I glance at his body on the bed and there it is—I see the blood on his pale dawn-tinted lips. The blood has made his lips darker than they were before. How could I have not noticed such a thing before? *"You were so busy with your blood tears that you didn't see the other blood,"* Michael whispers into my mind. He is right. I did not care to even observe his body, to certain that he would not be condemned as I am. But I had thought: *Surely Kathleen would never go to such great lengths just to torment me.* But I underestimated her again and it led to this notable alteration in Michael. *How could she?* It was horrible enough that she had made *me* into a vampire, she had to do it to the man that I loved as well? This war had *nothing* to do with Michael. He should have never been a part of it. But now that he is, what can *I* do about it?

This agonizing reverie is over and I bring myself back to the new Michael, standing before me and truth slaps me in the face.

"No ..." I begin to sob. "This isn't right."

"It's true, Sophia," he tells me. "You can deny as much of it as you want, but it doesn't change the facts. I drank before I died. I drank Kathleen's blood."

I run past him, but he seizes me by my shoulders and forces me to stare into his blood-red eyes. *He truly is a vampire.*

"Kathleen told me everything," he whispers into my ear, forcing the words into my mind so that they may never be forgotten. "All that time that you pretended to be human when you were really a bloodsucking little bitch—"

I break out of his grasp, crying, "No," but he catches me again with a speed that I have never possessed.

"You slaughtered your family the night that I found you—"

An image of my whole entire family sprawled on the carpeted floor invades my mind and I nearly shriek in horror.

"—And you killed Preston Bennington—"

"*In league with Satan!*" Preston accuses me. The picture of him flashes to the next scene: he is running to the door and I grab him. The next moment cuts this one abruptly. I gaze into the ceiling, altering my eyes and my teeth, and I viciously stab Preston with my fangs.

"—And you didn't even *try* to stop Kathleen from killing Christine."

"*No!*" I cry out, steeling myself for what I knew would come next.

Kathleen brushes hair from Christine's neck and drives her fangs into Christine's virtuous skin. I see my devastated face again, grieving out in vain attempts, "Christine."

Michael finally releases me and I stumble onto my knees like the awkward fool that lies in all of humankind. Michael giggles with a raw savagery that I thought I would never hear in his voice.

I struggle to rise while Michael continues his torture on me.

"But you still don't understand, Sophia, you just don't get it," he utters. "They say that youth is wasted on the young; well, Sophia, immortality is wasted on *you*."

My heart breaks at the harshness of his words and though I have my back turned to him and he wouldn't see it, I refuse to shed anymore blood tears.

"I mean, all this time, you had *all* that power, and you just *wasted* your time with it! You were so busy *bitching* about the hardships of immortality and the curse of darkness when you *should* have had the whole world bowing down to your feet. But *no*! You just couldn't let it go."

The "curse of darkness" has made Michael something beyond unrecognizable and I curse under my breath at the knowledge that if Michael had never known nor met me, his life would be full of light and not darkness.

"You have *no* idea what it feels like to feel what I feel everyday!" Michael bellows to the listening sky and stars above. "To have this…this *power* coursing through your veins every *single day*! To walk among the mortals knowing that you are above them and that you have the power to massacre all of them in a split second. The devil is not the one to be afraid of; it's what's in this world that's truly terrifying. We are the bogeymen that make children jump onto their beds after saying their prayers. We are the very things that thrive on life. We are the earthbound gods!"

I chuckle to myself at his foolishness, causing him to stomp his feet over to me and lift me from the ground. His hand is wrapped around my neck and his grasp is tight, though this does not intimidate me.

"*You think that this is funny*!?" Michael roars at me, his vampiric face no longer having any affect on me. "*Will you laugh when I dance on your grave?*" His tone is ruthless and demonic. I have no heard such a voice on *any* creature before.

I laugh right in front of him. "You know that we're both damned, don't you?" I ask him, my voice the exact opposite from Michael's; calm, soothing, and relaxed.

"I know no such thing of damnation," he says. "I know only a godhood that rivals the Creator."

"Such arrogance," I return, irking him with my controlled repose. "You think that you are a god...What happens when you fall down to earth?"

Infuriated, Michael yells, *"Never!"* as he throws me across the amusement park, until my back slams against the locked gates and I am sitting on my rear end. Before I know it, Michael is looming over me.

"There's a reason to everything, Sophia, just as there's a reason to why Kathleen chose .you." Michael squats gracefully in front of me. "Why do you have to struggle against it? Can you not accept your true nature?"

I reply, "I *have* accepted my true nature. *My* Michael taught me how." I say each word vehemently, to slice through his coolness the way he did to me, to *wound* him with my own truth. "But just because I have accepted what I am, it doesn't mean that I am or will become evil." I clutch my stomach. The force of Michael's throw and the power of the collision with the gate has injured me internally. He must have broken something.

"We are vampires, Sophia, not the devil's children," he explains to me.

"Aren't we?" I doubt. "We aren't God's anymore, so who do we belong to if not the devil himself?"

"No one," he responds quickly as if he has rehearsed this scene over and over again. "We belong to no one. And just because we drink the blood of the living, it does not make us evil."

If I were not in pain, I would begin to cackle. "We are the epitome of evil, Michael."

"Not so. We have souls, Sophia."

"You just choose not to use yours," I finish for him, sparing him the need to elaborate on the matter of human souls.

"Your stubborn nature will be your downfall, Sophia," Michael warns me. "Change your ways and *join* us. We will be great. All of us, we can be the source of fear for everyone in this world. We can be the embodiment of God."

My eyes meet his. "You honestly think that I would do something that involves Kathleen?" I am sickened by the mere thought of it.

"Hatred is a seed, Sophia," Michael informs me. "Will you nourish and allow it to spread in your heart?"

"I have no use for my heart," I tell him. "Why should I care anymore?"

"Because with no heart, there is no life," he counters back to me. Michael's curious gaze locks with mine. "How does it feel to be dead?"

"It doesn't hurt as much as living."

CHAPTER FOURTEEN

εφ

MICHAEL IS TRULY DEAD AND that hellish monster has replaced him. But even *with* his soul, he is not Michael. The darkness that I never wanted Michael to know has possessed him and all his morals and virtues have been incinerated. Tonight, I stared into his eyes and I saw no remnant of my sweet Michael there.

I ENTER BRIELLE'S APARTMENT THROUGH the door and I close it. I still have not figured out how to lock a door. The magick behind it is still unfathomable to me. Michael let me off easy tonight. He vanished after I answered his question. I find the couch in the living room easily and I lay down. My legs are weak and my mind is exhausted from thoughts and memories I wish to forget.

I feel a string tug at my heart when I think of Michael. I should have known that it is usually the innocent ones that become the cruelest vampires when changed. That is how it always works. The alteration from good to evil is done quickly when the victim was once righteous. The righteous ones are always the first to fall because they suppress their *inner demon* for too long that when the occasion rises, that demon will tear through flesh and bone to emerge to the surface for a chance at momentary freedom.

I see my blood tears again. They spill from my eyes as if I have stabbed them with daggers. I cannot hold back the tears any longer. I attempted to hold my bravado of strength in front of that beast, but now, unto the darkness, I release all my pain with the redness of color that pours from my eyes in ceaseless rivers.

I have not wept like this since I was imprisoned in the stone room. I remember crying for Michael when I found his body on the bed. Rather, I distinctively recall falling apart when I saw the fleshly shell of the physical remains of the Michael that I once knew and loved—*still* love.

I WAKE TO THE SOUND of a familiar presence opening the refrigerator and pulling out a bottle of water. I look up and see that it is Brielle. She is dressed in a short dress with equally short sleeves. There are light red stripes against a white background printed on her dress and her light brown hair is braided into two pigtails. She looks every bit the vivacious young girl that my ancient eyes first saw after centuries of imprisonment.

"Good morning, sleepyhead," she greets me with her peculiar vocabulary. I am still adjusting to this new age. "Did you get any sleep last night?" She pauses at the counter, holding the bottle in her hands.

"Very little sleep," I say, "but enough."

My rendezvous with Michael kept me up, troubling me with thoughts of what would happen next.

"You went to see him, didn't you?" Brielle suddenly asks me and I am in shock. Her voice is much too serious for her to playing some kind of twenty-first century joke on me. *But how could she know?*

"I heard you go out last night and come back in. You're still having problems with that lock, obviously. You made a lot of noise trying to open it."

I should have gone through the window! I curse to myself.

"I was standing right behind you when you started crying," she continues and her gaze can no longer hold against mine. "I thought that maybe you'd sense me, but you were too swallowed up in your tears to notice me." In a barely audible whisper, she adds, "I've never seen a person—human or not—cry like you did last night."

I fend myself. "I am a vampire," I remind her. "I feel things a great deal more intensely than you do."

"I don't argue with that."

As the silence builds up to a time-standing moment, I glance at the couch. My blood tears have stained the cotton and I am ashamed of myself, that I allowed myself to break down so easily and lower my mind shields to perhaps Kathleen. Even more so, I am furious over the fact that I truly did not sense Brielle behind me last night.

"I have to go to work," Brielle informs me. "You should probably stay inside to be safe. You should probably change your clothes, too."

I watch, mute, as Brielle throws the bottle into a black bag and saunters over to the door. Her back faces me as her hand touches the knob and she regards me solemnly: "Be careful, Sophia."

Then she is out the door before I have a chance to ask her what she means.

I AM RESTLESS ALL THROUGHOUT the day. I changed into some more black attire that Brielle purchased for me the day before. But this change of clothing does not assuage the roaming beast inside of me. I have been pacing in front of the couch since dawn till dusk. I catch another glimpse of the neon-green clock. Brielle told me that it was a digital clock and it was an easier way to tell time. The clock's bright greenness burned into my mind the numbers: *seven, forty-eight.*

The sun set almost an hour ago.

Brielle did not leave a time for when she would return, but I assumed that she would be back long before the sunset. To be bluntly honest, I was surprised to even hear that Brielle needed to go to work. Back in the sixteenth century—*my* time—a woman's only job was to look pretty and hope a nobleman would marry her. *But you are no longer in your time,* I remind myself. *What could she be doing that is keeping her from me for so long?* I instantly regret my thought. I sound so selfish. Brielle is a human being, she has free will, and she can choose to do whatever she wishes. That seems to be the creed of the twenty-first century.

I walk over to the window and peer out of the curtains. The dazzling lights are radiating throughout the city. I can see the jumbo-sized television in Times Square from here. This New World is still able to maintain its awe on me, even though I have been living in it for a little less than three days. Humankind has developed such marvelous technology, but one must begin to question—as I have—if this advancement in machines will somehow lead to the destruction of civilization?

While humankind is creating new and improved ways of doing certain things, it also seems as if they are creating new problems to go along with their new ideas.

Brielle told me a little bit about the energy crisis back in Sundry, California. She explained to me that even though Californians didn't hear as much about the crisis as before, it is still going on. Apparently, humankind learned how to capture energy and change it into some other form to benefit their own needs. Humankind has harnessed the powers of the sun and mastered the art of nuclear destruction. What shall humankind do next? — Seize the power of vampires and bend it for their own twisted uses? Brielle told me not to worry about this. Humans hardly believed in vampires anymore. Mostly, vampires were just fictional characters that existed only in paperback novels and classic black-and-white films. Hmm...how wrong they are.

The street is ridiculously bustling. I open my mind to gather the thoughts of the mortals running rampant on the pavement. I am thrown back by the combined pressure of their minds, hitting me all at once—the equivalence of plunging headfirst into icy waters. I immediately seal up my mind to prevent the continuation of this pounding knock to my head and I sit back down on the couch.

I sit on the couch for a few moments, collecting myself after the overwhelming power of the mortal minds. Mortals these days have become more strong-willed and forceful in their ways. But I cannot blame them. For it is a savage time and survival is only for those who are fit for it.

I lay my head down on the pillow and stare up at the ceiling, wondering when Brielle will get back.

I RISE FROM THE COUCH the moment that I hear arguing voices approach the door. Without needing to see her face, I can tell that the person on the other side of the door is Brielle and she is with a male companion.

"*This* is *exactly* why I ran away from home!" Brielle howls at her male companion.

"A normal college student would have stolen their dad's car and driven it three miles until bringing it back," her friend says. "But *you* had to go all *dramatic* and take a Greyhound bus thousands of miles to another state across the country!"

Brielle unlocks the door and she steps through. Behind her is her companion, and I recognize him instantly from the photo. It is Andrew Kaleiho, the boyfriend Brielle wanted escape from. He has a squared off nose and dark brown hair, which corresponds with his dark-tanned skin. He is lean and I can nearly count all his ribs through the orange shirt he wears.

"Andrew, I want you to meet my friend," Brielle introduces, gesturing her hand at me. "Sophia."

Andrew grins awkwardly and motions his right hand in a small, hardly perceptible, meek wave. "Aloha," he utters in an exotic language, his voice rather soft in such a silent place.

Brielle closes the door behind him. "She's a vampire," she announces casually, as if this sort of thing happened everyday.

Andrew's eyes bulge out as he looks over at Brielle. "She's a *what?*" He looks over to me as if for some sort of verification.

I can only nod my head. I am not certain of how to respond to such an unexpected comment.

"Yeah, authentic sixteenth-century French vampire from Paris," Brielle adds. By this time, she knows my life story as if it is her own.

Andrew gives Brielle the most dubious of looks. "You're kidding right? Sixteenth-century? She'd be like …"

"Three hundred, ninety-nine years-old," Brielle finishes for him, sauntering over to the refrigerator, opening it, and then skimming its contents.

"But this isn't possible," Andrew protests, losing his conviction. "Vampires don't—"

"Exist?" Brielle cuts him off. "Of course they do. I've known all along and now I have living proof." She reconsiders her words and offers instead, "Well, sort of living."

Andrew smirks. "All you have is a woman who *claims* to be a vampire. There isn't any real evidence to her identity."

"She hardly knows what a *car* is!" Brielle exclaims. If it were not for my exceptional control, I would perhaps blush.

"Maybe she's mentally retarded!" Andrew returns in the same tone as Brielle's.

"She's pretty damn smart to be mentally retarded," Brielle defends me. "She knows everything about sixteenth-century Paris, but nothing about modern-day twenty-first century New York."

"Maybe she just reads a lot," Andrew suggests.

"Can we just not have this argument right now? I need to eat," Brielle intones, driving Andrew away from the subject.

I watch as Andrew closely follows Brielle everywhere she goes in the kitchen. It is obvious that, even though he does not believe that I am a vampire, he does not exactly trust me either.

He whispers tightly, ignorant of my sensational hearing.

"She could be a...a *Goth* chick for all you know! A cutter or something," he murmurs, though I hear every word clearly.

"Do you have a problem with that?" Brielle retorts. "If I recall correctly, when *you* first met me, I was a '*Goth* chick'. And stop whispering. She can hear everything we say."

Andrew glances at me and I return the stare. But my eyes unnerve him and he quickly looks away again. "You have to be careful of who you pick up on the streets, Brielle," Andrew warns her.

"First of all, I did *not* pick her up in the streets," Brielle informs him. "I found her in a little stone room in an abandoned construction site."

"Oh, and that makes it safe all of a sudden?" His tone is caustic. "If she was walled up like Elizabeth Bathory somewhere, then there's probably a good reason why she was there."

With her back facing him, Brielle notices, "I never thought you paid attention to me when I was talking about historical vampire figures."

"It's kind of hard *not* to pay attention when that's all you talk about."

Brielle freezes, darts around, and points a finger to Andrew's chest. Her eyes are menacing. "She was locked up in there by the same person who made her," Brielle tells him. "She did nothing wrong, but her maker hated her enough to build a special room for her and keep her in there for centuries. It wasn't her fault."

Brielle turns her back to him and Andrew continues to whisper, even though he still does not realize that I can hear every whispered word.

"I still don't think that this is a good idea, Brielle," he persists.

I FELT AS IF I was suffocating in Brielle's apartment, so I excused myself and informed her and Andrew that I wanted to take a walk outside. When I was human—way back when—I always loved taking walks outside, pacing around nowhere, destination nowhere. I did it as a means of opening my mind or clearing it.

I stroll around Times Square—such a strange name. I even pass by the abandoned construction site where Brielle freed me. I stand in front of the jumbo-sized television, mesmerized by the moving pictures and the colossal people. I stalk over to the tiny boutiques; all huddled side-by-side with another, as if terrified to stand alone in this vast and perilous city.

I press my hand to the glass window and the coldness of the pane almost matches the temperature of my own skin. There are many people inside this spring-tinted shop for women's clothing. There are shirts and blouses with springtime floral prints of every kind, making the title of the shop appropriate: Spring's.

The electric lights inside of the shop are wondrously bright, illuminating the careless humans as if they are taken from some kind of angelic vision.

Watching these humans make me feel so detached and, indeed, I am. I am a vampire. I do not belong with the world of the living or their glorious light. I am as dark as the night I was born from.

I remove my hand and walk back to Brielle's apartment. There is nothing here for me in this world. All that I have ever loved is dead. My mind has been cleared.

I OPEN THE DOOR TO Brielle's apartment, finding it thankfully easy to open since it has not been locked. But at the same time I wonder why Brielle would leave the door so recklessly unlocked. This is not something of her behavior—someone that has studied and knows more about my own kind than I do.

As soon as I step into the room my senses are amply alert. My eyes scan the well-lit room and fall upon the female figure lying on the carpet floor. I recognize her instantly and I scurry over, turning her body over so that I can see her face and ascertain that she is alive.

"Brielle," I call out, pushing the words into her mind to wake her. She is unconscious and after examining her face I can see why. A circular grotesque blemish is appearing on her left eye, the result of a powerful blow to her face. "Brielle," I say again and this time there is a response. I wonder how long she has been here, lying benumbed.

Brielle's eyelids flutter as she struggles to unseal them. She winces when she attempts to open her left eyelid, unaware of the gradual bruise.

"Easy," I soothe her. "It's okay." I raise her head up, cautious of any injuries to her head.

"I'm okay," she assures me, beginning to stand on her own though I cannot help but assist her in spite of her protests.

"Are you sure?" I question her.

She nods her head, though I am certain it is painful to do even that. Brielle finally rises and her gaze sweeps around the room. Finally, she speaks again. "She took Andrew."

"What?"

"Kathleen...she came here and she...she and Michael took Andrew," Brielle explains, quivering.

I hold her by the shoulders and look her directly in the eyes. "Are you certain?" I ask her.

Brielle nods her head. "Positive."

"You've never even seen Kathleen before," I say, "how are you so certain that it was her and Michael?"

Brielle does not hesitate to answer, "Because she told me to tell you something."

"Tell me what?"

"The devil is waiting for the both of you."

SILENCE ALL AROUND ME AS I sit on the couch, closing my eyes, focusing my mind, reaching out through time and space to find Kathleen. Just as before, through my mind's eye, I can observe everything that is going outside without even having to physically look at it. All of a sudden, I hear Kathleen's repulsive voice in my mind, forcing the images of humankind out until all I can see is blackness and all I can hear is she.

Come, Sophia, come to me.

I see Kathleen and Michael now. They are on top of one of those massive buildings that humankind has erected over the years. There are many windows decorating the building and I see Andrew wriggling in Kathleen's grasp.

Ah, my immortal enemy. Kathleen has hardly changed though I notice a few alterations here and there. She is paler than ever and also slender than what I remember. She has modernized her look, but then again, so have I.

She has her hair pinned up in a stylish bun of brown braids and she is wearing a white shirt with thin straps and denim blue shorts that reveal her fair legs. The scars from the fire that I had once seen marked on her face before she murdered Christine are gone. There is no evidence of my victory over her several centuries ago. She is even more beautiful than what I remember.

But I also see Michael with her.

Almost as if they knew that I could see them, Michael and Kathleen roughly press their lips together and share a crude kiss. It is obvious to me that there is no love for any of them in their relationship. It is not what Michael and I had. But can the damned really love the damned?

I pull myself out of the trance and open my eyes to find Brielle sitting eagerly across from me on the glass table. Marvelous things to be able to withstand such enormous pressure.

"Well, what did you see?" she queries.

"She's taken Andrew on the top of a ridiculously elevated building," I retort. "Someplace immense." I

223

strain to recall the surroundings of the dream. I was so preoccupied with seeing Kathleen again for the first time in three centuries that I did not pay much attention to the setting or anything else for that matter. "It was next to the jumbo-sized television box."

Brielle grabs her car keys and bolts up from the table. I see the affection in her eyes for Andrew. In spite of what she dislikes about him, she truly loves him, even if she refuses to admit it at times.

I rise as well and I lead the way towards the door, but Brielle calls me back by my name. "Sophia," she says.

Ironic, though, that I have told Brielle everything about my life, except for my real name, the name that I was given at birth by my parents: Catherine Diana Opaque. She knows me only as Sophia, the Vampire. Sophia, the Sufferer, the Martyr. She will never see me as Catherine, the Human, because I have abandoned that identity so long ago that not even I can grasp those departed memories. But nothing human of me remains. My family is gone, my home, even my name. So am I truly *not* Sophia, the Vampire? I suppose some part of me is desperately clinging onto Catherine.

"Yes?"

"I want you to make me a vampire."

Her boldness with her words never ceases to amaze me.

"What?"

I step closer to her.

"I want to become like you," Brielle elaborates.

"You wish to become a damnable beast as I am?" When I told Brielle the story of how I was reborn into darkness, I tried so hard to make her see beyond the godlike powers of the vampire to the doom that we must all confront eventually. But I have failed. I only glorified her outlook on vampires. She thinks my suffering is beautiful and that vampires are beautiful when, most of the times, we are the most savage of all creatures on earth.

Brielle approaches me and I stop. "I don't want to be a helpless mortal anymore," she implores. "I'm tired of being human. I am *tired* of being a walking meal for the immortals. I'm tired of *life*."

"You do not truly appreciate life until you realize that it is about to be taken away from you," I tell her. "I learned that far too late and look at what I have become."

"A child of darkness, a lonely vampire, I see that."

"No, you do not see it," I protest. "You only see the appeal that loses its glamour when you become an immortal."

Brielle shakes her head, lost in her belief that she truly understands what I am. But she does not. No one can. No one does unless you are one of my kind. "There's a reason I sought out vampires," Brielle begins. "I was just so sick and tired of being this pathetic human and how everyone sees me that way. I don't want to be a normal, average Joe. I want to become something. Something greater. Something more than what I am right now."

"You do not have to have inhuman powers to do something inhuman," I explain to her, though I have not the experience to support this statement. "I would give up *anything* and everything to be what you are, Brielle. You take your humanity for granted, as does the rest of your kind. But I see humanity different than what you do. I see meaning behind every scrape and cut that scars. I see beauty behind the crystal tears that I shall never be able to have again. I see strength behind every painful moment that humans experience."

"But you said it yourself," Brielle insists. "You said that vampires feel more than humans do. I want to feel what you feel, to see what you see."

"You haven't the slightest notion of what you are asking!" I plead with her.

"I know what I want," Brielle declares and I cannot help but to be shaken by her firmness.

I try again to reason with her, though I am beginning to see that all my efforts will be futile in the end. "The devil will take you and he will keep you and he will *twist* you into something beautiful on the outside, but monstrous on the inside."

"I want what you have!" Brielle bellows at me and, caught up in my frustration, I seize her by the shoulders and draw her in close so that she may see my blood eyes and threatening incisors.

"You want to have the suffering, the regrets, the *miseries* of an immortal!? Life is brief, compared to death, which is eternal. You will die and you will be dead for the rest of eternity. Humankind will hunt you down to alleviate their fear. You will fall from God's Grace and He will not accept you into Heaven. Is that what you want? To die and stay dead? To never again experience the inexplicable human mysteries that make you human? To never know the worth of change? To never know the true value of love? Is that the curse you wish to have upon your head?"

Brielle writhes in my capture. She is terrified as she stares into my eyes. I can see her fear as I have never seen it in her before. But if I must scare her to turn her away from this death wish, then that is what I shall do.

When I realize that she is beginning to suffocate and her face is turning tomato red, I release her and her body clunks to the floor. She massages her neck, coughing to begin to restore her scattered breathing.

"You look into my bitter gaze and all you see is beauty," I spit out at her, my voice calming, my eyes and teeth returning to normality. "I look into your uncorrupted face and all I see is a humanity that shall never be returned to me."

Brielle coughs some more and I walk over to her, helping her to stand. Surprisingly, she accepts my help.

"You're right, Sophia, all I see is the attractiveness of being a vampire," she confesses, "but sometimes I forget, too, that being human can be beautiful."

"We need to rescue Andrew," I remind her. "Put him before yourself for the moment. But before we close this subject forever, remember this, Brielle: the devil cares not whom he damns, only that he damns."

CHAPTER FIFTEEN

εφ

DARKNESS BLANKETS THE CITY IN an oddly resplendent light. The world seems to come alive at night. The streets appear as if they are paved out of gold and the multi-colors of the civilians and their dresses are brilliant. Countless shining lights cast a small, nevertheless undimmed, radiance throughout Times Square.

As Brielle pushes her car to the speed limit—a phrase I learned from the college student herself—I lean my head out of the rolled down window, studying the colorful scene in the darkness.

As we approach the center of Times Square, I hear voices from the jumbo-sized television and then I turn my eyes to the left where I see the sky-touching structure—and three small figures on the roof.

I point to the miniature figures and shout to Brielle, "There they are! I see them! They are on top of the building!"

Brielle sharply turns the steering wheel to the right and I stumble back inside the vehicle, holding onto the armrest.

"Is Andrew up there?" she questions me.

"Yes," I answer.

"Did you see him?"

"Yes, I did."

Brielle stations the car at the entrance of the building and we simultaneously exit out of it. Brielle is immediately overwhelmed by the immense height of the building. Her gaze travels upward to the roof, as does mine. But she fails to see what I can see with my magnified vision.

"Are you sure they're up there?" she asks me.

I nod my head. "I am sure. How do you propose we get up all the way to the roof?"

Brielle looks at me, curiously. "Can you fly?"

I shake my head. "I do not think so."

"Then we can try the stairs," Brielle suggests.

I FOLLOW BRIELLE INTO THE inside of the building. It is dark inside because there is no one there, but Kathleen probably unlocked the entrance when she came before Brielle and I.

There are shadows on the walls and I easily blend in with them, seeing that I am clothed in black: a black long-sleeved shirt and black jeans. Brielle has a harder time concealing herself in the darkness. She is wearing pink shorts and a white shirt.

We stop a foot away from the staircase. We lean against the wall; both of us enclosed with ghostly shadows.

Brielle regards me cautiously. "You do realize that this is a trap, right?"

"I figured that, yes," I say to her. "Kathleen would not have allowed you to live unless she wanted to tell me something."

"Good, then," she intones. "Just wanted to get that out of the way."

We ascend the staircase. I am astonished by Brielle's nimbleness as she lifts one foot at a time and plants the other down. I am also agile and together, we are a deft pair.

It takes us only minutes to finally reach the highest level of the building and there we see a door with a red sign above it reading, *roof access.*

Brielle stands by the door and displays it with her hands. "We'll take what's behind door number one," she announces, opening the door as soon as she finishes the sentence. She gestures for me to go inside. "Vampires first."

I cannot help but smile in spite of myself. I enter the door and Brielle follows behind me.

The wind thrashes my face, whipping my cheeks the moment that I step onto the spacious roof. The view from this roof is remarkable and not only the height, but also the magnificence of this location awes me. I scan the area and I see three figures standing a great distance in front of us. I recognize the three figures instantly: Michael to the side, Kathleen next to him, holding struggling Andrew in her grasp. They are mighty close to the stone ledge, which is almost as high as my knees.

"I see them," I whisper to Brielle, who is still searching for them. I dash off and Brielle follows me blindly, with the same kind of faith I once had in Kathleen.

My hair flows out behind me like ocean waves and I ignore the wintry feel as I run.

I see Kathleen perfectly now and I am stunned by this. I have not seen her in centuries and this encounter is made impeccable by the location.

I slow down and eventually stop about three feet away from Kathleen with Brielle trailing behind me. Even with her human swiftness she is no match for my preternatural speed.

"Ah, Sophia, you've finally come to glorify this long-awaited occasion," Kathleen states, her voice cutting into my heart and slicing it into infinite pieces when I remember that this is the same voice that has tormented me for almost four hundred years.

I cannot even begin to describe with words what this meeting feels like for me. It is lacerating, liberating, and loathing. It is all these things and more. You cannot even begin to comprehend what this fated moment means to me. How *should* one feel after being betrayed by a "friend" who also destroys your last shred of humanity, murders and then condemns the man you love, slays your innocent daughter, and then locks you up for countless years with no hope of ever being freed? *Yes, there must be a book somewhere about how to react after this sort of thing*, I think cynically. Nothing could have ever prepared me for all the stirred emotions that beat me all at once. Animosity. Woe. Misery. *Pain*. So much pain.

"Let him go," I tell her forthright. This is not the time nor place to speak openly about all the suffering she has put me through. I have a profound feeling in the pit of my gut that this is not the final encounter between Kathleen and I. That we shall truly meet again. In truth, I honestly believe that the "final encounter" between

Kathleen and I will end up with one or both of us dying. Only then will I rest.

"Why should I?" she throws back at me. "You are in no position to make any demands, Sophia."

"If you refuse to release both him and Brielle, I will cut out your heart and carve my name in it," I threaten her, but I know that she is neither scared nor intimidated by me.

Kathleen chuckles and Michael spares a grin in my direction.

"Oh, Sophia, you do amuse me," Kathleen laughs. "So much fire and passion all going to waste."

I step forward and Kathleen steps back, closer to the ledge now.

"Come any closer Sophia and this boy *falls*," Kathleen warns me.

I can tell by the sanguinary gleam in Kathleen's eyes that she is not afraid to live up to her threat.

Andrew is turning blue. He is suffocating and he will probably go unconscious before this agonizing night is over.

"What do you want, Kathleen?" I ask her, hoping to strike some kind of deal with her. I do not wish to wound my pride by bargaining with the devil, but for Andrew and Brielle's sake, I do not quench my thirst for pride.

"I brought you here for a reason, Sophia," Kathleen informs me. "I wanted to tell you everything, to tell you the truth."

Just like how you wanted to show me the world? I think cynically, mocking her promises.

As soon as I am finished with the thought, Kathleen pulls her forearm back on Andrew's neck, tightening her grasp, choking Andrew.

"I heard that," Kathleen hisses.

Brielle comes to my side and watches helplessly as Andrew is losing his supply of breath. I see terror in Brielle's eyes. I know what she is feeling right now, what is running through her terrified mind. She is desperate to save Andrew and she would do it at all costs, including risking her own life—or sacrificing it. But I will not permit such foolishness. If anyone should be sacrificing his or her life, it should be me.

I put my hand in front of Brielle. I feel her rage mounting and I try to restrain her, though I know that if I were in her position, I would have already attacked and died trying.

"Do you want to know the truth, Sophia? Do you want to know everything, or do you want me to just get to the point and kill the little child?"

"What are you talking about?" I finally wave to her subject, rather reluctantly though. But I would do practically anything to stall her, to delay the disastrous ending she has in mind.

"You want your vengeance, Sophia, I can feel it," Kathleen commences. "Vengeance is the way only walked by dead men. But you're dead, so that all works out."

I have to bite back from telling Kathleen to hurry it up and get to the point.

"Do you remember the scarf?" Kathleen asks me.

I blink. "What scarf?"

"The *scarf!*" she yells as impatiently as a child throwing a temper-tantrum does. "The black scarf! Do you remember?"

I have to force myself to think under urgent circumstances. I am attempting to recall anything about a scarf. Memories flash past me, going forwards from the past to the present, in my mind and indeed, I do see a scarf!

I see the slim white arm holding the black silk scarf and then releasing it, allowing it to gently hit the ground.

I am in my dream again, watching Michael rock Christine. I hear their cavernous words echoing in my ears.

"Do you remember the scarf?"

"I remember the scarf. It was like silk."

"Do you remember how it fell to the ground?"

"I remember."

"Yes," I say. "Yes, I remember the scarf. The black one. Silk."

"Do you remember how it fell to the ground? The way it hit in a silent motion that screams forever in your mind?" Kathleen questions.

I close my eyes, picturing this again. "Yes, I remember how it fell." I open my eyes. I have stepped closer to Kathleen, shortening the distance between us. Brielle stands behind me. She has not moved.

"Good, you remember ..."

"Why is it so important for me to remember these things?" I ask her, unable to retain myself from doing so.

"Because there is something important about that moment," Kathleen tells me. "Have you ever wondered why I named you Sophia after you were changed? Did you ever think there was a reason why I chose that name?"

I reply truthfully, "I thought you just did it on a whim, like how you do all your other things."

"No, there is a reason why your name is what it is," Kathleen insists. "Sophia was the name of my daughter."

"What do *I* have to do with your daughter?" I interrogate.

"Think about it," Kathleen tells me. "That night when we first met, outside the theatre, after you saw my play...I had been waiting for that moment for seventeen years."

I am bewildered by her words. What is she trying to tell me? "What are you saying?" I voice out loud in askance.

"You were there the night that the scarf fell," Kathleen said. She pauses. "...Sophia, I am your mother."

I am taken aback. My first impulse is to laugh at the absurdity of such a thought. My second is to consider the possible reality of her words, if such a preposterous idea can be true.

I remain silent. Many thoughts hasten across my mind, but I struggle in vain to grasp any of them. This cannot be true. This cannot be possible. Kathleen cannot be my mother. I know who my mother was. Her name was...Come to think of it, I never really knew her name. She, nor my father, ever told it to me. I always referred to her as either "mother" or "Lady Opaque", but never by her first name *and* last name.

Yet still, this sort of thing is impossible. What kind of game is Kathleen playing now? What is she trying to do? What a low level she has stooped to.

All these thoughts and yet I say nothing.

It is not necessary. Kathleen continues anyway.

"I know it sounds crazy, nevertheless it is true," Kathleen persists. "Allow me to explain, Sophia."

This...I allow her.

"In the year 1585, I met a woman who was to change my life forever. I met her outside of a play as I was leaving. I loved to go to plays. It was my favorite thing to do and I promised myself that I would one day write a play of my own, though I had no inspiration for it. This woman was kind to me. She taught me things about ancient histories that I could have never learned on my own. And then, months before you were born, she revealed to me that she was a vampire and she wanted to make me into one.

"I refused at first, and she was fine with it. For she knew that if she were to change me at the present state, she would damn both my child and I.

"I gave birth to you in the year 1586. I loved you beyond any words that human or vampire could ever say. You were my pride, my joy, my one true source of happiness. But she, my maker, took all that away from me.

"You were young, *too* young to remember such a thing. You were hardly a week old when the terrible event took place and the Vampire Kathleen was the result of it.

"It was dark and you had fallen asleep. I was putting you into your cradle when, like a bat out of hell, she grabbed me from behind and wrapped her arms around my neck. She whispered to me to relax, but I refused to.

"I fought long and hard for my immortal soul that I was taught to believe in and to shield from any outside harm and evil. But mostly, I fought for the sake of my daughter, for you, Sophia.

"It wasn't enough, though. She ripped the silk black scarf I had around my neck and I snatched it from her hands and I held onto it as she sank her fangs into my neck. All I could think was what would happen to my tiny infant? Would she kill her too? Or worse, would *I* kill her?

"I tightened my grip on the scarf, but when she began to drain me, I grew so horribly weak that I released the scarf.

"I dropped the scarf the moment that I died. The moment that the old Kathleen was killed and the new Kathleen was ready to take over. And I could not fight any longer. I had not the strength, the power. So I allowed her to change me. I drank from her as she drank from me and I was damned.

"The reason why I did this was because I thought, at least I could still be alive. At least I had a chance to see my daughter again. At least it was better than the alternative to die and never be able to see my daughter ever again."

Her eyes have grown misty with tears from these recollections. Surely enough a blood tear slides from her left eye and rolls down past her mouth to her chin where it hits the ground, where it will make its permanent home.

I remember Kathleen's play now, the one I had just seen the night that we first met. I remember the part where she returned to find her daughter gone.

"I came back the next night. I was a vampire now, of course, and I hoped to find my baby. But when I returned, she was gone. I went mad looking for you. I had no idea where to begin. No one knew where my child was and no one knew where to find her. This grieved me and I even attempted to put a blade through my heart to end my sorrow, and I would have succeeded, had my maker not stopped me.

"My life was different now. It had been changed in a way I could have never conceived. I spent seventeen years looking for my long-lost daughter; mourning for her, hating my maker for what she did to me, and the rest of my time was spent contemplating my own death.

"This inspired a play. Thus, I wrote one and found a talented, yet unknown, group of actors to be in it. My actors performed the play throughout Europe and I sat in the theatre every night, among the audience, always lost in my sadness as I watched my life in a scripted reenactment. The names were slightly altered to conceal the true identities, but everything else was the same.

"But that night...In 1603 when my actors were performing my play in France and I was sitting in the balcony, watching it, I sensed you. At first, it was a familiar presence that I recognized with grief in my heart. I tried to figure out who it was. But there were too many people and I did not want to strain myself to reach out to the mind. Besides, I was sitting next to the owner of the theatre and I wanted to make a good impression. So I decided to find the person after the play was over. It would be easier that way. Most people would be distracted and either talking about the play or worried about getting home.

"So, when it was over, I left the theatre and sought out the familiar presence. I found her in the form of a seventeen-year-old young woman who was heir to a fortune from an aristocratic family.

"Even when I spoke to her, I was not precisely certain of who she was until I *fed* on her.

"I told you once, Sophia, that when you drink the blood of the living, you catch glimpses of their lives. You see things that they have seen; you share their experiences. Oftentimes, what is seen are things long forgotten or not remembered by the conscious mind. When I drank your blood, I saw my hand dropping my scarf and I knew that it was you. No one else had seen that image.

"I was incredibly happy, Sophia. You could never understand my content. I thought that I was now reunited with my daughter and now I could show you everything you have always wanted to see and more. I could show you what I had seen and I could teach you what I had learned.

"But it did not work out that way, as you recall. You resisted the way of darkness and were determined to follow your morals and virtues. I tried to do the same but I was not strong enough to do so and I failed in my attempts.

"I tried everything that I could think of. I tried to isolate you from humankind by destroying the last remnants of your humanity and by slaughtering everyone left in this world that was a part of your human life. But none of it worked.

"So I imprisoned you, for many reasons actually. To punish you for trying to kill me. To allow your emptiness to consume you until your will was weak enough to be bent to mine. I wouldn't have put you in there unless I knew that you would be freed eventually.

"And now, here we are, mother and daughter, both hating each other for the wrong reasons. I did what I had to do all for your sake, Sophia. And you did what you had to, to avenge yourself. I don't blame you. And now, all that matters to me is for us to be a family. For you to be my daughter and me to be your mother. It's never too late. Blood is thicker than anything else in this world, Sophia, we happen to know that's very true."

I am blown away into oblivion, stunned into helpless silence. I do not want to believe her but she knows all the details too well. I do not want to even think about this. Kathleen, my mother? What an abominable thing! A cruel god gave me this life, this vile fate.

"Why should I believe you, Kathleen? Why should I believe anything that you have to say?"

"Because you know that what I said was true," Kathleen declares. "Why would I make up such elaborate fabrications? Why would I want to go through so much trouble rewriting your entire life story just to taunt you?"

"I don't know," I say bitterly. "Why would you want to consign me to hell? Why would you want me to kill my own family? Why would you want to kill my loving Michael so you could turn him into something as revolting as I am? Why would you want to take my daughter's life right in front of my eyes? Why would you want to *lock me up* and leave me there and allow my hatred to grow and grow and grow? I don't know why. You tell me, Kathleen, *you* tell me why."

Kathleen speaks up. "I already told you why. I did it for you. I did it because I love you and I want us to be together, like family."

"If you really loved me, you would've left me in peace," I snap at her. "You would've seen that I was better off where I was than where I could have been with you. You would've said your goodbye, left my family and I alone, and mourn for your dead daughter. And so it is, that I have died twice in my life."

Kathleen is startled by my response, but somewhere deep inside, she knows that it was to be like this. She can't honestly believe that once she reveals to me a revelation of enormous proportions that I would just simply accept her into my heart and forgive her for all the pain she has caused me.

"Never hope to hear the name 'mother' on my lips to you, Kathleen," I hiss at her, lowly, dangerously, forcing the sentence into her mind where it will torment her.

Kathleen stares at me. She gives me an expression that I cannot read. But I sense pain, or at least anger, at my words.

Without warning, Kathleen releases Andrew and shoves him backwards, causing him to fall over the ledge.

Kathleen and Michael step aside as I run to the ledge. From behind me, I hear Brielle shouting, "No!"

And no, Andrew will not die.

241

I run to the right side of the ledge, opposite from where Andrew fell, and I dive from my location, aiming with my body in Andrew's direction. I am accurate as my body slams into Andrew's while we are soaring in the air and I latch onto him.

The momentum of my body forces Andrew to the left where we both crash into a glass window from a building next to the one we just fell from; my body shielding Andrew's so that I hit the glass first and spare Andrew the several lacerations.

We fall to the ground and I imagine that Andrew is either in shock or has gone unconscious. I look at his face in the dimness of the room. He has not even a scratch on him. I have taken all the brutality for him and that is fine with me.

A tremendous droplet of glass becomes a piercing waterfall behind us and I listen to hear Andrew's beating heart. He is alive, nonetheless unconscious.

Fortunately for us there is no one inside this business room where there is a metallic desk and several papers on it.

I lift Andrew's resting body into my arms, ignoring the blood from the myriad cuts on my skin. I do wince a little when I feel one of my cuts open and a tiny piece of glass drops out. I imagine that there are infinite fragments of glass embedded into my flesh.

But all pain is mental, even the ones caused by physical things. And if all pain is in the mind, then it can be conquered.

BRIELLE WRAPS THE ADHESIVE GAUZE around my right hand, all the while giving me a gracious look. Andrew rests on the couch, after I insisted to Brielle that he needed the couch more than I did. However, the various incisions on my body tell a different story.

We sit across from each other at the kitchen table, underneath the fluorescent light.

"That was one dive you took," Brielle offers. "You should've been on the swim team."

"It was nothing," I lie. It was actually one of the most exhilarating things that I had ever done. But I practice humility.

"Are you kidding me? It was tight," she says in the slang that I am still struggling with.

I gaze at my bandaged hand. My right hand took most of the beating. "I did what was necessary," I tell her.

Before wrapping the gauze, Brielle had to apply ointment on my cuts to prevent an infection. Even though I told her I did not need it, she insisted on doing so anyway. Even vampires weren't invincible. The ointment stung just a bit but I pushed the pain out of my system. My aching mortal shell is nothing compared to my wounded immortal soul.

Brielle finishes wrapping my hand. "There, all better," she chirps, patting my hand. "You can take it off tomorrow if you want but leave it on for now."

I draw my hand back from the table.

"Sophia...thanks, for what you did," Brielle credits. "You didn't have to stick your neck out for us and you did. I don't know how I can repay you."

I stretch out my good hand and stroke Brielle's face. "You don't have to repay me. Just do one favor for me."

"What?"

"Promise me that, when this is all over, when my quarrel with Kathleen has ended, you must go back to California, to your town Sundry, with Andrew and be happy," I request of her. "And try to mend things with your family for my sake, because it was too late for me to do anything with my family. Promise?"

Brielle nods her head. "Promise." And she removes my hand from her cheek and holds it in her hands.

We sit, looking at each other, studying each other's placid expressions. The tranquility is only disturbed when someone knocks at the door.

I sense the presence and it is not Kathleen. Whoever it is, she is no threat to us.

I follow behind Brielle as she rises from the chair to answer the door. Even if the visitor is no threat to us, we must be cautious.

Brielle unlocks the door and opens it and I receive a good view of the visitor.

She is beautiful, not in the way that a human can be beautiful, or a vampire for that matter, but beautiful in its purest form, in a divinity not known to any earthbound being. It is as if she was taken from some kind of heavenly vision from God. She appears before us as a divine angel. Her crow black hair creates an otherworldly halo above her head and her mesmerizing emerald eyes make me feel as if I am staring into the eyes of a powerful black panther. She is also wearing a long leather skirt and a bright red shirt—too bright for my eyes—with thin straps like Kathleen's. Perhaps I *am* envisioning her. A creature as angelic as her cannot be seen anywhere else but by a vision from God.

"Friend of yours?" Brielle asks me.

I shake my head. "No. Never seen her before in my life."

"My name is Bridgette," she introduces herself. "I have come to speak with you, Sophia, about Kathleen."

CHAPTER SIXTEEN

εφ

"**W**HAT DO YOU KNOW ABOUT Kathleen?" I ask her, curious as to why anyone would want to educate me on the person who calls herself my mother.

"I'm her maker," she tells me. "And I know other things, as well."

"Come in," I say to her, and Brielle and I simultaneously step off to the side to allow the visitor to pass.

Brielle closes the door while I lead this visitor—Bridgette, did she say?—to the kitchen table where we all take a seat.

Almost instantly I begin to pry Bridgette for information on Kathleen and for an explanation as to why she has come here just to talk about a woman that I intensely abhor.

"Who are you?" I ask her, though I already know part of the answer, but I feel that there is much more behind the name.

"My name is Bridgette," she says again. "I am a vampire, like you. I was born in the year 1140 in Ireland. I am over eight hundred years old."

Brielle bursts out loud, "*Cool*! *Another* vampire!? This is the coolest thing ever!"

I see Bridgette shoot Brielle a slightly annoyed expression and then it changes to something more pleasant.

"When I first saw Kathleen, she was nothing more than a harlot, a prostitute living on the shabby streets," Bridgette begins. "I took pity on her, I really did, so I began following her, pursuing her and finally, I met her in the year 1585, while we were coming out of a play. We spoke then and we continued to speak.

"I traded her pathetic, pitiable life as a prostitute for one more suiting as a noblewoman. I gave her gold and extraordinary dresses. I showered her with gifts of beauty. She liked things that sparkled, so I often gave her exotic jewels and rare gems. She was very grateful. And she was especially grateful when she met a man who truly loved her, not for her body, but for her soul, her inner beauty. They got married and she became pregnant. I was genuinely happy for her. For I would never be able to have children.

"A few months before she gave birth, I revealed to her my true identity. I told her I was a vampire and I offered her the gift of immortality.

"She refused, and it was good that she did so. If I had changed her while she was carrying a child, who knows what would've happened to the child? —Only that the child could never be born.

"But a few weeks before she gave birth, her husband was killed in a tavern brawl. He was out having a drink with a friend and a riot exploded between others and he was killed in the crossfire. Kathleen was devastated when she learned the news and I was there for her, comforting her anyway I possibly could, reminding her that my offer still stood.

"She refused, and again, it was good that she did so. A week or so after the death of her husband, Kathleen gave birth to a little girl who she named Sophia. I was there that night she was born and I even had a cradle specially made for her infant. I felt even more sorry for her when her husband died, so I did anything I could.

"Five days after Sophia was born, I made a decision to do something that I would regret later on. I decided to turn Kathleen into a vampire, even if it was against her will. I do not know why I chose to do this, perhaps out of a whim or boredom—Who knows what?

"I waited until nightfall and I attacked her right after she had just finished putting her child to sleep. I fed on her and she drank from me, and I condemned her. I took her to my chamber and I waited for her to wake.

"When she did, all she could ask was, 'Where is my daughter? Where is my Sophia'? I told her that we would go back to the house and get her and we did, but Sophia was gone and we could not find her.

"To say that Kathleen was angry with me would be an understatement. She was furious, enraged. I could understand her pain. For what is a mother without her child?

"I searched for her daughter, helping her anyway I could. I sent several search parties and spoke with agents all over Europe, but in the end Kathleen had to face the truth. Sophia was gone and there was no hope of ever finding her.

"Kathleen went stark, raving mad and who could blame her? She was nothing without her precious little daughter. Twice, she tried to take her life and twice, I stopped her. But maybe I shouldn't have. Maybe it would have been better just to allow her to kill herself and end the suffering there, instead of prolonging it any further.

"In one of many vain attempts to appease her, I took Kathleen to Greece, so that she could see the plays she had come to love. We saw Sophocles' *Antigone*; Homer's *The Iliad*, and his well-known sequel, *The Odyssey*. But none of this mattered to her. None of it. Eventually, just like how I had predicted, Kathleen left me. She ran off to some undisclosed location, presumably to take her life."

There is a concluding note to Bridgette's speech and I realize that the tale of Kathleen's past is over, but another chapter is about to be written.

"Lately, I've been having dreams about Kathleen, about our past together. I have not thought about Kathleen for decades, but a dark mother always has a strong and deep connection to her dark daughter.

"Through these dreams I saw what she did to you, all the anguish, and I felt such guilt—not pity—but guilt. I made her and she made you and then she put you through all that hell. So I came here, in search of you, to tell you the truth about Kathleen and to give you this."

Bridgette reaches her hand across the table and I allow her to take my hand. She unfolds my fingers and drops something cold into my palm. I pull my hand back and open my palm. It is a gold chain with a small square gold pendant. There is a quotation engraved onto the gold pendant. I read it out loud: "'There is no way to peace. Peace is the way'." And underneath the quotation is a name: "'A.J. Muste'."

"For good luck," Bridgette adds.

I nod my head and put on the necklace. "Thank you," I tell her after I have the gorgeous piece of jewelry around my neck.

"When Kathleen was first changed, she swore off blood," Bridgette continues. "She still hoped that her daughter was still alive and she would one day be reunited with her. She fought against the corruption I presented her with, and believe me, she fought with all the fire in her soul. But in the end, she was convinced that she would never see Sophia again and that hope that was her fire was extinguished and she gave way to the darkness."

I gaze at Bridgette, boring into her ancient soul. "Is Kathleen my mother?"

Bridgette returns my solemn look. "I'm afraid so," she tells me, and her confirmation is all I need.

I lean back against my chair, not knowing what to think. I feel Brielle's comforting hand on my shoulder.

"The devil dances with those he damns," Bridgette says. "And he's been dancing with you and Kathleen and I for a very long time. It's time to end the waltz. But evil is not overcome with evil; it is overcome with good. Know this, Sophia, if not anything else: forgiveness is the greatest act of mercy that any individual can show."

"Someone told me that once…He was wrong." I am, of course, referring to Michael Vandalius.

"It's not enough to just forgive someone, Sophia," Bridgette tells me. "You have to have faith in what you are saying. You have to sincerely forgive someone. You have to forgive yourself."

"I forgave her once...I will not make the same mistake twice," I growl at Bridgette and she is shocked at my response, as is Brielle.

"There is no mistake made when you forgive someone," Bridgette declares, as if she speaks from experience. "Forgiveness is forgiveness. There should not be any strings attached."

"And what if I can't?" I fling back at her. "What if I have lost the instrument that is capable of forgiveness?"

Bridgette shakes her head, doubtful. "You can never lose the power to forgive, Sophia."

Bridgette's words ring true in my ears. She sounds as if she is the female version of Michael. There is a strong conviction in her words and for just a second I am convinced that I still have the power to forgive Kathleen once more...but then I lose that power.

"What if all I have is my hatred and sorrow? What if there is no room for forgiveness or love?" I beseech her.

"Then you are as good as dead," Bridgette says. "No matter how painful love is, it makes you alive. If you can do neither, then you are the dead creature that legends speak of. If you feel pain, you are alive. Without pain, there is no humanity."

"Then I have no humanity," I voice. "Kathleen stole that from me the moment that she killed Christine."

"Pain will devour you, if you let it. Pain destroyed Kathleen long, long ago. You must learn to live with yours," Bridgette informs me. "If I had not changed Kathleen, she would have been a wonderful mother to you, Sophia. She had a mother's heart, until I corrupted it into despicable evil. If you should hate anyone, if you should take your vengeance out on anyone, it should be me."

"You were not the hand that struck down my soul," I argue.

"I might as well have been."

"But you weren't," I insist. "Thank you for everything. But I need time to think this out for myself."

I rise from my chair, followed by Brielle and Bridgette.

"I just wanted you to know the truth about Kathleen," Bridgette briefly notes. "Put yourself in my position. Would you not have done the same?"

"I guess we'll never know," I conclude coldly, ending this discussion for good.

Bridgette receives the implication and she heads towards the door. She stops after she has opened it and she keeps her back to Brielle and I while she speaks.

"Samuel Clemens once said that forgiveness is the fragrance the violet sheds on the heel that has crushed it…Will you be the fragrance or the heel?"

Leaving me with that thought, as well as many others, Bridgette steps out and closes the door.

I lean my back against the door and look at Brielle.

"Can you kill her still, now knowing that she's your mother?" Brielle asks me.

I think about it and a sadness washes over me with my answer. "If I had to…yes, I could."

"But *can* you? Can you honestly kill your own flesh and blood?"

"Yes, I can."

MIDNIGHT EMBRACES ME AS IF I am his friend. Indeed, I truly am. I belong in this dark realm.

How do you expect me to rest after such a rousing discussion that has brought out the worst possible questions in me?

Is Kathleen truly the enemy or is it I? Have I wrongly antagonized Kathleen? Does she deserve my malice? After all, she is my mother and all she wanted to do was to be with her daughter. Have I hated her for all the wrong reasons?

I do not have any answers to these questions as I stalk the lonely streets of Times Square. The twilight has brought a cessation to the herds usually thronging the streets.

I gaze up into the sky and I see the gloomy clouds overhead. A storm is coming.

I see my shadow underneath the glowing street-lamp. This shadow is my reflection. It is without face and full of darkness. My shadow shades the path wherever I go and I realize that I can never leave it behind, even in the brightest hours of the day.

I walk around in circles, retracing each step repeatedly. Perhaps this way I can receive answers to my questions.

Who is the villain here? Or is there a villain at all? And if there is, would it be me?

For the first time in my life I question my vengeance.

That is a bizarre thing to do. Vengeance is never questioned. It should not have to be. Vengeance is a kind of hatred that is bent on being executed upon someone. Vengeance should be easy and simple, like hate. But I have now just learned that it is not. Nothing is easy or simple in this world.

I RETURN TO BRIELLE'S APARTMENT near dawn. I am not exhausted or threatened by the imminent daylight, but I shall not find my answers outside. Answers always come from within you.

Since Andrew is still sleeping on the couch and Brielle in her room, I take a seat at the kitchen table, recalling the conversation between Bridgette and I.

Bridgette is a vampire and she is obsessed with the concept of forgiveness. She has faith in the hearts of every being, or so it seems. I wonder if she has faith in the devil's heart? I laugh to myself. Evil is not found in the heart of the devil; it is found in the hearts of men.

That has not changed since 1610, when I left my old world for this new one that took centuries to arrive.

But I do not care about forgiveness. In fact, I do not know what I care about now. I am looking back into the past, examining it to see if I am truly correct in my convictions and after I take this introspective scrutiny, I find my convictions to be a little blurry.

I sigh to myself. My world is fragmented. There are missing pieces wherever I look and there is hardly any adhesive for me to piece them all back together.

Perhaps my life will always be this way…broken.

MORNING COMES AND I SIT at this table, making no motion to move. Brielle and Andrew pass by me several times on their unfruitful quest to find food. Brielle explains to Andrew the reason for my sudden detachment. I still sit at the table with no will of my own.

I periodically glance down at the gold pendant I wear around my neck. It is a kind gift given from a stranger.

Brielle and Andrew constantly shuffle pass me, both knowing better than to stop and have a jaunty conversation with me about the birds singing. They do well to leave me alone in my past.

My past…it is all that I have left, isn't it? It is my past that builds the foundation for my future and for my present. My past outweighs any other thing.

NIGHT SITS ACROSS FROM ME, yet I say nothing. I have nothing to say to him, he who has been my constant companion. Brielle and Andrew have gone out. They told me where they were going but I do not recall the name of their location and for the time being, I can only think of Kathleen and myself.

I have not moved in the past sixteen hours and I do not plan to do so anytime. I have not paid attention to what has been going on outside either. I do not care. The sky could fall down at any minute and I will sit here, impassive. The whole world could be destroyed at any second and I could care less.

Brielle and Andrew have not returned and I have not seen them since the dawn. Whatever happens to them…it does not matter to me right now. I suppose you think that this is terribly selfish of me, but I do not care what you think either. Leave me be in my solitude until I find the strength and the courage to move again.

AURORA SEEPS IN THROUGH THE window and I am still sitting here on the chair, frozen to the spot, too afraid to leave it for the fear of what the world will hold now that I know what I know.

Brielle and Andrew have not returned and I have heard nothing from them since yesterday morning. My concern grows just a tad, but not enough for me to care yet.

Without warning, a vision hits my mind's eye. I close my immortal eyes and I watch carefully with my psyche.

I see Kathleen and Michael capturing Brielle and Andrew, both of them fighting strenuously to pry themselves from the vampires' deadly embrace. But Kathleen and Michael overpower them and finally, they both deliver blows to the humans that knock them into unconsciousness.

Kathleen turns and looks at me, as if I am actually standing there. She says simply, "Come tonight where you were freed by the young girl or they both die."

I open my eyes and still I feel nothing. A puny and irking voice in my heart tells me to go and save Brielle and Andrew, but I do not listen to it. Instead, I ignore it and gaze at the empty chair across from me...until it is suddenly no longer empty.

IT IS WELL PAST TEN 'o clock when she appears and the chair is no longer vacant. She has not changed at all. She looks the same way that she did the last time that I saw her: gold tresses, azure eyes, and porcelain-white skin.

I gawk at her timeless features as if I have never seen them before. I study each detail on her face so that I may never forget them.

"Christine," I whisper under my breath when I have finally found it.

She smiles sweetly at me. "Yes, Mother, it is I," she returns.

"Have you come to take me to the devil? Has he been waiting for me? I am ready to leave. Tell him he does not have to wait any longer."

Christine shakes her head. "No, Mother, that is not why I have returned."

"Then why?" *If not to deliver me to hell, then why?*

"Oh, Mother, I came here to return something to you that you believe you have lost," she tells me.

I laugh quietly. I have lost so many things over the years that I do not know most of them. "And what might that be?" I query.

"Compassion," Christine replies.

"*Compassion?*" I mock. "How will *compassion* help me now? Must I *love* my enemies in order to defeat them?"

Christine shakes her head again, disapproving of my response, compelling me to understand. "This is not about defeating your enemies. It is about you."

I am silent now.

"Kathleen succeeded in what she wanted to do. She imprisoned you so that it would allow hate to consume you over the years and something even worse happened. You lost hope and compassion and mercy. You lost all sense of humanity because you allowed it to happen," Christine declares. "You have forgotten the lessons taught to you long ago. The greatest power on earth is love, and it is not about loving your enemies, or loving your friends, but loving yourself. You have never loved yourself and if you cannot love yourself, you cannot love anything else. Back then, you had everything to lose. You lost your family, you lost Michael, and you lost me. Then you had nothing else to lose except yourself. And you lost that, too. But now, two people who care for you are about to be lost and you do not even care. A great force of good is giving you another chance at redemption, but you are too narrow to see it. They gave you Brielle and Andrew to protect in order to atone for the people you could not protect long ago, and you are simply giving up on your one last chance! Do not give up. That is not what you were put on this earth for."

I slam my fist onto the table, rattling it. "Then what?" I snarl. "To suffer?"

Christine's voice remains calm against my ferocity. "Everyone suffers. Some continue, and some don't. Not everyone changes afterwards. Suffering can be put behind you, but it can also consume you if you let it. I know what you have wanted all these years. You have wanted salvation, not from love, not from God, but from yourself. You must make peace with yourself before you can make peace with anyone else."

"Have you only come here to tell me to save Brielle and Andrew?"

"I am giving you a choice. Either you save them and free yourself or you can stay here, locked up in a stone room once more. But this time, it will not be by Kathleen; it will be by your own doing. The choice is yours."

I am stunned by everything that she has said. It is all true. A blood tear mists my eye, yet it does not fall.

Christine speaks again. "Remember this, Mother: before you can save anyone, you must save yourself."

Then she vanishes from the chair, dissolving right before my very eyes until she is gone as if she was never there in the first place.

Perhaps she was not there at all. Perhaps that little aggravating voice finally took form before me, but it was not real.

It no longer matters, however.

The blood tear that has been waiting in my eye finally drips onto my cheek.

Christine was right. Without even knowing it, I lost my ability for compassion when Christine was murdered. But what is in the past is in the past, where it rightfully belongs. Even now, in the darkness, I hear Michael's precise words chime in my ears.

"Study the face of innocence and you shall find compassion."

CHAPTER SEVENTEEN

εφ

STORMCLOUDS TOWER MY PATH. BUT they do not threaten me. What are stormclouds but gray materials that produce the beautiful rain? I am fearless, as I have never been before. I walk onto the streets with recovered courage and a newfound prowess. I am strong again, alive and coursing with power and spirit! I have the gold necklace and pendant that Bridgette gave to me around my neck, for good luck, as she said. I wear a black long-sleeved coat that descends to my ankles. I have a taut black tank top and black jeans. One might say that I am dressed to kill. They are right.

I APPROACH THE ABANDONED UNCOMPLETED building with caution. I take in all that is around me—the people hurrying from place to place, the cars jammed in a standstill passage, the tremendous structures that stretch to the vault of heaven—fully aware that this will perhaps be the last time that I shall ever see the outside world. I might meet my death here tonight, in this damning place where I was incarcerated.

They say that everyone will come around full circle. Perhaps I will not die here, but Kathleen will. Then that will make up for the death I have suffered twice.

Kathleen died when she first became a vampire and she shall die again here in this place. I died when Kathleen killed me and I died again after I was imprisoned here, but I am alive once more. Her first death was at the hands of others; but our second deaths have been or will be at the hands of one another, as it should be. Mother and daughter...how appropriate.

I enter the building and my senses go on full alert. I survey the area from where I stand. It is pitch black and a human would not be able to see a single thing. But I see everything and so far, I see no sign of Brielle, Andrew, Michael, or Kathleen.

I close the door and step further into the darkness until I hear Kathleen's recognizable voice speak to me: "The guest of honor has finally arrived."

All of a sudden, torches are ignited throughout the frail walls and I see Kathleen and Michael, each of them holding Brielle and Andrew, standing in front of the entrance to the stone room.

Kathleen holds Brielle and Michael is holding Andrew. It is strange that Michael has a knife pressed against Andrew's throat and Kathleen is without a weapon. I assumed that both of them would use their fangs to kill them.

"How could I resist such a tempting invitation?" I counter. I am not rash, in spite of what my actions may say. I am in a playful mood. I am finally taking on Kathleen's qualities for amusement.

"I thought you would have come sooner," Kathleen points out.

I grin at her. "I was preoccupied at the moment. I hope you will *forgive* my tardiness." I stress on that word, "forgive", out of a pure whim.

Kathleen beams at me. "All can be forgiven, Sophia," she intones, lowering her head down to Brielle's neck.

"Sophia!" Brielle cries out, probably wondering what kind of game I am playing.

I lose my smile. Game time is over. "No, it really can't, Kathleen," I proclaim.

Kathleen lifts her head up and shoots me a curious expression.

"Let them go, Kathleen," I demand in a firm, apathetic tone.

"Let me think about it...Hmm...no." Kathleen bares her fangs and brings her head down to Brielle's neck.

"This isn't about Andrew or Brielle or Michael even," I inform her. The strength in my voice surprises her and causes her to stop. Even Michael, who stands emotionless beside her, is astounded. I continue. "This is about you and me, Kathleen. It's personal, so let the rest of them go."

Kathleen considers this and when she begins nodding her head, I feel a sense of relief wash over me. "True, true," she agrees and then she trades her agreeing face for a cruel one. "But I work better with an audience," she finishes, her fangs too close to Brielle's skin for Brielle's comfort.

"You hide behind innocent and defenseless humans, Kathleen? You *are* a coward."

And this makes Kathleen stop. For a moment, I see a flicker of anger on her face much similar to the one I saw hundreds of years earlier when my father called me his "baby girl", then it disappears, replaced by interest. "And what if I am a coward? At least it is better than being a weak, pathetic creature like you are."

I laugh out loud at Kathleen's words, upsetting her a great deal. "You really think that will work on me, anymore? You're wrong, Kathleen, and your miscalculations of me will be the end of you."

"Is that a threat, Sophia?" Kathleen questions me.

"I can make it one," I reply sharply. "You didn't want me to come here just so I could watch my friends die. You wanted me to come here because you wanted to beg with me, for one last chance to be with your daughter. Is that right?"

"And what if it is?"

I saunter a little to the left, pressing my palm against a wooden beam. "Then that means I have the power to hurt you," I answer. "The same way you hurt me all those years. Now, the tables have turned *favorably* in my direction."

Kathleen narrows her eyes until they are nearly slits. Michael's eyebrows knit. Brielle is confused. Andrew is still terrified.

"Your arrogance will cause your friends to die," Kathleen hisses at me.

"And if my friends die, you will suffer an eternal damnation for it," I return, abruptly.

"Don't make promises you can't keep, Sophia," Michael speaks out loud.

I turn my eyes to him for a second and then back to Kathleen. "I'm not," I notify him. "I'm merely giving you the facts, plain, simple, and direct."

"And I wonder, what could have caused this sudden change in your behavior, Sophia?" Kathleen asks.

"And I wonder, what could have caused such cowardice in you that you would hide behind humans, Kathleen? Perhaps you *are* afraid of me." I retort and she is miffed for a second, then she chuckles devilishly.

"This is rich," my maker laughs at me and then I realize something. Kathleen is my maker in more ways than one. I do not know if I should be comforted by that or disgusted at it. "Sophia has finally reached her rebellious age."

I tire of this banter. "Let my friends go and I will allow you to walk out of here alive."

Michael and Kathleen exchange looks before busting up into insane cackling.

"*You* are threatening *us*?" Michael mocks incredulously.

"If you harm my friends in any way, you won't have to wonder if it's a threat," I retort.

It is Kathleen's turn to speak. "She is serious, Michael. She is dead set on her way. Perhaps we should consider her threat. As a matter of fact, I have an idea. I challenge you, Sophia, to a battle…to the death. If I win, you will kill your friends and you will join us."

"And if *I* win?"

"I will release your friends and allow you all to walk out of here in peace," Kathleen answers.

It is my turn to laugh. "Do you think I am that stupid, Kathleen? You never keep your promises."

"That is the only way, Sophia," Kathleen says, gravely. "There will be no renegotiating. Either you fight me and win, or your humans, and maybe even yourself, will die."

I exchange glances with Brielle and Andrew. Brielle is afraid for her life, but even more afraid for mine.

I have to do it, I whisper into her mind.

Are you crazy? What if you lose? she questions me.

It is better to go down with a fight than to just go down, I remind her.

WE STAND THERE FOR HOURS.

It is well past midnight, Devil's Hour, and I still have yet to make a decision. The last time I fought Kathleen, I succeeded in torching her, but not in killing her. I do not know if I have that same power inside of me and I am not quite willing to risk Brielle and Andrew's life in order to find out.

Another hour goes by.

"TIME IS RUNNING OUT, SOPHIA," Michael informs me. "Make your decision."

"Why so urgent, Michael? We have until forever," I remind him.

Michael presses the blade against Andrew's neck just enough so that Andrew can feel the sheer deadliness of it. "But your friends don't," he points out.

"What will your decision be, Sophia?" Kathleen asks.

I look at Brielle again and then back to Kathleen. Reluctantly, I announce my decision. "Battle...to the death."

CHAPTER EIGHTEEN

εφ

KATHLEEN SMILES AT ME, GLAD that I have come around to seeing things her way. "Very good choice, Sophia," Kathleen congratulates me. "Now, pick up that bag over there."

I walk over to the left where I see a black bag lying on the ground.

"Open it," Kathleen instructs.

The bag is already opened. I just reach inside and I feel two sharp blades. I take out two swords and I hold it up, analyzing them. *It is a rematch*, I realize.

Kathleen throws Brielle over to Michael and now Michael is holding the both of them. But Michael is strong and he will be able to retain them.

"The last time that we fought with swords," Kathleen commences, "you beat me. But we shall see if we have improved."

I toss one of the identical swords to Kathleen and she puts a firm grip around the hilt. She surveys the fine and long blade. "A blade through the heart will kill a vampire," she reminds me. "Whose blade will go through whose heart, first?"

"We'll find out," I tell her.

We stand a foot away from each other, circling one another with our swords. We wait and wait. I do not plan on making the first move, but if I did, I would have the advantage. But everything I do must be done with care and precision. This is the final battle and I cannot permit any room for error or carelessness.

But someone must initiate the battle and unfortunately, I see that it must be me.

I extend my sword out, hoping to get a good incision to Kathleen's stomach. But she hops backwards to avoid it and then I try again, this time, I raise my sword to the right and bring it swiping down to the left, in a diagonal direction. Kathleen's sword blocks mine from finishing the path, and she pushes my sword back. Now Kathleen seizes the opportunity. She cuts the air with the sword every time that she attempts to slice me. But every strike that she attempts, compels me backwards. My back is nearly against the wall when Kathleen swings her sword at my neck. But I duck and she misses, knocking off one of the blazing torches on the wall instead.

Fire leaks onto the floor from the torch.

I rise quickly and I attempt to stab Kathleen at her side, but she brings her sword there and stops me. She kicks me in the stomach, forcing me to bend over slightly. She elbows my back, impelling me to fall onto the ground where she has positioned herself so that she can gore my back through with her sword.

Before she can lower her sword all the way down, I reach out and grab Kathleen's feet, knocking her feet from her, causing her to fall backwards and slam against the ground where the fire has spread some more.

I regain my balance as I stand, but Kathleen is quick and she is already up before I am.

As my struggle with Kathleen continues, from the corner of my eye, I see Brielle take the initiative. Her sharp elbow collides with Michael's nose vigorously and the surprise hit forces Michael to release Brielle and Andrew.

I pray that they will not kill themselves attempting to escape.

In the meanwhile, Kathleen kicks me in the chest, sending me flying backwards into the stone room. My back smashes against the stone wall and I slide down. I recover my ground as Kathleen enters the room. I hop onto the box, which has not been moved since I left it.

I kick Kathleen in the face when she approaches close enough to me and then she swerves the blade at my feet.

Artfully, I jump and avoid the oncoming blade. I seize the advantage and strike out at Kathleen with my mind. She is taken off guard and she is dazed for a moment before she regains her senses.

Behind Kathleen, I see that another torch has been dropped during Brielle and Andrew's struggle against Michael, who is lying unconscious on the ground.

I see Brielle smile at me for an instant before the flames create an impenetrable barrier between us. The ever-growing fire has blocked even the entrance to the stone room.

Kathleen duplicates a move I did to her; she seizes me by my ankles and pulls my feet from underneath me and I hit the ground hard.

Kathleen is on me in an instant. My body is in between her legs as she drops her sword at my neck. I bring my sword to shield against hers. Our blades struggle against each others for what seems like everlasting seconds until I lift my legs and kick Kathleen in the stomach, causing her to collide with the same stone wall I collided with.

I rise from the ground and I see Brielle and Andrew.

"Get out of here!" I shout at them, wary that the fire is swallowing the building and will eventually bring it down into ashes.

"No! Not without you!" Brielle yells back at me.

"I'll be fine!" I swear to her, even though I am not certain of my fate. "Just get the hell out of here!"

"Behind you!" Brielle screams.

I turn around too late. Kathleen spears her blade just a little beneath my right shoulder. I cry out in pain for a moment. The pain is brief compared to my next fate.

Kathleen hovers over me, smiling evilly at me. "So, this is the end," she tells me—*as if I didn't already know.*

Kathleen's sword comes down rapidly at me, with a lightning speed I have never quite seen before.

I close my eyes, steeling myself for the moment and I ponder what it is like to die.

The next thing I hear is Brielle shrieking: "*No!*"

And then I wonder why the blade has not fallen on me yet and why I have not died.

I open my eyes and see Brielle on top of Kathleen, after tackling the vampire down.

I recover my ground and I scurry over to Brielle, fearing the worst, but not quite believing it.

I lift Brielle up and I see that there is blood on her stomach where the sword has punctured her skin.

"Did I stop her?" Brielle asks me.

I look over to where Kathleen is lying on the ground. She is still alive. I avert my attention back to Brielle and her bleeding wound. I examine it. I sigh relief.

"It's only penetrated a little," I inform her. "A few more inches and it would've killed you. You're lucky, but you still need help."

She shrugs it off, as if it is nothing. "Nah, I'll be alright. Besides, that was totally tight. Did you see what I did?"

"No, unfortunately, I didn't," I tell her. I hold Brielle by her shoulders and force her to look into my eyes. "Listen to me, Brielle. I want you to get out of here. Get some medical help and then I want you to take Andrew and leave this place."

Brielle shakes her head, refusing. "No, I won't."

"*Listen to me*," I repeat. "I'll be fine. You need to worry about yourself. Get out of here. Do you hear me?" Brielle nods her head, finally agreeing. "Good. Now *go!*"

Coincidentally, the flames have gone down enough so that Brielle can pass through them by vaulting over them. But as soon as she leaves, the flames roar up.

I turn around and Kathleen surprises me. She hits me in the face, aching my jaw.

She slices my arm—a minor cut in the long run compared to what I *might* have if I lose—and then my other arm—another minor cut, but that is not to say that it did not have a brief moment of pain.

"Sophia, you disappoint me," Kathleen declares. "And now you make me angry. But I am going to give you one last chance to redeem yourself. Take your rightful place as my daughter or die here right now."

"I'd rather die before I ever call you mother," I respond.

Enraged, Kathleen clutches my shirt and raises me higher than what any average human can do. Her teeth have elongated into fangs and her eyes sear me with their scarlet hue.

"*That* can be arranged!" she bellows at me before she flings me across the flames back into the empty building.

I slam onto the ground and every organ in my body trembles with the force of the throw. Kathleen advances towards me.

The same murderous gleam is in her eyes, just as it was in mine when I was about to kill Preston Bennington.

I look over to my left and I see a flaming torch that must have fallen when Brielle and Andrew were fighting with Michael. I turn my gaze over to Kathleen, who is standing in front of me and kicks me in the face.

I recede just a little bit back. I roll over so that I am on my stomach and I can see the torch clearly, in spite of the haziness from the charcoal smoke.

My fingers are sprawled out in front of me. I slowly reach for the torch, my movements subtle so that Kathleen will not notice.

"Looks like you're going to die, Sophia ..." she points out.

Well, duh, I say to myself, still reaching for the torch.

"Any last words?"

Yes! I have a good grip on the torch.

"Yes, as a matter of fact," I reply. "Tell the devil Sophia says hi."

271

I see Kathleen's eyes widen when I finish the sentence. She has an assumption as to what will happen next.

I hurl the torch at her and the fire immediately catches onto her pale body. Kathleen shrieks and dances around the building like a madwoman.

The flames engulf her almost instantly and before I know it, I can no longer see Kathleen; her body is now composed of flames.

Yet she is still scurrying around the building like a blind mouse searching for its home.

I must stay and make sure that Kathleen is dead. The last time something similar to this happened, I left too soon and Kathleen was able to extinguish the fire. That mistake must not be repeated twice.

After a few moments, I have a firsthand account of what Kathleen once told me about. Fire will kill a vampire and indeed, it does.

For Kathleen is no more. Her ashes are scattered about the earth and I feel at ease for the first time in a long while.

"… Now *that* is tight," I say under my breath.

CHAPTER NINETEEN

εφ

FIRE ENCLOSES ME AND I see no possible way of escape. One of the many wooden beams from the ceiling collapses right in front of me, after it has been eaten away by the flames. I turn to my right and the flames stretch out to the ceiling, as if they have arms. I look ahead and the fumes from burning cloud the entrance and I can no longer see the door at all.

I turn around, my back to the door, and inspect the area. Perhaps there is a back door somewhere. Indeed, there is! But there is no way that I can make it there.

The flames lower themselves to allow me to catch a glimpse of the exit that I shall never reach, as if taunting me. Then they rise again, heavy and blazing, and my path is blocked.

Surrounded by fire, I am certain that this is how I will die.

I see Kathleen's ashes on the floor. *At least she is dead*, I say to myself. The heat of the flames has become almost unbearable, a raging inferno, a version of hell on earth.

Without even thinking about it, my fingers touch the coldest object amidst the heat. I feel the letters underneath my fingers, tracing them, I can read it without even having to look at it. *Peace...is...the...way.*

Perhaps it is the way, but I do not think it is for me. We all walk separate paths, each creature on earth. My path has just reached its end.

I gaze into the fire, entranced by it. This is possibly the same thing that I shall experience when I am delivered into hell. If I burn in hell, so be it. No fate is worse than the one I have suffered here on earth.

I stand alone in the fire, just as I have done all my life.

DAWN HAD ARRIVED, YET IT still felt like the darkness enveloped them. She had shed many tears in the darkness. He remembered that she had nearly hit hysteria. He had to restrain her from jumping into the flames, which she severely wanted to do. She sobbed onto his shirt like she had never sobbed before and he could not help but feel sorry for her. He could not quite understand her anguish—he had not bonded with her comrade the way that she had. He had an insignificant understanding of the sorrow she felt, but not enough.

She had cried out her name so many times throughout the night, when the firefighters were arriving to douse the unquenchable fire. As they worked tirelessly to keep the fire from spreading to other places and maintain control of it, she had wandered from location to location, searching for any sign of life.

The building had crumbled, slowly at first, and then so quickly that no one would even remember where it once stood.

But still, she looked. She looked and looked, and hoped and hoped. They interrogated the firefighters about it, but all they would do was lower their gaze sadly and turn away.

The paramedics arrived to take care of her hemorrhaging wound, but she turned away from them and stood so close to the building that a police officer had to tell her to back away.

When dawn approached and the soft colors of the morning replaced the black waves of the night, she had grown silent. He was uneasy about her silence, but it was better than listening to her woeful wailing. He held her in his warm embrace, both of them wrapped around by a single gray blanket.

They looked on as the firefighters stepped onto the ground where the building once stood.

News reporters came with their insatiable craving for the latest stories. They wanted to interview them, but none of them could speak. They had nothing to say.

She gazed into the sky and saw the overbearing stormclouds. But she could not be mad at them. The sky was weeping for them, for their loss.

Moments after dawn, they were finally allowed near the wreckage when the firefighters had declared that they had found nothing in the debris.

He released her and she stepped towards the fragments of the building. Each step she took was full of heavy sorrow and graveness. He was certain that her somber mood was so potent that it caused the sky to turn gray; a mirror image of her mourning soul.

She knelt down a few yards away from him, the exact place where she had last seen her. There was nothing on the ground but ashes. She was ready to turn away when a flicker of light revealed a glint of gold underneath the ashes.

Curious, she dug her fingers into the ashes and uncovered a gold necklace with a gold pendant. She knew this necklace. She remembered this necklace! She ran to her boyfriend and displayed it for him. She was stunned, incredibly happy! The

Catalina Chao

inscription on the pendant was difficult to read because there were tiny specks of soot. She brushed it off and the message was clear: Peace is the way.

276

CHAPTER TWENTY

εφ

*S*HE LOOKS TO THE RIGHT and then the left, *positive that she heard her voice once more, whispering to her, calling out her name. But her hope of that vanished when she saw no one and heard nothing more.*

Trick of the wind, *she thinks to herself.* Or trick of the mind.

She was going to do as she had promised. She was going to return home with her boyfriend and be happy and even aspire to amend things with her family. She had told her that when her quarrel was over, she had better leave New York for California and that was what she was going to do.

It took a few days before it could actually happen. The day after it happened, she was much too upset and he gave her time to grieve. She would never forget that he did so.

After two days, she remembered her promise and she knew that she could not fail to keep it.

For her sake, *she had said.* In her memory.

She returned the car and he called the Greyhound and booked two tickets to Sundry. The rest of their time was spent on packing up the things from her apartment.

She fingers the gold chain around her neck, as she stands in front of the apartment building, on the sidewalk to the street, waiting for the taxi to arrive.

One week has gone by since it happened, *she recalls.* God, it feels like only yesterday that I was talking to her and now she's gone. I guess it doesn't matter. As long as she's at peace and no longer at war.

She feels his arms around her and she welcomes the touch, the comfort it brings to her.

"Time to go," he informs her, as they simultaneously see the approaching taxi cab that will take them to the bus stop, which is about two and a half miles away. "You ready?"

He notices her hesitate and he quickly reassures her. "She would've wanted it this way, remember?" he reminds her.

She stares into his eyes and she can recall her exact words and her exact facial expressions when she told her this promise. She nods her head. "Yeah," she says with a hint of sadness. "She did."

He nods as well, hoping to strengthen her and he bends down to kiss her. It is a brief kiss, but it is the last one that they will share here in New York.

He opens the door and allows her to enter first—much like what a proper gentleman should—and then he closes the door and opens the passenger side.

She had requested that she wanted the window view where she could gaze out at the apartment building one last time. And this she did.

Her eyes survey the multiple windows on the front of the building and she can see her window. Then she looks up at the unhappy clouds above. They are ready to weep. She smiles at them, hoping to brighten them, but she knows that a storm is coming. She feels it.

She is saddened that she will never gaze at the building again, but perhaps she would return here later on in her life and remember everything that had taken place.

For the blink of an eye, she could swear that she sees a dark figure—clothed in black—perched on top of the ledge of the apartment building, looking down on her, protecting her still.

She shudders, though it is a welcomed thought, even if she knows it is impossible. Then the figure seems to vanish, a mere illusion, one that was never there at all.

Trick of the light, *she tells herself.*

Then the car begins to move and rolls lazily down the street, exiting this scene forever.

I WANTED TO SAY SOMETHING.

I wanted to tell her that everything was okay, that I was alive, but I couldn't. I would not allow myself to do so.

Yet still, I wanted to say something then and I still want to say something now. She is looking from right to left, thinking that she has heard my whisper carry with the wind. It is but a trick of the wind. I still want to say something. But I know I cannot, because if I do, it would be terribly selfish of me.

I have been keeping a vigil over them, to make certain that they will be fine until they leave New York. Then, after that, I can no longer protect them, as much as I want to.

The flames had seared into my skin just a bit, but when the fire began to die down, I made my escape—after I took off my necklace and left it there for Brielle to find.

Brielle plays with the pendant around her neck and I am glad that it gives her comfort, hope, and strength. Andrew approaches her and puts his arms around her.

He informs her that it is time to go and asks her if she is ready.

She is silent at first and this somewhat scares Andrew. He is quick to remind her of the promise and she remembers it too. They kiss and they go inside the car—lady first.

She gazes out of the window at the apartment building one last time. For one evanescent second in time—one insignificant moment—I allow Brielle to see me, just to give her a sense of security. But I quickly vanish again so that she can leave in peace.

I watch sadly as Brielle and Andrew exit my life forever. They are probably the only friends that I have ever had. This is for the best. Everyone that I have known is dead. And Brielle and Andrew have nearly lost their lives already. I will not let it happen again and if it means never seeing them again, then so be it. They got off easy, very fortunate of them. Other lives that I have touched have died. I refuse to allow it to happen to Andrew and Brielle. They are still innocent and have so much potential for the future.

They think I am dead. It is better for them to think of me that way—better to remember me fondly in death than to know that I escaped and their lives are in jeopardy because I am alive.

But alas, I cannot die. Not yet. Life weighs too heavily on my soul. Things I did and didn't; things I should have done and couldn't...or wouldn't.

There is still much for me to do before I can—what is that old saying?—"rest in peace".

My quarrel with Kathleen—my mother—has ended, true enough, but I fear another one shall begin.

I am sitting on the ledge of the apartment building, on the roof, in the same clothes that I wore the night that I finally avenged myself when I took Kathleen's life.

As horrible as it might sound, it feels so good to finally do what I have been talking about for centuries. I have my retribution.

I have sat here on this very ledge so many times since that night when I finally killed Kathleen. I feel no remorse for doing so. I suppose you think that is monstrous of me, but I am a vampire.

I also suppose that that is no excuse for what I did and you are right. There are no excuses to justify what I did, maybe except for the fact that she was going to kill my friends and I if I did not accept her challenge.

Kathleen was my birth mother, true—and she was my dark mother as well—but flesh and blood is nothing compared to love. She never loved me. If she had, she would have left me in peace with my family. She would have never brought such evil into my heart.

No, Kathleen was my mother, but not in the way that she wanted to be. I feel no guilt over my actions even though I have committed a blasphemous crime. Not only did I kill my own flesh and blood, but I also killed my maker. Ah, well…all I can do now is shrug it off.

When I feel a bead of rain—the sky's way of weeping—I look up into the vault of heaven and I see its gloominess as I have never seen it before. The sky is mourning for a loss that was never lost!

A great storm is approaching. I feel it in the pith of my heart and soul. It is strange, though, that another storm should be impending so soon when a tempest has just passed so recently.

Ah, perhaps it is not so strange after all. Just because one great thing happened it does not mean that it will stop another great thing from happening. That is Mother Nature and life, I fear.

The rain is showering down on me. It feels unbelievably wonderful to have these tears on my body. I hold my right hand out, open my palm, and observe the raindrops gathering into my hand in mere seconds.

These raindrops remind me of the human tears I was once able to cast so long ago—saline and lucid, brilliant and beautiful.

Conceivably, I could cry these tears again one day. Anything appears possible in this time—a vampire was freed after centuries of solitary confinement; a vampire befriends a human and regains compassion and mercy; a vampire overcomes a great evil that has tormented her for century after century; a vampire remembers what it was like to be human.

Yes, I sincerely believe that anything is possible in this time. If all that has taken place, then surely one day I just might be able to shed diamonds from my eyes again, instead of the garnets that have substituted them.

It is a hope. And sometimes, hope is enough.

IMMORTAL BLOODLUST WILL CONTINUE

. . .

ABOUT THE AUTHOR

Born in 1987, Catalina Chao currently lives in Antelope, California with her family, where she is a sophomore at her high school. *Immortal Bloodlust: Retribution* is the ninth novel that she has written and the first that she has gotten published. She writes vampire novels because of several reasons, one of them being that she has always been fascinated by the stories surrounding these "creatures of the night". She is very in-depth with her writing and is always eager to begin a new story. She enjoys writing her friends into her novels as well. She is very passionate—and extremely intense—when it comes to friends, family, schoolwork, and her writing. Outside of the worlds she has created within her stories, Chao relishes the challenges of everyday life and sees them as an opportunity to learn more about everything around her and to expand her understanding of humanity. She is deeply devoted to everything she does and none of it is ever done halfway.

Printed in the United States
764300003B